SUPERPLANE

'Bob Powell means to have your ass in a sling,' Terry said.

Stirling looked around the country club dining room, aware of how eyes dropped as his glance traveled. 'Well, he's got it,' he said. 'I'm president of a company with which I have no contract. I'm not bringing in my own management team. I'm committed to manufacturing and marketing an experimental aircraft. And the first thing I've got to do is sell some banks on the idea they should lend the company a lot of bucks.'

'And you've got another problem, Mac.'

'Which is?'

'There aren't ten people in this room who don't entertain at least a small suspicion that you're the new president of Powell Industries because you're sleeping in my bed. There are some who *want* to think that, who don't want to try to explain you any other way.'

He shrugged. 'Well . . . anyhow, I'm flattered.'

Terry laughed. Her eyes met his. 'So'm I,' she said.

HAROLD ROBBINS

PRESENTS

Superplane

CARL F. FURST

NEW ENGLISH LIBRARY
Hodder and Stoughton

Copyright © 1987 by Pocket Books, a division of Simon and Schuster, Inc.

First published in 1987 in the USA by Pocket Books

New English Library Paperback edition 1988

HAROLD ROBBINS PRESENTS is a trademark of Harold Robbins

British Library C.I.P.

Furst, Carl F.
    Superplane.—(Harold Robbins presents).
    I. Title
    813'.54[F]   PS3556.U76/

    ISBN 0-450-42170-8

Printed and bound in Great Britain for Hodder and Stoughton Paperbacks, a division of Hodder and Stoughton Ltd., Mill Road, Dunton Green, Sevenoaks, Kent TN13 2YA (Editorial Office: 47 Bedford Square, London WC1B 3DP) by Richard Clay Ltd., Bungay, Suffolk.

"WHO THE HELL'S the civilian?" the line mechanic asked.

His terminology was of habit, not of fact. He was himself a civilian, though it would have been difficult to tell from his government-issue blue coveralls, his close-cropped hair, his oversized dark sunglasses, or from his ramrod bearing and demeanor. He was in fact a retired Air Force master sergeant. He stood with his hands planted on his hips and was direct in his curiosity about the silver-gray Mercedes that had somehow managed to penetrate security and now cruised along the ramp, under the tailpipes of a line of six varied and majestic jet fighters.

Curiosity changed to astonishment when the Mercedes stopped finally under the tail of an F-16, a chauffeur hurried out to open the door for his passenger, and that passenger emerged.

She had to be the most beautiful hunk of woman Sergeant Magruder had ever seen. She was maybe six feet tall. The wind caught her honey-blond hair and whipped it around her neck and jaw for a moment—which she ignored and simply let it fall back in place, as if she were hardly conscious of it. She wore western-style blue jeans, Levi's maybe from the look of them—anyway, nothing that would have turned her fanny into a billboard for some New York designer. Her sweat shirt was raspberry colored, and though she was a slender piece of cake, he could see she had boobs under that loose sweat shirt. She reached into the car and pulled out a big pair of binoculars.

He had hardly noticed the man who had been in the back seat of the car with her. Now he saw it was General Harris—they kept to their old military titles, though no one on the field was active anymore—General Ralph Harris, vice director of the Mojave Aeronautical Research Center. The general came around the car and stood beside her, pointing up. She raised her binoculars and began to scan the sky to the east.

"Put two knuckles right under your chin, Sarge, and push up. Your mouth's hangin' open."

The mechanic grinned and mimed the action suggested. "Hey, Buck. Who's the broad?"

The other man—a young pilot clad in an orange flight suit—laughed. "You don't know? You are staring at a legend, Sarge."

The mechanic turned his eyes back to the woman. "Who the hell? Some Hollywood bimbo? The general's—"

"No, Sarge, not at all," said the pilot. "And shame on you. You're going to be embarrassed when I tell you."

"Well, tell me, goddamnit."

The pilot put a mock-sympathetic hand on the mechanic's shoulder. "She's Terry Powell, Sarge. You know—wife of the late Stan Powell, Powell Industries."

"*She*—"

"Right. That's the one. As rich as that car looks. If you figured the general had picked himself up a girl

2

friend, you can forget that. She could buy and sell the old boy out of pocket change."

"Well, what the hell's she doin' here?"

The pilot shrugged. He squinted up into the brilliant mid-morning sun. "Well now, nobody's taken me into their confidence. But my guess would be she's here to see Mac bust up the X-41A. I mean, she's in the airplane business, after all."

The mechanic fixed an even more intent stare on the striking, statuesque woman, who was still scanning the skies with her binoculars. "Sure she is," he said scornfully. "Sure she is."

"You're familiar with the term *envelope*, Mrs. Powell," said General Harris. She nodded without taking down her binoculars, and he continued. "Well, Colonel Stirling is going to fly outside the envelope this morning. We have to know what the X-41A will do when it's flown outside the envelope. We wouldn't be at all surprised to see him eject and let the airplane go."

"I didn't come here to see him get killed," she murmured.

"No, of course not. But we have little to fear on that score. Colonel Stirling has ejected many times."

"Statistically, then, he is in little danger," she said dryly.

General Harris looked up as if studying the sky to look for some anticipated danger. "Colonel Stirling," he said, "has almost ten thousand hours flight time, including more than sixty-five hundred in high-performance jet aircraft. He flew more than a hundred sorties over Vietnam. He holds records for time-to-altitude. He—"

"I am well aware of his record," she said.

"Well, then . . ."

"And he has often been called on to fly outside the envelope," she said. "Even so, it is no enviable job."

"But one that has to be done," said General Harris. "And I can't think of anyone I'd rather have up there doing it."

"Spoken like a brigadier general," said Terry Powell.

"Have you got him yet?" the general asked. "See the contrail?"

"I've got him," she said. "What? Forty-five thousand feet?"

Flying outside the envelope meant forcing an aircraft beyond the limits for which it was designed: flying it higher, faster, maneuvering it more sharply, subjecting it to greater G-forces than it was built to take. Occasions would arise in the life of any aircraft, whether it was a supersonic fighter or a ten-passenger twin, when it would be stressed to its operational limits. To be sure it would stick together at that limit, you had to know it would stick together *beyond* those limits. It was essential to know what it would do when it was stressed beyond what it was designed to take.

And that was what Colonel McDonald John Stirling, U.S.A.F. (ret.) was doing with the X-41A that late-summer morning.

This was maybe his twenty-first or twenty-second flight in the X-41A, and from the beginning he had never had much confidence in the airplane. It was a long, thin beast, its clean lines broken by immense rectangular air scoops on both sides of the fuselage. The wings were flat and thin and stubby. The tail ended

in two fat stovepipes, where the two turbofans shot
forth an enormous blast of power. Though it had the
insignia of the U.S. Air Force on its wings, it was
painted garish red and blue, with the initials CAC, for
Consolidated Aeronautical Companies, emblazoned on
its vertical fin.

He had set a climb record in the X-41A, climbing
from runway to 40,000 feet in 51 seconds. On the other
hand, it had nearly killed him twice. Once it had
developed uncontrollable oscillation on the takeoff roll
and almost skidded around and disintegrated on the
runway, where the ejector seat would have done him
no good at all. Another time the port turbofan overheated and began to disintegrate; and before he could
stop it, the whole left rear of the airplane tore open.
That time he had been forced to eject at 48,000 feet.
His nose and jaw were broken in the ejection, and an
ankle in the landing on the rocky Mojave Desert. The
X-41A was no friend.

He had flown worse for less money. For twenty years,
almost, he had test-flown or combat-flown just about
everything the Air Force bought. Since his retirement
from the Air Force in 1984, he had worked under
contract as an engineering consultant and test pilot,
first for General Dynamics and lately for MARC, the
Mojave Aeronautical Research Center. It was an independent test and research facility that had contracts
with the Defense Department, eight aircraft manufacturers, and several foreign governments to evaluate
aircraft—everything from a four-place twin-engine
family plane whose manufacturer hoped the MARC
imprimatur would create confidence in a new concept,
to the X-41A.

Now, encased in a silvery pressure suit, complete with fishbowl helmet, Mac Stirling was strapped tightly into the ejection seat, in the middle of an orderly tangle of lines and tubes.

The configuration of the cockpit was unlike anything in any other aircraft; it was almost wholly lacking the familiar instruments a pilot knew how to read. Instead, it communicated everything he needed to know by displaying numbers and images on three square cathode-ray tubes—television screens. The most vital information was projected on the surface of the bubble canopy right before his eyes, so he could see it without taking his eyes away from the sky ahead. The throttles were at his left hand. The stick—instead of being between his legs as it was in almost every stick-flown airplane—was to his right, so as not to interfere with his view of the large center CRT that displayed his altitude, speed, compass heading, and course and distance to whatever navigation facility he had tuned in.

This X-41A carried none of the armament it was designed to carry. The weight was made up by the load of instruments mounted throughout the airframe. Most of them offered him no readout but sent their signals directly back to the monitoring station at MARC Field.

"X-four-one, we show you passing through five-niner thousand, two-point-four Mach, climbing at two-five thousand per minute. Advise."

"Uh, Roger, MARC. Onboard instruments agree."

"Temperatures, sir?"

"Normal."

He was well above all haze, and the sky above was dark blue and cloudless. From the ground the sky looked perfectly clear, he knew, but from up here the earth was half obscured, and it was difficult to fix the horizon with any precision. It was quiet. He was outrunning the shrieking roar of his engines.

"Uh, X-four-one, we are getting normal indications. The F-15 is at your twelve o'clock position, altitude one-zero-zero."

"Roger, MARC. I'll roll out at niner-zero."

The F-15 was his chase plane, carrying cameras to photograph whatever happened. It was competent at speeds in excess of Mach 2.5 and could keep close to him for a while. Shorty Bellows was flying. He had been up here five minutes, waiting. Stirling knew exactly where Shorty was; he showed up dramatically on the X-41A's target-finder display screen.

"Got you on screen, Shorty."

"Got you with eyeballs, Mac."

At ninety-thousand feet, a little more than sixteen miles above the surface of the Mojave Desert, Stirling eased his stick back and made the X-41A level off inverted. When he was streaking across the sky at Mach 2.9—about 1800 miles an hour at this altitude— upside down, he rolled the aircraft over. This maneuver, instead of terminating his climb simply by pushing the nose over, was habit. Pilots not wearing pressure suits did it to relieve themselves of the painful experience of red-out, the rush of blood to the head.

He noticed that the plane was sluggish coming out of the climb, responding only slowly to his back pressure on the stick, and developing a tendency to wallow.

Shorty Bellows had turned the F-15 to the east and was flying level at Mach 2.75.

"Going into my right turn, Shorty. Will be coming by to your left at about two thousand yards. Will initiate climb in five seconds."

"Roger, Mac. Give 'er hell."

The F-15, making more than sixteen hundred miles an hour at an altitude of one hundred thousand feet, would be overtaken and passed by the X-41A, even though the X41-A would be climbing at a seventy-degree angle of attack. Shorty's cameras would be rolling as the X-41A swept by, flying out of its envelope.

Outside the envelope here was too much climb at too much speed, too high. The computers had suggested the X-41A would develop problems in that situation, but future pilots had to be told it did or it didn't—based on real flying experience, not just what computers said.

Stirling raised the nose and pushed in the throttles. Intent on his instruments, feeling every shudder in the airplane, he did not look for the F-15 except on his screen.

"Altitude established."

"Roger, X-four-one. Readings within acceptable range."

The beast had more power than it could handle. He knew that at lower altitudes it was capable of climbing eleven thousand feet straight up; he had done it. Up here, its nose raised to a seventy-degree angle, it hardly lost speed. He passed through one hundred thousand in seconds. He had had the X-41A up as high as a hundred twenty, where it had begun to resist, as any airplane would as it reached its operational ceiling; but today it felt as if it could fly right on out into orbit.

"One-ten, X-four-one."

"Roger. Here goes."

This was the test: to see if he could now arrest the climb without throttling back, just by lowering the nose and slipping into level flight. It was what he had not done at ninety thousand. That was why he was wearing the pressure suit: because this time he was going to try to force the nose down, to transition into level flight at full power without the inversion maneuver. The suit, its sensors reacting to the G-forces, would tighten the belts on his arms and legs to restrict the flow of blood. It was too bad, he thought grimly, the X-41A wasn't wrapped in a big pressure suit to hold it together. Here was where the airplane might fail.

Stirling drew a deep breath, glanced over his instruments one more time, then pushed the stick forward. Nothing. The plane shuddered and wallowed but did not respond to the controls.

"The computer was right, boys."

"Okay, throttle her back."

"Try again. That's what we brought her up here for."

"One-two-oh thousand, X-four-one."

"Roger."

This time he pushed the control stick as far forward as it would go. He turned his head and looked back. He could see the tail from the bubble canopy. The elevators were hanging down like two trap doors, and they should have raised the tail, depressed the nose; but the only reaction from the X-41A was to porpoise a little and shudder, and the nose began actually to rise. At this angle of attack, in the thin atmosphere at 120,000 feet, the tail control surfaces were in an eddy of burbling air behind the wings, with insufficient pressure on them to rotate the hurtling airplane on its horizontal axis.

Stirling jammed in a rudder pedal. The same thing was almost equally true of the pressure on the rudder. The X-41A swung gradually around, but only reluctantly. And the nose kept rising. The fuselage was almost vertical. He was flying a blowtorch, out of control.

He reached for the throttles and eased them back. But the nose did not fall. The X-41A began to buffet, to stall. He pushed the throttles in again, but the airplane stalled. For a moment it stood on its tail, shaking, fighting gravity; then it fell away to one side and went into a cartwheeling spin. Suddenly it was no longer an aircraft supported seventeen miles above the earth by the pressure under its wings and the vacuum above them; it was a heavy hunk of metal that the earth compelled to return.

He felt himself cramp with terror, as if the pressure suit had malfunctioned and tightened on him. This was what every pilot feared, no matter how experienced, after no matter how many ejections he had survived: a stalled airplane, falling out of control. Instinct overwhelmed reason when this happened; it always did. His stomach had hardened; his hands were weak on the controls.

"Don't stay with her too long, Mac."

That was the voice of Shorty, strangely calm.

"X-four-one, we are showing all readings out of range. Confirm. Are you out of control?"

"Affirmative," said Stirling. "Violent spin."

"Structural disintegration?"

"Not yet."

"Eject at your discretion, sir. Don't ride her down."

Another voice came on the air. "Don't ride her down, Mac. She's scrap metal now, anyway."

"Say altitudes," Stirling snapped, aware that his voice had broken. "Keep saying altitudes."

"You're passing through eighty, sir."

The X-41A was tumbling. It was not just spinning; it was rolling, porpoising, turning violently around all three axes. Stirling made a quick scan all around. Oddly, it had not begun to break up, though it was taking stress from angles it had not been designed to take, with immense pressures on the wings and stabilizers.

He read his gauges. Engine temperatures were not excessive. Neither were pressures. Hydraulic pressure was normal. He had electrical power.

"Visual contact lost," said Shorty.

"Six-five thousand, sir. Rate of descent far outside tolerances. Eject at discretion."

Ejecting above sixty thousand feet—almost twice the altitude at which commercial airliners flew—did not appeal to Stirling. He had hung on chutes at high altitudes before, half conscious, stunned by the explosive ejection, freezing, bleeding. Better to ride the airplane down to twenty-five. Still better—to bring it to a landing.

Power. That was the key. Standard procedure was to throttle back in a situation like this, not to propel the aircraft forward in its buffet and spin, not to break it up. On the other hand, with the blowtorches blasting out the rear, the beast might straighten out and fly in one direction, even if that direction was straight down.

11

He decided. He forced his trembling left hand to push the throttles to maximum.

The buffeting increased. The X-41A, caught between the forces of gravity and the power blowing out behind, whipped and yawed. Stirling put his hand on the EJECT switch, ready to go if the wings wrenched off or the fuselage began to disintegrate. But, as he had expected, the plane slowly stabilized—rushing nose-down toward the earth at Mach 3.7—more than twenty-two hundred miles an hour.

"Twenty thousand, sir. Eject!"

"Get out of there, Mac, for Christ's sake!"

Stirling eased the stick back. Very gradually. The wings would come off for sure now if he tried to jerk it up at this speed. The nose came up a little. The airframe groaned under the strain. He eased the stick back a little more.

Theresa Powell stared, frozen to her binoculars. For some time the X-41A had been almost beyond her vision, even through these powerful lenses. She had been following only the flashes of reflected sunlight at the head of its contrail. Now it was rapidly growing in her field of vision, and with horror she realized it was not flying but falling. In the magnified image she had, it seemed to be falling straight at her: tumbling, spinning, obviously totally out of control.

"Oh, my God!" she muttered weakly.

A voice she did not know—it was Sergeant Magruder —began to yell "Eject! Eject, you stupid son of a bitch! *Eject!*"

"Hasn't he ejected yet?" she asked the general.

General Harris shook his head.

Terry Powell heard the emergency siren scream, drowning out even the coarse voice shrieking "Eject!" She watched, not aware that her mouth now hung open. She dropped back weakly against the door of her car. The image of the X-41A grew in the field of her binoculars until it filled them; and finally she put them down, to see the crash—though she might not see it, since her eyes had filled with tears and she had begun to shake with sobs.

The overwhelming roar of huge engines reached them here on the ramp. She forced herself to stare, in renewed horror. The X-41A wasn't tumbling anymore. It was just diving. It was coming down faster than she had ever seen an airplane dive before. And now it was too low for Stirling to eject. Terry closed her eyes and wept.

"Christ-All-Jesus-Mighty!" shouted the general. "He—"

She opened her eyes and saw what he meant. The X-41A was almost level. Then it *was* level. It shot across the base at maybe five thousand feet, maybe ten—who could tell?—at an unbelievable speed. The sonic boom struck her like a fist. Every window in every building on the field shattered and fell in a shower of glass.

The X-41A entered a climbing turn, still flying at three times the speed of sound. It swept out over the desert, and she put the binoculars to her eyes to follow it again. It flew miles and miles away, almost out of sight; and then it turned and settled into an approach for Runway 28. It came in straight and level. Flaps came down. The gear came down. It settled to the runway, touched with a shriek and a puff of smoke, and the drogue chute went out.

"Mrs. Powell," said General Harris. He gestured that she should enter the Mercedes. "Let's go see the man."

Terry Powell wiped her eyes with her sleeve. She nodded dumbly, then found her voice and said, "Yeah. A man who flies like that . . . that's who I came to see."

The sonic boom had cracked the window of her car. As the driver turned and drove back along the line of fighters, she could see it had also cracked canopies and maybe had done structural damage to some of those aircraft. The airfield was chaotic, with some people running around hysterical over the damage and others running to the ramp where the X-41A would taxi in.

The field's emergency trucks surrounded the airplane as Stirling taxied to the ramp. Their foam nozzles were aimed at it. It was strange to see how big the thing was, how it dwarfed the trucks. Its huge engines, throttled back almost to idle now, whistled authoritatively. Her Mercedes was not the only automobile on the ramp. A MARC station wagon with a flashing blue light on top had pulled to a stop beside her. A Porsche Targa came in on the other side.

She stepped out of the Mercedes. General Harris came around the car and stood beside her.

"Let me introduce General Wurst, the director of the center," said General Harris. "And Mr. Sullivan, the president of Consolidated Aeronautical Companies. Gentlemen, this is Mrs. Theresa Powell. She has an appointment with Colonel Stirling today, which I'm afraid he almost missed."

While they were all shaking hands and exchanging pleasantries, the X-41A came to a stop and fell silent as Stirling cut the engines. Terry Powell watched as the mechanics pushed up rolling stairs. In a moment three of them were on top of the plane, opening the canopy, helping Stirling extricate himself from the wires and tubes on the pressure suit. One took his helmet and tossed it down to a mechanic on the ramp. Two lifted him from the seat.

He stepped out on the platform at the top of one of the stairs, and she saw that Colonel Mac Stirling was a red-haired man: compact, not very tall, trim but certainly not athletic of build. She was not certain if his face was pink because of what he had just experienced or if that was the color of his complexion. He ran his hand over his head, possibly to press down his thinning hair; and then he trotted down the steel stairs.

"You're Mrs. Powell?" he said immediately, extending his hand.

"Yes. And very pleased to meet you. For a while I was afraid I wasn't going to."

"Yeah," he grunted. "For a couple of minutes there, I was afraid you weren't going to either."

He was matter-of-fact about what had happened, not grim but certainly not flippant, either. If he had been afraid, it didn't show now. What, she wondered for an instant, had she expected to see? She would not believe this had been just an all-in-a-day's-work kind of thing. She searched his eyes for something she could not find: a residue of terror. It wasn't there.

"We're having lunch, right?" he said to her.

"Yes. Though I don't know where. Nobody seems to be able to suggest any place but the center cafeteria."

Stirling smiled. "I know a place. I'm going to want about eight martinis. Give me about"—he glanced at his watch—"thirty minutes. Have you been shown around? Ralph can give you the VIP tour if you haven't. That's good for about half an hour."

General Wurst and Stephen Sullivan, were pressing close, waiting for a word. Stirling turned to them. "Steve," he said to Sullivan, "if that was you on the horn, telling me the X-41A is scrap metal, kick your own butt. That son of a bitch is an *airplane*. Don't scrap it, fix it."

As she walked away with General Harris, to begin her half hour's tour of MARC, she glanced back at Stirling, who now stood in gesticulating conversation with Wurst and Sullivan. "What kind of man is that?" she asked Harris.

"What you call a professional, Mrs. Powell," said General Harris. "I think that's the compliment he'd like best." The general grinned and added: "One hell of a man, too."

Terry Powell nodded. "One hell of a man," she murmured.

2

"On the house, Colonel. Drinks on the house." The tall, slack-jawed owner of the Silver Wing ("Steaks, Chops & All Legal Beverages") laughed loudly. He grinned at Theresa Powell. "That's the fourth goddamn time this S.O.B. has broken my windows, busted my bar mirror. Fourth goddamn time! And every time he's made history. I don't believe this story, though. Three point . . . Nah! Nobody that's flown that garbage can at 3.7 Mach is sitting here asking for martinis."

"Hot-shot flying makes a man thirsty, Dan," said Stirling.

"Right. On the house. Be right back."

"The place really is damaged," said Terry Powell, looking around. It was true. The big mirror behind the bar was cracked, every window in the place was shattered, and two light fixtures had broken and fallen. "I'm surprised he takes it in such good humor."

"He's paid for his damage, promptly and without argument," said Stirling. "Besides, he only opened the Silver Wing to provide a watering hole for the staff of the aeronautics research center. There aren't three customers in here right now who don't work there. Anyway, Dan's an old airport bum. He's never flown an aircraft in his life, but he's got flying in his blood and has cadged rides in everything from the Wright Flyer to the X-41A."

17

She laughed.

"Actually," said Stirling, "he's been taken up in everything from a Piper Cub to the Grumman Tomcat. I took him up in the Tomcat myself. He knows what Mach 2 is. He's done it."

The previous owner of the Silver Wing had tried, apparently, to re-create an old-fashioned cattle-town saloon as he had picked up the image from movies and television. Dan's dozens of model airplanes, hanging from the ceiling, were in jarring contrast to the mounted animal heads on the walls, the long oak bar, the heavy oak tables and chairs, and the brass light fixtures with green glass shades.

Their host returned, bringing a beer for himself as well as two Beefeater martinis—Stirling's on the rocks, Theresa's up. He sat down with them.

"Seriously speaking, Mac," he said. "I hear you almost bought the farm this morning."

Stirling shook his head. "Ask Mrs. Powell. She saw it."

"Did he?" Dan asked.

"No," she said as she took a sip of her drink. "He was just putting on a flying show for me."

"Yeah, he's always been a showoff," said Dan.

As Dan and Stirling bantered, she took the opportunity to study him more closely. His sandy red hair had retreated a little, giving him a high pink freckled forehead. His sun-bleached brows were almost white against the pink. His eyes were pale blue. His face was square, and his mouth was wide. He was not as tall as she was, by three inches. He was a solid, stocky man, muscular and obviously in good physical condition. He was wearing Levi's, a blue and white checkered cotton

18

shirt, and a khaki nylon windbreaker with COL MC-
DONALD stenciled on the breast with black ink.

She knew his age; he was forty-four, twelve years
older than she was. She knew his marital status: twice
married, twice divorced, no children. He was a career
pilot, but he was also an aeronautical engineer with a
master's degree from the University of Texas. He had
won the Flying Cross and the Silver Star during his two
tours of duty in Vietnam.

In the Mercedes on the way here she had decided he
was the most direct, straightforward man she had ever
met. It was disarming.

"What do they call you?" she asked after Dan had
left the table to return to the bar. "Colonel McDonald
John Stirling. I've heard Mac, Don, and Colonel. What
do you prefer?"

He shrugged. "Call me Mac," he said. "That's what
my friends call me."

"Well, I'm Terry," she said. She raised her glass. "To
you, Mac. I wish Stan could have seen the piece of
flying you did this morning."

"I met Stan a few times," he said. "One hell of a
guy."

"He mentioned you. He'd have liked for you to come
to work for him."

"Yes, I know. He made the offer. I figured Stan and I
would have mixed like oil and water."

"I suspect you're right," she said. "Stan wanted
things done his way. You impress me as a man who
wouldn't do anything anybody else's way."

"You're wrong about that," said Stirling. "I spent
twenty years in the Air Force, tucked into my slot in
one of the world's most rigid hierarchies."

"On the other hand . . ." she suggested with a sly smile.

He nodded. "On the other hand, twenty years was enough."

"You'd have made general by now," she said. "On the other hand . . ."

He laughed. "On the other hand, you spent the morning with one brigadier general and got acquainted, as I understand, with a major general."

"Anyway," she said, more seriously, "Stan had a lot of respect for you. He'd have made you a vice president."

"Another term for brigadier general," said Stirling. "Actually . . . I'm sorry. I'm flattered. I was honored when he made the offer."

Theresa Powell lifted her stem glass and drank the rest of her martini in two quick swallows. "How much do you know about the situation of Powell Industries since Stan's death?" she asked.

"Not a whole lot. What I read in the newspapers. Rumors. I understand you're going to try to revive the Flying Pencil project."

"What do you know about the Flying Pencil?"

Stirling frowned and drew a deep breath. "It was Stan's—"

"Brainstorm. Dream. Revolutionary concept . . ." she said. "I've heard it called all three—and more. He was right a whole lot more often than not. Wasn't he? He was called a fool at every turn in his career."

Stirling nodded. "For sure."

"Well, why was he wrong about this one? He had a lot of faith in this one, Mac."

"Airplanes don't fly on faith," said Stirling. "And

faith doesn't raise the financing companies have to get to make them fly."

"Stan had a record of success. Nobody ever lost money by investing in a project Stanley Powell believed in," she argued.

"That's not exactly true," said Stirling.

"All right," she conceded. "But you know what I mean. People who stuck with him did very well in the long run."

"The Flying Pencil . . ." Stirling mused. "An airplane that's going to look like it's flying backward. Fabric skin. Graphite and epoxy frame. A thousand engineering concepts that haven't been tested. Promises that maybe can and maybe can't be kept." He shook his head. "Stan made things work by his enthusiasm and his powers of persuasion. Without him . . ." He shrugged.

"People who know, people who know a lot about aircraft engineering and the economics of the industry, say it's Stan's most brilliant concept," she said.

"But it's never flown."

She nodded glumly. "Stan died during the taxi tests."

"To inject a new airplane into the business-aircraft market today is a risky proposition at best," said Stirling. "One that's chock-full of radical new ideas—"

"Could make all the difference," she interrupted. "Three hundred fifty knots plus, on half the fuel—"

"*If*—"

"Well, we'll never find out," she snapped, "unless somebody has the guts to take the chance."

"According to the press reports, there's talk of the company scuttling the Pencil," said Stirling.

"Yes. That's what Bob Powell wants to do. Stan's

son. Stan would hardly let Bob in the plants while he was alive. I exaggerate, but it's true that Stan had no confidence at all in Bob, for imagination or skills as an engineer or manager. Now Bob wants to take over the company. And the first thing he wants to do is scrap the Flying Pencil."

"But he doesn't own the company," said Stirling.

"And neither does anybody else," she said. "I'm the largest stockholder, between what Stan gave me while he was alive and what he left me in his will; and Bob is the second largest, with the twenty-five per cent Stan left him. The rest of it is divided among loyal employees who received stock from Stan for their services, some of the old investors, and some banks. None of us can force through a decision about anything. While Stan lived, what he said went. Now . . ." She turned down the corners of her mouth and shrugged.

"What does Bob want?" Stirling asked. "I mean, in the long run. What motivates him?"

"Cash," she said. "Dividends. Maybe a sale. He wants to go on manufacturing the Cirrus as long as possible, taking the profits we can while we can. The Pencil would be a risk, as big a risk as Stan ever took. Bob is not willing to take it."

"And the other stockholders?"

"Some are loyal to Stan's memory and would do anything they thought he wanted. The banks . . . well, you know banks. Right now, it's a standoff. But it's got to come to a head soon. Either we're going to build the Flying Pencil or we're not. The industry won't stand still forever, waiting to see what move Powell is going to make."

"I've read a good deal about this," said Stirling. "In

the *Wall Street Journal,* in *Aviation Week,* and so on. I'm surprised to hear you call the plane the Flying Pencil. I didn't understand the term to be a compliment."

"It's not," said Terry. "Stan hated it. But it's gotten stuck on the project. Stan called it the Nimbus. Flying Pencil is what Bob calls it."

"And so does the aviation press," added Stirling.

"Right." She picked up her glass, looked at the olive drying in the bottom, and frowned. "So you can guess why I've come to see you."

Stirling snapped his finger at the bar. Dan snapped back.

"I think you had better tell me. I wouldn't want to guess and guess wrong."

"I came to offer you an executive position with Powell Industries," she said, looking directly into his eyes.

Stirling nodded. "Why me?"

"I think you would carry enough weight with enough stockholders to commit the company to the Pencil. You know my background, and I hardly need to tell you what some of them think of me. Right now the only weight I carry is that I vote thirty-five per cent of the stock. If you came aboard, evaluated the project, and told the board of directors you believe the Pencil should be built, I think that might be enough to save the project." She paused, sighed. "On the other hand, if you came aboard, evaluated the project, and told me the Pencil was an old man's pipedream, maybe I'd accept that and back down."

"You've got a prototype," said Stirling. "It's built."

She nodded. "Stan got it that far. But it's never

flown. It makes you think of Howard Hughes and the Spruce Goose. It's a project that depended on one man's enthusiasm, and when he died there was no one left with enough faith and clout to carry on with it."

"Who has evaluated it?"

"Nobody. That's another point. No one has flown it. No one has evaluated it but some aviation writers, who have been divided about half and half. Bob doesn't want anyone to get near it—for fear someone might like it too much, I think."

"Stan bet the company on it, right?" asked Stirling.

Terry nodded emphatically. "As he bet it on the Cirrus. That was Stan's way. He bet his career and his personal fortune on things he believed in."

"But when you bet a corporation, you bet other people's careers and fortunes," said Stirling.

"So I'm constantly told," she sneered.

"I've read the specifications," he said. "I mean, I've read what's been published."

"Stan was an enthusiast," said Terry soberly. "I know that. He could get all wild about things. But when he talked about facts and figures, it was different. He said—he told me again when he was dying—that the Pencil can fly at three hundred fifty knots at forty thousand feet, carrying eight passengers and two pilots. It can be manufactured and sold for half the price of one of today's bizjets, and it will burn one-third of the fuel. He didn't get those numbers out of his head; they were from his designers and engineers. It would be *criminal* to let the project die."

Stirling lowered his eyes, grinned, and shook his head. "He made a believer of you, didn't he? He could do that. It was Stan's specialty. That's one of the problems. He ran a very personal operation."

"Do you know Stan's history, Mac? I mean, do you know it all? And mine? Some of it's personal stuff, but I'm willing to tell you if you are interested in betting some of your time and reputation on Stan's last baby."

"Terry, I . . ."

"No commitment from listening," she said.

"All right."

"Stanley Powell wasn't his real name, you know. He was Stanislaus Pawel Bierniacz. On August 20, 1939, when Stan was seventeen, his father decided that a Swiss vacation might be a very good idea for the Bierniacz family. They weren't Jews. In fact, Stan was a faithful Polish Catholic all his life. But his father was nervous about what might happen to Poland if the Polish colonels and Hitler kept on spitting at each other, and he took the family to Switzerland to sit out what he guessed was a coming crisis. He took along as much of his assets as he could and deposited them in Swiss banks. In May of 1940, the Bierniacz family arrived in New York, a family without a country—but a family with money and sponsorship and a warm welcome. Stan's father was a surgeon, and a Boston hospital was glad enough to get him.

"Stan learned English, cast around for an American university where he could complete his education, and had finished a year at Boston College at the time of Pearl Harbor. He enlisted in the army and was sent to Europe to fight the Nazis. Sergeant Stan Bierniacz. He had some romantic idea that he would lead an infantry platoon into his old Warsaw neighborhood, take over the Bierniacz family home, and send word to his parents and sisters to come back to Poland."

Terry stopped, took a sparing sip from her second martini, smiled faintly at Stirling, and shook her head. "I suppose that was typical of the kind of ideas that Stan got into his head, all his life."

"A beautiful idea," said Stirling respectfully.

She sighed. "Yes. Well . . . He came back to the States. He had a Bronze Star. He didn't go back to Boston College. He took his credits to M.I.T. He changed his name, applied for citizenship, and in 1947 he got married to a Boston barmaid. That was another element of Stan's character, Mac. He was in his cups in an Irish bar one night, made a play for the barmaid, was successful—as he always was, with that appealing personality of his—and bedded her secretly, in his students' boardinghouse in Cambridge. She was Bob's mother. It's likely he got her pregnant the night he seduced her."

"Bob was born in . . . ?"

"In 1947. Anyway, being a husband and father didn't slow Stan down. M.I.T. did. He finished his junior year but got interested in something else in his senior year, never finished, and never graduated."

"Flying," said Stirling.

"He had always been fascinated with airplanes," Terry went on. "He went to a field outside Boston with a friend of his to look at a Piper Cub somebody had bought as war surplus. And he flew it. That afternoon. He taxied it up and down the field, tried out the different controls. It seemed simple enough to him, so he shot the power to it and took off."

She stopped to chuckle and sip her drink.

"I wish I had been there to see that," said Stirling.

"Someone told him he was supposed to have a license, so after a while he got one," she went on. "But to Stan anything like lessons and licenses were irrelevant. He drove cars all his life, and I happen to know he never did have a driver's license. He never had an accident and never got a ticket.

"Oh yes, he commonly flew in instrument conditions, but he never had an instrument rating. He dealt with air traffic controllers with such confidence that they never thought to ask him if he was instrument-rated. Later on, of course, they simply assumed the man who manufactured the Cirrus, who was calmly bringing it down through fog and drizzle, surely had the right license to fly the thing."

"Jesus!"

"He wasn't reckless, Mac," she asserted quickly. "He never did anything stupid. I never heard a controller call him for wandering off his assigned heading or altitude. He was a precision flyer, with a perfect natural touch for it. It was just that he never got around to picking up the instrument rating. He never had time."

"One of the reasons the Cirrus is a pilots' favorite," said Stirling, "is that the man who built it flew it. You can feel that when you're at the controls."

"You'll feel it in the Pencil, too, if we ever get it in the air," said Terry.

"You want me to test-fly it, too, I suppose."

"Yes. I want you to fly it." She glanced around. "Can we order a steak? Anyway . . . Stan married Margaret O'Neill in 1947. The marriage stuck for twenty miserable years. Margaret would never have flown without a

27

license. Or driven. Or bet everything she had on something she believed in."

Terry stopped. "No, that's not right. That's a romantic cliché. Let's put it this way and let it go—she was an impediment to him. For twenty years she tried to anchor him to something. At least that's how he told it to me."

"And they were divorced," said Stirling.

"They had Bob and one more child, a girl named Mary. She's a nun, teaches school in Boston. Sister Maria Immaculata. After the divorce, she refused to see Stan. He never saw her the last nineteen years of his life."

"Rough," said Stirling. "Steak rare?" He ordered their steaks by hand signals to Dan. "Is Bob as unforgiving as that?"

Terry shrugged. "He talks tough. About everything. Including his stern Catholic morals. But it's nothing but talk. Reserve judgment until you meet him."

"Okay. Anyway, Stan—"

"Going back to 1947," said Terry. "Stan was obsessed with that Piper Club. He bought a half interest in it for $300 and flew it every time he could, everywhere, all over the Northeast, as far as its range. Of course, it was too slow for him, and pretty soon he sold out and bought an interest in a Fairchild. He borrowed a thousand dollars from Dr. Bierniacz to buy part of that Fairchild, on the understanding he was to find some way to make money with it and repay the loan. His first job with it, he contracted with a hatchery to deliver baby chicks. He'd take off with a thousand peeping little chicks in crates and fly all over, delivering them to country airfields where farmers would pick them up.

Sometimes he'd come back from a trip with crates of lettuce or carrots. Or even eggs. One bumpy landing broke more than two hundred eggs. They were all night cleaning the plane out."

Stirling shook his head. "I never heard any of this."

Terry sipped her drink. "He wasn't born an aircraft manufacturer, big-time entrepreneur," she said.

"The first Powell aircraft I ever heard of was the Twin Beech," said Stirling.

"If you'd been a drinking buddy, you'd have heard about the Cub and the Fairchild," said Terry. "And about the girls who waited for him at the country airfields and gave him quickies while he waited for the farmers to drive over to pick up their chicks. Stan never turned a girl down. Incidentally, he and his partners kept the Fairchild after they bought the Beech, and Powell Aircraft continued to deliver baby chicks until 1955. That airplane smelled so bad inside that pilots wouldn't fly it without a window open. Stan never sold the Fairchild. It still sits in a hangar at the plant. He flew it again once, the year before he died."

"It was a success story from the time they bought the Beech," said Stirling. "Right?"

She sighed. "It's always easy to suppose so when you haven't been a part of something. Stan had to struggle and fight every year of his life, Mac. There was always something—banks, unions, bureaucrats . . . and he saw every frustration as a personal attack."

She finished her second martini. Stirling was a little surprised at how much her reminiscences of Stanley Powell's life seemed to affect her. From what he had read of her, he had gained an impression that Terry was an opportunistic young woman who had married an aging businessman and inherited much of his fortune when he died five years later.

"He might have lived a lot longer if he had been able to lay off a little, take it easy. Well, you know," she went on. "But he couldn't. We had a hell of a five years, Mac. I'll tell you that." She grinned and shook her head. "He played as hard as he fought."

Stirling grinned, too. "There are great stories about him."

"I was his third wife," she said. "After Margaret, there was Lana. Lana was everything Bob thinks I am—a grasping, mercenary bitch, a sexual athlete, a trophy a man can display to prove his prowess in middle age. Lana would have taken everything he had—"

"Except for the accident," Stirling interrupted.

"Except for the accident," she said. "Call me another drink, will you?"

Dan had anticipated. He sent two fresh martinis the moment Stirling looked toward the bar.

"If you take my offer seriously, you're going to hear a lot about me," said Terry.

"You're under no obligation to give me an autobiography," he said. "I'll make my own judgments."

"You know how Stan met me?"

"I've heard the story. Stanley Powell was a very public man."

She poked the olive in her martini with a toothpick, pulled it out, and ate it. "I was a showgirl at The Sands, in Las Vegas. I'd been working there two years, dancing in the chorus you might call it if you want to give it respectability. Actually, all the chorus did was walk around the stage, sort of rhythmically, striking wooden poses. We wore fixed smiles and a few feathers. And, of course, monstrous hats. For some reason, they think it's sexy to have tall girls in the chorus. Well, I'm six feet. I was in demand. I could have moved on to another club anytime."

"You were in *Playboy*—"

"Big deal," she said quickly. "I was at Ohio State, sophomore year—this was 1974—and the guy from the magazine came around to shoot some pictures for one of those things they do with college girls. You know. 'Girls of the Big Ten' this one was called. I had been a beauty contest winner. I was runnerup for Miss Pennsylvania in the Miss America contest. Anyway, posing for *Playboy* was nothing special for me and no big thing. I was glad when they picked one of the shots of me to run in the spread. I was just topless. Really rather modest.

"Anyway, Stan came to The Sands, saw me, and decided he was going to have me. I worked every night, so I agreed to meet him for lunch beside the pool. When he found out I'm Polish—"

"You, too?"

"Sure. I mean, I was born in Pittsburgh and grew up there. But my grandparents are Polish, from Cracow. My family's name is Kielce. I was Theresa Kielce. I gave *Playboy* the name Terry Keel, and that's what I was using at The Sands."

Stirling raised his glass. "Theresa Kielce," he said, toasting her.

"I never changed my name. Legally, that is. Stan changed his in a Massachusetts court. He was officially Powell. And now, so am I."

"How long did you know him before you married him?"

"Ten weeks," she said. "Damnedest ten weeks I ever spent. He didn't have to marry me, of course. I mean, I was sleeping with him anyway. And I didn't get pregnant. He had his own personal Cirrus, you know. Most of the time he flew it himself, but he carried a pilot with him to fly when he wanted to do something else."

"Like drink," suggested Stirling.

She laughed. "Sure. He took me to Acapulco. To Aspen. To New Orleans. To New York. For a while—I wouldn't kid you—it was a fling, just a fling. But as I got to know the man better . . . God, Mac, what a wonderful man he was! When he asked me to marry him—" She shrugged. "I couldn't believe it. We talked a long time about it. I told him I hadn't planned to be a showgirl all my life, and I wasn't interested in being a rich man's trophy or ornament, either. For the time being, maybe. But . . . you understand?"

Stirling nodded.

"Some people can't get over it that I spent some years having a great time and making good money, just showing off my body. Well, what'd God give it to me for?"

"Stan made you a vice president," said Stirling.

She nodded. "After a couple of years. Bob was bitter about that. Stan told him I'd learned more about the business in two years than Bob'd learned in ten. I do know a lot about the business, Mac. I really do. But not enough. And I need an ally."

"To do what?" Stirling asked bluntly.

"To see the Pencil fly. And make money. To prove Stan was right."

Stirling lifted his glass, sipped from it, then held it

before his face for a long moment and frowned over it. "And . . . ? You've got more in mind than that."

Her expression hardened. "Stan was right about something else," she said, fixing her eyes coldly on his. "Theresa Kielce is a lot more than a naked showgirl."

"Uhmm . . ." Stirling agreed. He sipped again from his martini. "Smart. Ambitious."

"So?"

"So we understand each other," he said with an amiable smile.

"I can make you a vice president," she said. "I'm sure the board will go along. Even Bob Powell might agree to it."

"Let's go at it in stages, Terry," said Stirling solemnly. "Let's sell your board the idea of giving me a contract to test-fly the Pencil. If it flies—"

"It'll fly," she said firmly. "If I could, I'd fly it myself. I'm not afraid of it."

Stirling sighed, nodding. "Okay. I'm sure it will fly. But will it give us anything like the performance Stan expected? We can't go to the banks for the financing unless we've demonstrated its market feasibility, and we can't determine that without a series of test flights. Let's see if we can get a deal to test it. I want to bring it over here to the center. I'll fly it from here."

"It'll fly," she insisted. "Just like Stan said it would."

"We'll see," said Stirling. "Nobody ever flew one like it before."

3

THE MAIN PLANT and executive offices building of Powell Industries, Incorporated was some fifty miles from the Mojave Aeronautical Research Center. It was in the same desert, though nearer concentrations of human habitation, since Powell had not yet experimented with supersonic aircraft whose sonic booms would damage homes and businesses. The town was, in fact, called Powell, California; it had grown up to provide housing and amenities for the employees of Powell Industries.

Stirling arrived there the next morning, flying across in a Beechcraft Bonanza that MARC made available to its test pilots for short trips. The silver Mercedes, still with a cracked windshield, was waiting on the ramp. Terry Powell was waiting, dressed this morning very much the way she had been yesterday, in tight blue jeans and a sweat shirt, this one gray.

"It's in Hangar One," she said. "It hasn't been announced yet that you are here. Or that you are coming."

"Any problem?" he asked.

Terry shrugged. "With this company, everything's a problem. I've heard some of them argue about who gets to piss in what pot."

Stirling wore a dark blue nylon windbreaker this morning, with a MARC patch on the left sleeve. His eyes were covered by dark sunglasses. His pants were khakis. He could have been any MARC pilot.

Terry stopped the Mercedes at the closed doors to a big hangar. It was early. The sun was up, but very few workmen were about. She was out of the Mercedes almost before it stopped and strode ahead of Stirling, toward the security shack at the entry to the hangar.

The security guard was half asleep in the shack. She gave his door a kick.

"Hey! Who the hell are you?"

"You better know who the hell I am, my sleepy friend," she snapped. "Who's your supervisor?"

"What the hell business is that of yours?"

She gave the guard a shove, pushed into his shack, and picked up his telephone. "Security! Get somebody's ass to Hangar One on the double. This is Terry."

"Uh . . . you Mrs. Powell?"

"Right on, Rip van Winkle."

"Nobody could'a got by me."

She grinned. "True. Open the goddamn doors, Laker," she said, reading his name from his uniform badge. "And ass on the ball here after. Right?"

"Eyeballs like two ice cubes, Mrs. Powell," the young blond guard promised.

"Deal," she said. "Switch on the lights."

The big doors rolled back, admitting the morning sunlight into the hangar and the lights came on overhead, killing the shadows and filling the endless space of the outsized building with white light. There were ten or more airplanes inside, some with ladders up to them, some with cowlings open and parts lying about.

35

One of them, sitting toward the front, where it was receiving service on its radar, was a Cirrus, the business jet that was the mainstay of Powell Industries.

Sitting toward the rear of the hangar, a little out of the light and traffic but dramatically unique and unmistakable, sat the Flying Pencil.

Stirling had seen pictures, so he was not much surprised by the appearance of it. It was smaller than his image of it had suggested: less than forty feet from nose to tail, with even less wingspan. It was sleek and gleaming white, with no markings whatever: no stripes, no deltas, no logo, only an aircraft registration number on the wings and vertical fin. The wings were straight and thin, not swept back as they were on so many high-performance aircraft. A small stabilizer slanted up and out from each wingtip, as if someone had seized each wingtip between thumb and index finger and bent it up.

The position of the horizontal stabilizers and elevators was a conspicuous departure from conventional design; they were at the front—where the Wright brothers had put them on the Wright Flyer—and angled up at 20 degrees. The vertical fin and rudder stood in the conventional position, a bit forward of the tail.

What was radical was the power system. The Flying Pencil had four sleek pods on its fuselage, equidistant around the rearward quarter, just forward of where the horizontal stabilizers would have been on more conventional aircraft. At first glance they looked like small jet engines. But they were only intake-exhaust ports for two big turbo engines encased in the rear of the fuselage. Connected by shafts and a transmission, they drove a huge six-bladed propeller on the tail. That was how the Wrights had powered the Flyer: with pusher propellers toward the rear of their airplane. That was how most jets flew: by pushing the aircraft forward instead of pulling it by the nose. Stan Powell had returned to basics, in some ways.

It was called the Flying Pencil because the basic component was not aluminum, as it was on ninety-nine per cent of the airplanes in service, but a graphite-epoxy composite that had tested stronger than aluminum, at a fraction of its weight. Graphite. The "lead" in pencils was graphite. The Flying Pencil.

Why graphite? Why the pusher propeller? Why the whole odd configuration, why a radically different airplane?

Stirling had studied Stanley Powell's engineering projections, sent to him by messenger from Terry, and if they were correct, the Flying Pencil would carry eight passengers and two pilots at a cruising speed a little above four hundred miles an hour. Its cruising range was fourteen hundred miles. It could, for example, carry eight businessmen from New York to Chicago in roughly an hour and forty-five minutes.

The typical business jet could make the same flight in twenty minutes less. So what was the appeal of the Flying Pencil? Very simple. If the projections were correct, the Pencil could be manufactured to sell for less than two million dollars—compared to three or three-and-a-half million for the comparable bizjet. What was more, on the New York–Chicago round trip, the Pencil would burn $520 less fuel than the bizjet. In the course of a year, when the average bizjet flew a quarter of a million miles, the Pencil would fly the same distance on $92,000 less fuel.

Why? How? Because the graphite-epoxy Pencil would weigh less than half the weight of the aluminum business jet, and its twin in-line turbine engines would operate at an efficiency unheard-of for conventional jets.

Transatlantic flights? No way. (Few bizjets could do it, either.) Coast-to-coast, non-stop? Again, no way. But Stan Powell had estimated that ninety per cent of all business flying involved distances within the range of the airplane he wanted to call the Nimbus. Why, he had argued, buy a jet for twice the money, burning almost three times the fuel, when the plane would get you from New York to Chicago, or from Washington to St. Louis, in only twenty minutes more?

And there it sat: the Nimbus, the Flying Pencil, never yet flown because its designer and builder had died during taxi tests, before it ever lifted off the ground—and, if Terry Powell was right, because the shortsighted managers who had been left behind by Stanley Powell were afraid to risk what it would take to make it fly, get government certification, and manufacture it.

Somehow, it looked like an *airplane:* sleek, low, powerful, like a brilliantly designed flying machine, impatient with sitting on the ground, just begging someone to take it into the air.

Stirling walked around the Pencil, still fascinated by its small size. Under the tail, a skid extended on a rod some six feet long. It was there to prevent the pilot from over-rotating—that is, pulling the nose up too sharply on takeoff—so lowering the tail too much and hitting the propeller on the runway; and it would retract when the landing gear were retracted. Walking on around, he noticed that the turbine exhaust would shoot back into the arc of the propeller. He wondered how that would affect performance. It was something to watch for when the plane was tested.

He touched the fuselage and wings. The graphite-epoxy skin was actually a sort of cloth woven of fiber; still, it felt as hard and rigid as aluminum. He had pressed hard on the surfaces of planes like the marvelous Bellanca Viking and had felt the stiffened fabric yield. The graphite-epoxy fabric did not yield.

Even the internal structure of the airframe was made of this material, layered and bonded. That was why Stan Powell's Nimbus weighed less than four thousand pounds sitting here empty, while the empty Cirrus sitting not far away probably weighed ten thousand. It was difficult to believe that this little airplane could get you—and nine other passengers—to San Francisco in forty-five minutes while the forceful-looking Cirrus would take only fifteen minutes less.

He wondered if it could really do it. It was an exciting idea.

As Stirling had walked around the Pencil, Terry had spoken with the security supervisor and exonerated the young guard. She stood now just ahead of the nose of the plane, staring pensively at its handsome lines. One of the hangar mechanics stood beside her, talking quietly. She nodded.

"Mac," she said when Stirling completed his circuit

of the plane. "I'd like you to meet Bill Carey. He was with Stan for twenty years, and he's been telling me something about the Nimbus."

The mechanic shook Stirling's hand. "Engines haven't been fired up in three months," he said. "If we don't—"

"I know what you mean," Stirling said. "You'll begin to get corrosion."

"And worse," Carey said. "Right now, I'd want about five hours to get 'er ready. I wouldn't want you to fly 'er, Colonel, until I've looked inside every inspection panel, checked every control rod and cable, run through the operation of every system. If she sits here much longer . . ." He shrugged.

"Beautiful thing," Stirling said pensively.

"It'll do everything Stan promised it would," said Carey. "If it ever gets a chance."

"I read you," said Stirling. "I'm beginning to believe it. Anyway, it'd be fun to find out."

"Want to look in the cockpit?" Carey asked.

Stirling nodded, and they walked around the plane to the wooden stairs that led up to the wide door behind the cockpit. Carey unlatched the door and swung it up, and Stirling stepped inside.

The passenger cabin was configured with three wide, deep seats in line across the aft bulkhead, faced by two separate executive chairs, on the two sides of the aisle. All the upholstery was of dark blue plush. A sixth full seat stood back-to-back with one of the executive chairs and faced the bulkhead separating the passenger cabin from the cockpit. There were two more seats: a jump seat inside the door and a seat that folded over to uncover the toilet—which could be isolated from the rest of the cabin by pulling a ceiling-mounted curtain across it. The cabin also contained a microwave oven and a refrigerator, mounted over and under a small counter, and a square desk or eating table for the five passengers at the rear.

"Uh . . . Mac." Terry had stepped inside. "We've got visitors."

Through the cabin windows he could see two men in business suits striding purposefully across the hangar floor.

"Bob Powell," said Terry.

Stirling stepped outside and down the stairs in time to meet the two men as they came around the nose of the Nimbus.

"Terry—"

"Good morning, Bob," she cut him off. "Here's someone I'd like you to meet. Colonel McDonald Stirling."

Powell, who had been unsubtle about his annoyance as he hurried into the hangar, abruptly smiled warmly and extended his hand. "Well, Colonel Stirling," he said. "This is a pleasure. Terry didn't tell me you'd be here this morning. We'd have received you for coffee and had some of the engineers come along to show you the Flying Pencil. Let me introduce Lou DiAngelo."

If the son had not inherited Stanley Powell's best qualities, he had at least inherited another for which Powell had been well known: his disarming cordiality. He was forty years old but looked fifty. The graying hair was gone from his forehead, and he wore rather long and very full bushy sideburns. His face was tanned. His dark eyes, under heavy black brows, shone with the appearance of friendly good humor. Dressed

41

like a Harvardian, he had the appearance of a Wall Street lawyer or banker—and Stirling had no doubt he cultivated exactly that look.

DiAngelo was a tall, swarthy Italian, with a blue beard under his skin, darkening his newly shaved face. He shook hands without a word, with a reserved smile.

"Looking at Dad's brainchild?" Powell asked.

Stirling nodded. "Interesting airplane," he said.

Powell looked up at the Nimbus. "Damned interesting," he said. "My father put thirty-five million dollars in building what you see sitting here. Did you know my father, Colonel Stirling?"

"I met him a couple of times," said Stirling.

"An enthusiast," said Powell, casting a glance up at the polished nose of the Nimbus. "From a different era. If he developed an enthusiasm, he followed it—no matter what the risk or cost. This was the last one. An enthusiasm."

"So was the Cirrus, though, I suppose," said Stirling, nodding toward the big, shiny business jet sitting at the front of the hangar. "As I recall, they told him that one couldn't be done either: I mean, the original Powell bizjet."

"They told him he couldn't pay for an airplane by flying baby chicks from the hatchery to the farmers," said Terry.

"And he didn't, either," said Powell darkly. "He liked to tell that story, but the truth is that my grandfather subsidized the old Fairchild with his earnings from the practice of surgery."

"Anyway," said Stirling, breaking off that line of conversation, "the Nimbus is an impressive aircraft."

42

Powell nodded. "If we put another hundred million in it, we might—I emphasize *might*—have a business." He sighed heavily. "Which might, of course, kill the market for the Cirrus, which is the only aircraft that is making money for Powell Industries."

"The Cirrus killed the PO-35," said Terry. "Powell Industries competed with itself—and of course with others—by putting the Cirrus in the air. And the Cirrus became the mainstay of the fleet, making more money than the PO series ever did. Stan saw the Cirrus as his response to the changing technology of corporate aircraft—and that's how he saw the Nimbus, too."

"Yes. So he said," Powell agreed. "The problem always was that my father never analyzed the market—or the state of the economy or the international situation or the tax consequences or anything else. He saw the engineering principles, plus what he *guessed* the market might want—"

"And earned what you and I inherited," interjected Terry.

Powell nodded. "More often right than wrong. *In his era.*" He stopped and smiled. "Let me ask you, Colonel Stirling: Have you ever heard of the Powell Bug?"

"Bug?"

Powell nodded. "For his every success there was a failure. Maybe two failures. Maybe three. He was a genius. God, I'll never deny that. But he let his enthusiasms run wild."

"Bob . . ." protested Terry.

Powell smiled and put an arm around Terry's waist. "Here's one of his enthusiasms, Colonel Stirling." He smiled up into her face; Terry was four inches taller than he was. "I guess the best one he ever had. Any man who had the smarts to see the qualities in Terry Keel was an intelligent man."

"Put some stress on the word *man*, Bob," she said.

"Right," said Powell, not visibly offended. "If she weren't my stepmother, Colonel Stirling . . . well, you get my meaning. Jesus! Making money was Dad's smallest talent."

Stirling forced a smile. "Anyway, Mr. Powell, what is the plan for the Nimbus?"

Powell drew a deep breath. "Uh . . . call me Bob, Colonel. Uh . . . what's your best estimate of what it would take, in dollars, to get it certified, market it, and initiate manufacturing?"

"You spoke of a hundred million," said Stirling. "That might not be too far off."

"We haven't got it," Powell said flatly.

"On the security of this prototype—"

"No," interrupted Powell. "On the security of that beautiful airplane that stands in front of us, we couldn't raise a dime. We could raise the hundred million on the credit of Powell Industries. And if the Pencil failed, Powell Industries would be broke. That's the problem, Colonel Stirling. That's the problem I've explained to Terry. But she learned her business sense from my father and sees it differently. God, she's a honey! But she just doesn't see the business prospects in a realistic way."

Stirling turned away from Powell and looked at the Nimbus. "Would you sell it, then?" he asked. "If a group of investors—"

"*Colonel Stirling,*" Powell interrupted. He shook his head. "Suppose Dad was right? Suppose Terry's right?

The Pencil could kill the Cirrus—along with half the market for Lears, Cessna Citations, and all the rest of the bizjets." He grinned. "If we can't fund it ourselves, we'd be fools to let somebody else try it. Does that sound cynical?"

"Totally," said Stirling.

"Business," said Powell. "Anyway, we are not un-imaginative here at the new Powell Industries. We have another project in mind that will make more money than the Pencil ever possibly could—and it's not competitive. I'd like you to take a look at that, Colonel Stirling."

They walked into Hangar Two.

"Recognize them, Colonel Stirling?" Powell asked.

Sitting in the huge building, in various stages of disassembly, were six old North American F-86 Sabres.

"I bet you've flown one of those," said Powell.

Stirling nodded. Yes, he had flown more than one of those. Introduced late in 1947 as one of the first operational American jet fighters, the Sabre had shot down an astonishing number of MiGs over Korea. Amazing. He had been a toddler when the Sabres entered service; still, he had trained in them in the 1960s. They were subsonic, but just. They had been tough, serviceable fighters in their day.

"Walk over here," said Powell.

He led Stirling and Terry to a corner of the big hangar. There, being worked on, was a bright new small aircraft, polished and striped and painted with the logo MINK BAT. It carried two small bizjet engines on the rear quarter of its fuselage, and the nose ended in a long, pointed antenna.

45

"Guess what's inside," said Powell.

"You're going to tell me a Sabre," said Stirling.

Powell nodded and beamed proudly. "New engines. A new configuration of some of its external surfaces. But the basics are an F-86 Sabre: airframe, wings . . . all the basic structure. Forty years old, almost. They made them of aluminum in those days, and very strong and durable. Some of the newer fighters, made of sophisticated metals, can triple the Sabre's performance; but they are junk after twenty thousand hours' flight. A Sabre has unlimited life if you take care of it. And that's what's inside the Mink Bat."

Stirling walked around the gleaming, buffed little aircraft. What Powell said was true: The basic configuration of an F-86 Sabre was inside this sleek new plane. The old nose hole was closed, because air for the engines would enter through their own scoops, not through the nose of the aircraft; and the way the wings were faired to the fuselage had been modified a little in anticipation of new performance requirements.

"The whole rear third of the fuselage used to be full of engine," said Powell. "Now that the engines are outside, half as big and developing twice the power, we put fuel tanks back there."

"Not all of them," said Stirling.

"Oh, no. That would make it tail-heavy. There's a tank in the nose, together with today's more sophisticated electronics, and of course tanks in the wings. It balances out very well."

"Which makes it . . . ?"

"Basically, a trainer for the pilots of Third World countries," said Powell. "Countries that have the money to buy Mirages but don't have the pilots to fly them. Pilots can learn high-performance jet flying in the Mink Bat, which their countries can buy for a small fraction of the cost of a Mirage or F-15; and when they come to the big airplane, they'll be ready. Also, if they want it, the Bat can be equipped with machine guns, cannon, rocket launchers, or even bomb racks. For counterinsurgency work."

Stirling put a hand to the fuselage of the Mink Bat. "Impressive," he said.

"We have a market for them," said Powell. "A ready market. There are people who suggest we are sitting on our butts, waiting for lightning to strike." He nodded at the Mink Bat. "There's the immediate future of Powell Industries, as far as I'm concerned. We've got one ready to fly, Colonel, if you'd like to try it."

"What I'd like to fly is the Nimbus," said Stirling.

Powell shrugged. "It would cost a great deal to put it in condition even to sustain a test flight," he said.

"Stan had seen it through taxi tests," said Terry. "It—"

"I'm not sure of this," said Powell, "but I suspect my father actually had it in the air. I think he flew it one Sunday evening—one time around the pea patch, as they say. I have no doubt it will fly, Terry. What I very sincerely doubt is its commercial feasibility. And proving that is not just a matter of a test flight or two."

DiAngelo spoke for the first time. "FAA certification tests would cost millions," he said.

Terry flushed. "Stan believed the Nimbus would put the company in the forefront of general aviation for the next twenty years," she said.

Powell turned down the corners of his mouth, raised his brows, and nodded. "It might," he said. "It just might. But we'd have to bet the company to find out. Dad was willing. I'm not."

"Fortunately, Bob," said Terry angrily, "you don't run the company."

Powell remained smooth. "But I think the board of directors will go along with my judgment. Anyway, Terry, you can put it to them again, anytime you want to. They've tabled your motion—what?—a dozen times? The board's not ready to bet the company, either. I don't see that anything has changed."

"We'll see about that," said Terry.

4

"Where's that million-dollar automobile of yours, man?"

Stirling squirmed on his bar stool at the Silver Wing, trying to settle his backside a little more comfortably into the vinyl-covered foam rubber.

"Fuck subtlety, Dan," he said. "I know what you're talking about."

"You care?"

Stirling drew his breath deep, his chest swelling, his shoulders squaring. "Sure I care," he said. "What the shit? But I'll live."

"What's more important, the Porsche or the cowgirl?" Dan asked.

Stirling reached across the bar and picked up the martini the bartender had just mixed for him. "That's a highly personal question, my man," he said. He reached, too, for a handful of peanuts. "She been in?"

"Yeah, 'round noon. Hung around and waited for you. Went off and came back about two-thirty. Asked if you were back from Powell. You wasn't, so she said she figured you were gettin' your rocks off over there, so she wouldn't wait for you. Tossed some gravel when she shot that car off the lot and onto the road."

"She burns out my transmission, I'll burn out hers," said Stirling.

" 'Member the ol' song, Mac? Went—

"Shagged her once, shagged her twice,
Shagged her once too often,
Broke the mainspring in her ass,
And now she's in her coffin."

Stirling grinned. "Not exactly what I had in mind."

"No. You're a *gentleman*. An' you're bein' *had.*"

"I'm gettin' what I want, Dan. Don't worry about it."

"Okay, Mac. But you get tired of it and still want everything you're gettin' and more, jus' let me know. I can set up somethin' for you that'll be a hell of a lot less pain."

Stirling nodded. "'Kay, Dan. I'll keep it in mind."

He had spent the morning touring the Powell Industries facilities. Robert Powell and Louis DiAngelo had never left his side throughout the morning. It was only at lunch that he had been able to have a private conversation with Terry Powell. They had agreed that he would write a letter from Mojave Aeronautical Research Center to Powell Industries, proposing that Powell grant a contract to MARC for a series of test flights of the Nimbus. When that letter arrived, she would arrange a meeting of the board of directors, at which he was to appear and present the proposition.

He had not made it back for lunch with Bettyne at the Silver Wing, and he had expected she'd be pissed. It had been two-thirty before he took off from Powell, three-thirty before he checked in at MARC, four-thirty by the time he got out of there. Here it was five o'clock when he finally got to Dan's. He wasn't surprised she had driven off in his Porsche, in bad temper.

Bettyne had a short fuse. The fact was, she valued

herself highly, and she demanded faithful attention. His own appraisal of her was that she didn't have much to be proud of in this world except how she looked and what she offered to men, and anything that depreciated that was a threat to her. He had kept that in mind in the six months she had lived with him, and it had been a warm yet exciting time, for which he was grateful.

They had gotten along well, generally, because she was young, beautiful, erotically imaginative and vigorous, and glad to be seen in the company of Colonel McDonald Stirling; and he had received what she gave with genuine gratitude and constant praise. He had enjoyed showing her off at Dan's and around the tidy little community of airplane people that dominated this part of California. He knew what people said, how they speculated about him and Bettyne. Everything they guessed was true.

He was driving her car, a 1978 Chevy. As usual, she had his Porsche Targa, about forty-thousand dollars worth of sports car. He left the Silver Wing about five and set off for home in the smoky Chevy.

He could have lived in a better place. Bettyne had argued repeatedly that "we"—as she persisted in putting it—should buy one of the condominiums in the complex where General Harris lived, where they would have access to the condo swimming pool and tennis courts. She talked about having a cocktail party for the generals, test pilots, and engineers from MARC, in "our" new condo—as soon as they moved in. He hadn't told her he wouldn't buy a condo. He hadn't called the agent, either.

He liked the place he had. It was not a condo but a house, and it had the features he regarded as essential:

air conditioning that worked, sufficient distance between him and his neighbors that they would not complain if he had a loud party, a landlord who never called or came around so long as he got his rent on time, a big kitchen, a big master bedroom, a big, western-style living room, plenty of room for clutter. He had plugged around the world with the Air Force for twenty years, and this was as good quarters as he had ever had. He could afford better, but this little brick-and-stucco house was comfortable.

Three dogs were playing in the middle of the street when he turned the corner with the Chevy. No trees broke the dry and desolate character of Joshua Street. No one tried to grow grass. Some people watered shrubs and kept them lush and green so the neighborhood dogs could identify them and know where to lift their legs.

A pickup truck was parked just around the corner on Sequoia Street. The green Ford, the one he had seen before. Stirling parked the Chevy at the curb and walked up the unpaved driveway past his Porsche. He opened it and took the keys from the ignition. No matter how many times he told her, she still left the keys in the car. He walked around the house to the back door and opened it quietly.

"Ah hearn somethin'," a male voice said.

"Eddy . . . Ed-dy. You're always hearin' somethin'. This stuff makes you hear things."

Eddy laughed. "Yeah," he agreed. "What I never hearn b'fore."

Bettyne laughed. It was one of her things, that throaty, suggestive laugh.

They were in his bedroom. Stirling walked through the kitchen and into the living room, then into the hall that led to the bedrooms and bathroom. The bedroom door was open. They sat naked on his bed.

They didn't see him. They were so occupied that they did not notice him in the hall outside. They had lines of coke laid out on a plate; and just as Stirling reached the door and was there to watch, Eddy sniffed through the straw in his nostril and drew up part of a line of the white powder. He arched his back and grunted with satisfaction. Bettyne laughed.

Half angry and yet half amused, Stirling stood with his hands on his hips, waiting for them to become aware that he was staring at them.

He would miss Bettyne—and that was what he was going to do: miss her. She was a rare one. Her blond hair hung around her shoulders and lay on her forehead in bangs. She had big breasts and big shiny nipples. Her pubic hair was dark, as were her eyebrows and lashes, but there was not much of it; she kept it trimmed short and shaved off all of it but a narrow central stripe. Her belly and butt were flat; her legs were long and trim. She was really put together.

Eddy was tall and very thin. His body was hard, hairless, and smooth. It was oddly white, showing that he never hung around the swimming pools Bettyne thought were so important, never exposed any of himself to the sun except his deeply tanned arms and face. He was hung, too. His thick, circumcised penis stood erect out of his blossom of sandy hair, maybe eight inches, maybe more.

"C'mon," she urged impatiently.

Eddy bent forward. *"Man!"* he grunted.

She laughed again. "Okay, huh?" She drew back her shoulders and arched her back. "Aw-*right!*"

"Aw-right," he murmured.

"So let's get to it, buddy. Ain't got all night. I gotta get back to Dan's before the ol' man decides I'm not comin'."

It was odd, how she talked to the cowboy. She lowered herself to his level, even in her accent and inflection. ("Ain't got all naat.") Stirling had sometimes heard a faint residue of this, when she got excited or a little drunk and did not control herself. But she had never let him hear anything like what he heard now.

"'Kay," said Eddy. "Lick me up a li'l, hon. Get me goin'."

"You bastard," she muttered, but she went down on him readily enough, grabbing his big shaft in her hands and thrusting it into her mouth. She moved up and down on it, holding it tight in her lips, moving fast, grunting. "C'mon now," she said after a moment, as she pulled away and rolled over. "You come in my mouf agin, I'm gonna cut that son of a bitch off."

Stirling hesitated to interrupt. The more he heard from her and the more he saw, the easier this break was going to be. Anyway, it was hard to believe they could go on and still not notice him standing there at the door.

Eddy rose on his hands and knees. "'Kay," he said. "Grab ahold it there."

She helped him guide it into her, and as he lowered his hips onto hers she moaned and lifted her breasts in both hands. He took the cue and began to suck her nipples as he drove himself into her as deep as he could and she thrust upward to get as much of him as she could. Both of them grunted, and they rolled and pitched with his strokes.

Eddy's anus was lifted toward the bedroom door. His hairless white ass looked like the belly of a fish, except that it was marked by three or four pink pimples. His big brownish scrotum swung around violently. Sweat gleamed on his backside and legs. Stirling's thought was that he would have to wash and dry the bedclothes before he went to bed tonight.

He supposed this was how it looked when *he* did it with her—something like this—and if it was, he was glad no one had ever watched. At least she didn't talk like that. And didn't grunt.

And maybe didn't have as much fun.

He was not angry. Not really, not much beyond annoyance. But he'd seen enough.

"*Ed-dy!* Ooh, Jee-zuss Kee-rist! Oh Gawd, don't stop! Bang it to me, man! *Bang it,* goddamnit!"

Stirling could almost laugh. "Yeah, Eddy," he said. "Bang her good."

"*Jesus Christ!* Hey, man!" Eddy scrambled to his knees and backed toward the head of the bed, jerking at the sheet, trying to cover himself. "Hey, man. Cool it! Lak, I mean, hey man, it ain't nothin' lak—"

"Shut up, Eddy," said Stirling coldly. "Bettyne. Get up. You've got about two minutes to clear out of here."

"Mac . . ." she shrilled. "Mac, for God's sake!"

Stirling reached into his pocket with his left hand, pulled out her car keys, and tossed them toward her. She didn't reach to catch them, and they hit her belly and fell to the floor.

"Good-bye, Bettyne," he said coldly. "Your Chevy's on the street. I put a tank of gas in it this morning. And that's it. The deal's over. Get moving."

Eddy had grabbed for his jeans and was shoving his legs into them. "Hey, man. Don't get hard-nosed," he sneered. "Tough nookies, y' know."

"Yeah, Mac," said Bettyne. She reached for her panties and began to pull them on lazily, in no great hurry. "I mean, you know . . . things happen. Tomorrow—"

"There isn't going to be any tomorrow," said Stirling firmly. "I told you. You've got about two minutes to grab your junk and get out of here."

Eddy stepped menacingly toward Stirling. "Hey, ol' buddy," he growled. "Don't talk mean to the lady. You ain' man enough to play big, bad daddy." He shoved his face toward Stirling's, pressing forward to make Stirling back away.

Without a word, Stirling drove a fist into Eddy's solar plexus; and as the cowboy gasped and staggered, Stirling slammed a knee into his crotch. As Eddy bent double, Stirling struck him again with a fist to the ear. Eddy fell against the wall and slid to the floor, stunned and retching.

"Get your clothes on and get out, Bettyne."

"Mac, for Christ's sake!" Bettyne sobbed. "Mac . . . Jesus, honey, you can't *do* this!"

"It's done," snapped Stirling. "Just get dressed and get out. I'll drop the rest of your stuff at Dan's."

"Honey, honey . . ."

"*Go*, Bettyne! Fun's over."

* * *

56

He found more cocaine in the bathroom. She'd had quite a supply of it. He flushed it down the toilet. He put the bedclothes in the washer.

Everything she owned that she had not grabbed and taken with her he stuffed into two shopping bags. It was pitifully little, he realized, as he pulled it from the drawers and closet and jammed it in the bags. Except for a couple of skirts and sweaters and a cocktail dress he had bought her, her possessions were all tawdry: pants and shirts grabbed off the racks in discount stores, a lot of costume jewelry, not a piece of it worth ten dollars. (He'd given her an emerald ring, which she had been wearing when she left.) Her cosmetics . . . dime-store stuff. Pitifully little.

He kept five hundred dollars cash in the house, and on impulse—because she had been good for him for a while, after all—he decided to put it in one of the shopping bags. But when he went to get it, it was gone. She had helped herself already, God knew when.

He drove to Dan's Silver Wing. He left the two shopping bags with the cook in the kitchen, then went around front and walked to the bar.

"You say you got a girl for me, Dan?" he asked when he was settled on his usual stool.

"Uh-oh! You and the cowgirl . . ."

Stirling nodded. "I'm a free man, my friend."

"You always were, Colonel," said Dan, grinning. "Well, you know Valerie. She always has cottoned to you."

"You can spare her?"

Dan shrugged. "Sure. A little later. Let me get happy hour out of the way."

"I want to buy her a steak," said Stirling. "I want somebody to talk to over dinner."

An understanding frown crossed Dan's face. "Sure thing," he said. "I'll tell her. You know, she's gonna be real pleased."

Stirling knew Valerie. He had traded little jokes with her. She worked behind the bar most of the time, though sometimes she filled in as a waitress. Dan wouldn't have employed her if she had been inhibited, but it had amused Stirling to see her blush. He could make her blush, and more often she made herself blush, by blurting out the bold and sometimes coarse quips her quick wit constantly produced. She had long mousy-brown hair, full dark eyebrows, a thin nose, a tiny mouth with thin lips, and a full figure always boldly displayed in the tight red T-shirts Dan provided all his barmaids and waitresses.

"Thought you'd never ask," she said as she pushed a Beefeater martini toward him. She would work behind the bar a while yet, but she made a point of serving him herself. "I mean, you know I was interested."

"I had a problem," he said.

"That's what I'd call her," said Valerie.

Shorty Bellows—the pilot who had flown chase for him yesterday—climbed onto the next barstool. "You looked at the data from the X-41A?" he asked. "If you haven't, don't do it before dinner."

"Almost bought it, didn't I?" Stirling asked.

"It's scrap metal. Like Sullivan said. Everything was coming loose. I mean, Mac, it looks like ten ounces more strain on any component would have broke her apart. You're damn lucky, man. Take my advice, hero. The next time somebody yells 'Eject!' you by God eject."

Stirling lifted his drink. "It wasn't good judgment," he said. "I'm getting too old for that kind of work."

"Shit. You used the same kind of judgment twenty years ago. But you're gonna buy it if you go on like that."

"I still say it's an airplane," said Stirling. "It *didn't* break up, under a hell of a lot more punishment than it was designed to take. It's got a design flaw. Fix it and you've got a competent machine, one of the most competent I've flown in a long time."

"What was that? The third time the X-41A almost killed you?"

"Three design flaws, three fixes," said Stirling, tossing back the last of his martini. "That's what testing is for."

"The trouble with you, Mac, is that you fall in love with airplanes," said Shorty.

"I've always had better judgment about planes than I have with women."

By the time Valerie could get away from the bar and accompany him to one of the booths at the back side of the room, Stirling had drunk two more martinis. He was in a half-euphoric state, infected with a fuzzy optimism that suggested to him that all was right with the world, except what wasn't, and that could be easily fixed.

Valerie's boobs—which was the word for them that imposed itself on his mind right now—looked especially

59

pretty: round and soft and youthful. The red T-shirt was lettered in white—DAN'S above a pair of air force wings, SILVER WING below. Her boobs thrust the wings out and distorted them.

"I'm glad you didn't kill yourself yesterday," she said. She had carried a draft beer from the bar and sipped it as she smiled at him. "You're a day older and a day wiser."

"Wiser . . ." he mused. "Don't be a wise-ass. I mean, don't shoot me any more zingers about—"

"That's a deal," she said. "So forget it."

"Anyway, you're not so smart yourself. If you were, you'd get up and walk away from me."

"Is that what you want me to do?"

Stirling smiled and shook his head. "Hell, no." He went on shaking his head. "Hell, no, Val."

She reached across the table and put her hand on his. "Want a steak?" she asked. "Rare?" He nodded, and she gave Dan the sign.

"How long have you been around here?" Stirling asked her.

"I was born here," said Valerie. "I've been as far west as L.A., as far east as Vegas. That's me. I'm a high-school graduate, and I'm twenty-eight years old. I have clean habits, don't smoke, and don't drink much. I go to church about once a month. I give head if I like a guy well enough, and . . ." She stopped. Her face turned red. "And I talk too much."

He squeezed her hand. "So do I," he said. "But it all sounds good."

Her face remained flushed. "Well, that's me," she said quietly. "Also, I need glasses to see across the room—that is, if I want to see clearly." She opened her purse and took out a pair of shell-rimmed spectacles, which she seated on her nose. "Cute, huh?"

"Yeah," said Stirling. "Seriously, yeah; they're cute."

There was a certain innocence about her. He tried to remember if he had thought he saw the same thing in Bettyne six months ago or if he always deceived himself. Dan, you bastard, why didn't you fill me in more about this one?

"Mac?"

"Umm?"

"Y' okay?"

"You wanta mother me, Val?" he asked. "If you've got that in mind, don't let me order another martini. Shut me off firmly, and just let's have a glass of red wine or two with our steaks."

"Well, don't get too tough about it," she said. "I'll try. But I won't fight you."

"Ah, you won't have to, honey," he said. "I'm always a sucker for a soft-spoken but commanding young woman."

"Fuck you, Mac," she said. She poured much of her glass of beer down her throat. "How'd two wives ever put up with you?"

"How'd you know I had two wives?"

"Everybody knows," she said. "And what medals you have. And how you damn near killed yourself in that flying blowtorch yesterday. You got no privacy, man."

"Right . . ." he murmured. He shrugged. "Could be worse."

"You been married twice," she said. "Nice girls?"

"Oh, hell yes," he said quickly. "Nice girls. College girls. Country-club girls. I have visions of wool skirts and silk blouses. Very nice girls." He sighed loudly. "C'mon, Val. You've lived in this shit-ass quarter of the country all your life. How you think a Vassar girl, accustomed to the lush green countryside of Connecticut, would react to cockroach-infested officers' quarters on some stinkin' desert air base, with her husband home every third weekend and nobody to talk to in the meantime but other wives in like situations—most of whom are high-school graduates like yourself, from boondock towns in the South and Midwest? How you think she'd like it?"

A small smile spread across Valerie's thin little mouth. "You folks married the wrong folks," she said. "Simple enough."

He nodded. "Simple enough. And I did it twice."

"Same kind of girls?"

"Yeah . . . pretty much. Different schools. Connecticut once, Bucks County the second time. Daddies were climbing in big companies. Captain Stirling was a trophy each time." He grinned. "I mean, if you had a fag for a son or a guitar-plucking head, you might pray your daughter would marry an air force pilot. Shit, honey. I was a marketable commodity."

"So lately you've traded in marketable commodities," said Valerie.

"Ouch! Careful, Val. Nothing is tougher to take than criticism from somebody you know is right. Anyway, it makes you feel old, to think you've switched from selling to buying."

"Jesus! Do you talk like this after *three* martinis?
Hey. C'mon. I'm investing *tonight*. And not my virgini-
ty, 'cause I forget when I had it. Whatever, Mac.
Whatever. . . . Give me something to remember in the
next twelve hours. Anything after that—" She
shrugged. "We'll think about it later."

5

"It's ILLEGAL, GODDAMNIT," grunted Stirling.

"Don't tell me about illegal," said Terry. "I've got more at stake in this than you've got, and I don't give a damn about some chickenshit regulation."

"The plane's not certificated," said Stirling. "If something happens . . . if it won't fly—"

"It'll fly," she said bluntly. "Fire it up. For the moment, you work for me."

"That's true, boss lady. So, let's hope we don't bend your airplane—and you with it."

It had not been easy. He had not supposed it would be. He had sent the letter from the Mojave Aeronautical Testing Center and had been invited to appear before a meeting of the board of directors of Powell Industries to present the case for test-flying the Powell Nimbus, otherwise known as the Flying Pencil.

"You propose," Robert Powell had said, opening the discussion, "that this company spend one and a quarter million dollars to test-fly the Pencil. Since we have thirty-five million in it already, can you give us an estimate of what it will cost to complete the check flights the Federal Aviation Agency will require to issue the certificate necessary to allow us to sell the Pencil as a general aviation aircraft?"

"All flights at MARC," Stirling had said, "will be

64

conducted to FAA certification standards and will become a part of the test record for the certification process. Assuming those first tests do not indicate any major modification of the aircraft, we should be able to complete all certification flights and provide all demonstrations and documentation for three million dollars."

"Assuming . . ."

"If the aircraft is flyable, you can get it certified for minimal cost. If it is not . . . you see the point."

"Three million more," said Powell. "Thirty-five million to get it to this stage, three million to get it certified. What to get it manufactured, do you suppose, Colonel Stirling?"

"I have no idea. Fifty million, at least. Probably more."

"We could wind up with a hundred million invested," said Powell. "Of which we have only a little more than a third so far committed."

"Assuming success, how many could you sell?" Stirling asked. "If an airplane like this fulfills the promises your father made for it, what is the limit of its potential?"

Powell grinned and shrugged. "Could we sell *any?* A radical new airplane? What's *your* best estimate, Colonel Stirling?"

"The general aviation industry is selling a little more than five thousand units a year," said Stirling. "That includes everything from Cessna 152s to the Cirrus, everything from little trainers to mini-airliners. With any kind of penetration of the business-airplane market, you should be able to sell a hundred units the first year. Say you sell a hundred the second. Then competitors are going to see your success and offer their own graphite-epoxy aircraft. So maybe you can't sustain a rate of a hundred a year. But you don't have to. If you generate net revenues of, say, forty million in each year you sell a hundred units—"

"Most optimistic," said Louis DiAngelo.

"Without Stan's optimism," interjected Terry, "where would any of us be? What would I be? An aging showgirl? What would you be, Bob? An insurance salesman? In real estate? In Levittown? And you, Lou? Running a pizza parlor in an L.A. suburb?"

"All this is a little personal, Terry," Powell objected.

"We all sit here," she said acerbically. "Once more challenging the judgment of the man who gave us everything we have. Stan believed in the Nimbus and asked us to finish the job on it. And we've sat around—"

"We haven't sat around," snapped Powell. "We—"

"No," she interrupted. "We haven't. The Nimbus has. Called the Flying Pencil, to put it down. It sits and corrodes. Stan's last great project . . ."

The board of directors consisted of seven members: Theresa Powell, Robert Powell, Louis DiAngelo, and four others.

Theresa was president and chief executive officer. Robert was executive vice president and chief operating officer. DiAngelo was vice president and corporate comptroller. DiAngelo was in Robert's corner and had been since the death of Stanley Powell and the reorganization of the management of Powell Industries.

Of the remaining four directors, one was clearly on Theresa's side. That was Walter O'Connell, vice president for engineering. Stanley Powell had hired him away from Lockheed and made him a vice president and stockholder. He had been with the company five years and had developed a strong loyalty to Stanley Powell and to the Nimbus project.

· Stanley Powell had accepted a banker on his board— Richard Deering from California United Bank, to which the company was heavily indebted. He was a conservative, interested in preserving his bank's security. He had consistently voted against the Nimbus project.

That left two swing votes. George Binghamton had been with the company for thirty years, held his stock as the result of bonuses and options, and tended to revere the name of Stanley Powell. Terry's appeals moved him. Lola Weiss, the final director, had been a management consultant, brought in by Stanley Powell to advise him on how to run the company more efficiently. She had taken up her stock options, which had been part of her compensation, and had devoted herself to the company for six years. She tried to be objective. She had voted against spending more development funds on the Nimbus, but only because she felt she did not have enough information to justify her voting to commit the corporation to a project that might break it.

Lola Weiss spoke now. "I'd like your assurance, Colonel Stirling, that you will advise us and will suspend the contract the instant you discover any major defect in the airplane."

"The proposed contract says," Stirling pointed out to her, "that tests will be suspended if we find any defect that will require the commitment of any sum over a quarter of a million dollars to correct."

"On that basis," she said, "I will vote to execute the contract and initiate the tests."

"Now wait a minute, Lola," said Robert Powell. "We're not talking about a quarter of a million. We're talking about a hundred million, as Colonel Stirling will admit."

"Judgment to be made when we have the facts," she said.

The airplane can't—"

"Can't be put in the air as a money-making project for much less than the hundred million you're talking about," Stirling interjected. "But, Bob, for God's sake. Your father had a first-class mind and was a first-class entrepreneur. You'd be fools to walk away from a Stanley Powell project saying you can't see the value in it. I've stood in the hangar and looked at that airplane —as you well know. It's odd. It's radical. But it has the potential to revolutionize this industry and make Powell Industries a leader once again."

"On what basis do you say that, Colonel Stirling?"

"Two bases," he said. "One: an engineer's assessment. More than that, on the basis of a sense that Stan Powell was *right,* that he hit on something brilliant—"

"Didn't he always?" grunted Bob Powell, closing his eyes. "But will it *sell?*"

"You'll have to invest a little to find out," said Stirling.

The argument did not immediately end. The company, said Bob Powell, had a sure thing in the Mink Bat and only a speculative possibility in the Pencil, as he persisted in calling it. He was tired, he said, of hearing the ghost of his father invoked to defeat rational management decisions.

Lola Weiss brought the meeting to an end. "I am not," she said, "ready to commit a hundred million dollars or anything like it to the Pencil. But I think it would be bad business judgment to drop a project of this magnitude, already so far carried forward, for want of our willingness to put another two or three million in it."

Bob Powell drew in so much breath that his body seemed to expand unnaturally. "So be it," he conceded, his voice betraying the anger he meant to subdue. "I move that we accept the contract offered by Mojave Aeronautical Research Center to conduct another series of tests on the Pencil."

Bill Carey, the mechanic, had spent a week checking every system of the Nimbus. As Stirling sat in the cockpit going through the three-page checklist, Carey stood on the ramp, watching critically.

Terry read the list and heard Stirling's responses.

"Avionics master switch, off."

"Off. Check."

"Systems master, off."

"Off. Check."

"Power master, on."

"On."

"Fuel boost, on."

"On. Pressure coming up."

"Prop max."

"Set."

"Clear prop."

There was no way to see if anyone was standing around the propeller in the rear, so he pressed a button that sounded a horn on the rear of the airplane.

"Start one."

He pressed the button, heard the turbine revolving, then heard the fuel fire. "Oil pressure coming up," he said. "Temp moving up. Normal."

"Start two."

The second turbine turned and started. Oil pressure came up on the gauge, showing that it was being properly lubricated. Temperature edged up, not too fast. He had amps.

"Systems master, on. Avionics master, on," said Terry.

The cockpit was comfortably appointed—a Stanley Powell specialty. They sat in a pair of blue plush seats, strapped down by lap belts and X-crossed shoulder harness. The wide console between the seats afforded space for most of the dual sets of communications and navigation radio equipment, leaving room on the panel before them for the main flight instruments: altimeters, airspeed indicators, gyros, and engine gauges, the basic instruments by which pilots flew, regardless of how sophisticated the airplane might be. The flap and gear controls were centered at the junction between the console and panel. The throttles and fuel and prop controls were there, too, within easy reach of either pilot.

"Normal as hell," Stirling remarked after the engines had spun for a minute or so.

Terry nodded.

Stirling gave Carey a thumbs-up sign, released the brakes, and advanced the throttle a little to let the airplane ease forward. There was no control tower at Powell Field, but he picked up the hand mike and spoke to the communications center.

"Eight-seven Sierra Pop, moving on the ramp."

Sierra Pop. Correctly said, Sierra Papa. S P. For Stanley Powell.

"Sierra Pop, it's all yours. Ramp and runway clear."

As he taxied away from Hangar One, across the ramp, toward the runway, two hundred employees of Powell Industries came out to watch. The little airplane —and it *was* little, compared to aircraft like the Cirrus —rolled forward and turned into the taxiway to the south, toward the south end of the runway. They watched the ailerons go up and down, the elevators go up and down, as Colonel Stirling checked the controls. The Nimbus made S-turns on the taxiway as he checked the steering. He cycled the flaps again. The turbines shrieked as he cycled the pitch of the six-bladed propeller.

The sky was clear. It was his intention to make a VFR flight to MARC—that is, a flight under visual rules, without any need to get a clearance from air traffic control. That meant, too, that he would stay at a low altitude. This wasn't a real test of the Nimbus. It was a delivery flight. Still, officially it was the first time the aircraft would be airborne. Unless Stanley Powell himself had flown it unofficially, it had never been in the air before.

"Sure you don't want to get out?" Stirling asked Terry as he turned into the runway.

"It'll fly," she said, but it was clear she realized she was about to lift off, not just in an experimental aircraft, but in an experimental aircraft of radical design. Her proclaimed confidence in the Nimbus was being put to the test—she was betting her life on it.

"So I figure," said Stirling.

Sitting at the end of the taxiway, he cycled the propeller once more through its entire range of pitches, then spun up the turbines as he checked the temperatures and pressures one more time. He glanced at his altimeter once more, and at his gyrocompass. He picked up the hand microphone.

"Eight-seven Sierra Pop ready to go."

"Clear of traffic, Sierra Pop. Nothing reporting. Good luck, sir, and good day."

Stirling swung the Nimbus into the runway. He glanced at Terry, whose eyes were frozen on the pavement ahead. He advanced the throttles, and the airplane rolled forward. Acceleration was normal, nothing surprising.

"Read me airspeeds, Terry," he said.

"Uh . . . sixty knots."

He would continue to glance at his own indicator, but it gave her something to do.

"Seventy."

"Pressures, temps holding," he said. "Steering okay."

"Eighty."

No one had said at what speed the Nimbus would lift off the runway. He supposed it would go at a hundred twenty knots, something like that. It was his intention to let it fly itself off, without forcing it. Another time he would pitch the nose up and see what it could do, but this time he would let it accelerate until it was ready to fly.

"Ninety."

One of the instruments measured gear-box temperature, that is, the temperature generated by friction in the gear train that linked the two in-line turbines to the propeller. He was concerned about that and was ready to abort if the temperature rose out of the green arc on the gauge. It held.

"Hundred."

"Smooth," he said.

Terry Powell nodded. She was glancing back and forth between him and the airspeed indicator.

"Hundred ten."

If you raised the nose abruptly, you could destroy the airplane in an instant by jamming the propeller into the pavement. That was the reason for that ugly little crutch that hung in the middle of the rear quarter. If you raised the nose too high and lowered the tail too much, the crutch would bang the runway and set you right. Mac was acutely conscious of it.

"Hundred twenty."

They had used half of a fifty-five-hundred-foot runway. Okay. Was it ready to fly? He pulled back very gently on the control column. The nose lifted. And smoothly, so smoothly that it was almost imperceptible, the Nimbus lifted off the runway. He didn't force it. He let it fly. Free of runway friction, it accelerated noticeably and climbed briskly.

"Okay, it flies," he said to Terry.

She licked her lips. "Sure it does," she whispered. "What'd you expect?"

Stirling glanced around the sky and down toward the earth, which was receding. He grinned. "It flies smooth," he said. "It's got a lot to prove, but for now it's a honey."

"Bob'll crap," she said.

* * *

Over the next week the Nimbus was loaded with test instruments. Temperature, vibration, and stress sensors were installed. Temperature-sensitive decals, which would change color if temperatures exceeded a calibrated level, were affixed to the fuselage behind the engine exhausts. Instruments were installed in the fuel tanks and lines, in the oil lines, in the hydraulic systems. The airplane was weighed as each instrument was added, and it was hung in a sling to check its balance. Two FAA inspectors spent four hours examining the airplane. They spent six more hours reviewing the test procedures and methods of handling the data the tests would produce. After ten hours, they issued the documents that would allow test flights that would produce certifiable data.

Taking the Nimbus up to twenty thousand feet, its first altitude test, was a very different proposition from taking the X-41A to a hundred thousand. There was no ejection from the Nimbus. If something disastrous happened, Stirling would have to work his way back from the cockpit to the one door in the passenger cabin and throw himself out, just ahead of the wing. If the wing didn't hit him and injure him severely, then he would be out in the atmosphere, falling, not attached to a seat, dependent on his parachutes. If he was knocked unconscious by the wing, he would fall, unable to open a parachute. There were devices that would open a parachute automatically at specified altitudes, but an unconscious or injured man, landing out of control, was in immense danger.

Even so, Stirling looked forward with enthusiasm to the first tests. During the fifty-mile flight from Powell to MARC, the aircraft had handled beautifully. Shorty had said he fell in love with airplanes. He had quickly fallen in love with this one.

"Eight-seven, Sierra Papa, cleared for takeoff. Initiate a turn to four-five degrees at your discretion, sir. Your climb corridor is clear."

"Sierra Pop, Roger. Rolling."

This time he was alone. This time he would stretch it out. Terry Powell was on the ramp, watching through her binoculars. All the members of the Powell board of directors were there, too.

This didn't involve a pressure suit. He was wearing a dark-blue flight suit, with two parachutes strapped in place. He had earphones over his head—over a New York Yankees baseball cap—and a microphone in front of his mouth. He pushed in the throttles a little more confidently this time, and the Nimbus roared and surged forward on the runway.

At two thousand runway feet it was ready. He pulled back on the control column, raised the nose, and felt the airplane lift off briskly. He held the nose up, watching the airspeed, and the Nimbus accelerated on climb. He retracted the gear. The Nimbus responded by gaining speed and rate of climb. It was not underpowered. It was going to test out with a climb rate in excess of thirty-five hundred feet per minute.

He swung into his turn to four-five degrees and set the throttles and trim for what he considered a good cruise climb: three thousand feet per minute, a little less than seventy-five per cent of what the Cirrus could do.

His flight plan was to level out at twenty thousand feet and let the Nimbus accelerate to an operational airspeed, say three hundred knots. At that speed, the

75

instruments would check vibration, internal and external temperatures, and control pressures. Particularly, they would monitor the operating temperature of the transmission that connected the big propeller to the two engines.

"Uh, Eight-seven Sierra Pop, all transmitted data is within normal ranges. Instruments confirm?"

"Sierra Pop, Roger. Transmission showing niner-zero centigrade."

"Roger. Ten above optimum. Watch that one closely, sir."

That was a critical point. The transmission that conveyed engine power to the propeller was a new engineering departure. If it overheated, the Nimbus project was in immediate trouble.

He shoved the column forward and leveled easily at ten. With climb completed, the airplane gained speed. He raised the wing flaps and set the throttles and propeller pitch for a cruise configuration. As the Nimbus drew up to three hundred knots, it wanted to climb, and he had to trim it to hold the nose a little lower.

"Looking good, Sierra Pop. How's it feel?"

"Smooth," said Stirling. "Cutting back power to hold three hundred." That meant normal engine power would drive the airplane at well over three hundred knots, three hundred forty-five miles per hour. At forty-thousand feet, the Nimbus might well approach four hundred knots.

"Say transmission temp, Sierra Pop."

He frowned. "Okay. Passing through one hundred."

"NG, Sierra Pop." No good. "Throttle back."

"I want to try one-two-zero," said Stirling. "I want to see if rate of increase is manageable."

"Roger, Sierra Pop. But do not exceed one-two-zero. Repeat. Do not exceed."

"Understood."

He scanned his instruments, then looked around at the gray California desert from twenty thousand feet. The Nimbus was smooth, no question. At sixty per cent of power, it was holding three hundred knots at twenty thousand, which was impressive efficiency. The needle on the transmission-temperature gauge crept slowly to the right. The problem was developing only very gradually, but it was developing. At sixty per cent, it was developing.

One-ten. That was enough. He didn't have to take it to one-two-zero. He knew enough.

"Eight-seven Sierra Pop, throttling back for cruise descent. We are running too much transmission temp."

"Roger, Sierra Pop. Bring 'er in."

"So what will it cost to fix that?" Robert Powell demanded when the board of directors and two engineers met Stirling on the ramp behind the Nimbus.

"Not much," said one of the MARC engineers. "Scoop in more air, that's all."

Stirling nodded. "That'd be my judgment. Open the scoops a little wider."

"At a sacrifice in aerodynamic efficiency," said Powell. "Lose speed."

"Why?" asked Terry. "Why scoop in more air? Why not make better use of what you are getting?"

"Meaning?" Powell asked scornfully.

"If I remember the transmission-cooling system correctly," she said, "the cooling air is directed across a set of fins on the housing of the transmission. Before we make the scoops bigger and maybe lose speed, why not try making the fins bigger? If the cooling air is more efficiently used, maybe we don't need to scoop in any more. And since the fins are inside the fuselage, they don't interfere with the aerodynamic configuration."

"Since when did you become an aircraft engineer, Terry?" asked Powell.

"I'm as much a one as you are, Bob—as your father often reminded the both of us."

"Terry—"

"Reduce it to my level of experience," she said sarcastically. "When you're standing nude on a night-club stage, in the glare of the lights, you don't get much comfort out of the draft from the air conditioning. But if you've got a few feathers around your body, they slow down the cool air, and you sweat less. Could the principle be anything similar?"

Stirling laughed. "Damn right," he said. "Damn absolutely right. And we could add fins to the transmission for less than a thousand dollars."

"I'd try it," said Lola Weiss. "It makes a lot of sense to me."

"First test," said Powell. "First problem. What's next, Colonel Stirling? What assurance do we have that this is the last problem we'll have with the Nimbus?"

"None, Mr. Powell. In fact, I'm sure we'll have more problems."

"And Terry can give us some common-sense solution," muttered Powell.

"Sure. Let's hope so. Let's very much hope so," said Stirling.

6

ROBERT POWELL LAY on his back in the warm water of his swimming pool, floating in an inflated chair. A buoyant tray floated within reach, carrying his Scotch and soda and the morning's *Wall Street Journal*, which he had been scanning before the sun and Scotch made him sleepy. His twins, a son and a daughter, thirteen years old, whispered together at the edge of the pool, unsure if his eyes were open or closed behind his sunglasses.

They were open, though barely. "You do and I'll switch two bare bottoms," he growled at them, only half facetiously. He knew what idea had them laughing: jumping into the pool, making waves that would upset Daddy's drink and wet his newspaper. "You use this pool every day. I only get in it once a week. You make waves, I'll make butts smart."

The two ran away, laughing. They were cute kids, Robert Junior and Roberta, Bob and Bobby. Both had reached that age of acute self-consciousness about the development of their bodies, but they were still playful children. Robert reached for his Scotch. He was proud of the kids. Their grandfather had been proud of them too—and had treated them with all the self-indulgent carelessness that had characterized his personal life.

He picked up the *Journal*. The goddamned economy

. . . How could a man achieve any security—comfort with security—in a screwed-up economy like this? How could you know what to do when no one could guess what new tinkering Congress would do with the tax structure? If his father had left his estate to his family instead of leaving half to his doxy, everything would be simpler. The self-centered old bastard!

"Bob . . ." When the boy wasn't around, Ruth called him Bob. Otherwise, for clarity, it had to be Robert for him, Bob for their son, Bobby for the girl. "Bob, you've got a visitor. Were you expecting somebody?"

"About half," he said. "Bring him on out here."

Powell paddled to the edge of the pool, pushing his floating tray ahead of him with his feet, and climbed out. He was toweling himself with some vigor when the young man from *Aviation World* came through the patio door and walked out to poolside.

"Mr. Powell. Good to see you. I'm Bob Clark."

"Another Bob," said Powell, turning on his father's warmth. "Confusion . . . Sit down. Like a drink? If you'd like to get in the water, we've got some extra trunks."

"I'll take the drink," said Clark, looking at the wheeled bar that stood near the umbrella table. "You making gin and tonic this afternoon?"

"Sure thing. Bombay gin suit you?"

"Wonderful," said Clark. He settled into a chair of vinyl webbing and aluminum tubing. "Since I moved out here, I've learned not to start conversations by saying 'Warm, isn't it?' It's always warm."

"And dry," said Powell. "And the air is clear. That's

why so much of the aircraft industry is out here. The testing part especially. We can't just make aircraft; we have to fly them."

Clark nodded and watched Powell pour more gin into his glass than he had expected. He was an intense young man, only twenty-seven, maybe too young yet to relax. He was dressed in a jacket and slacks, white shirt and tie. He carried a small notebook.

"Well," said Powell when he had refreshed his own drink as well as mixed Clark's. He handed over the gin and tonic and sat down across the table. *"Aviation World.* You called about the tests."

"Yes, sir. We'd like to know how it's going with the Flying Pencil."

Powell leaned back and crossed his arms over his hairy chest. "You remember the story of Woodward and Bernstein and Deep Throat?" he said. "I'm sure you do. Every journalist ought to know that story well. We still don't know who Deep Throat was." He smiled and nodded. "Ethics. Journalists' ethics. And you know why I mention the subject."

"Certainly," said Clark.

"It would damage my position with my company if I were identified as the source of what I am about to tell you," said Powell earnestly, fixing his eyes intently on Clark's face. "What I'm gonna tell you is the truth, but I expect you to verify it from other sources. That's the condition on which I agreed to see you."

"Understood, sir," said the young reporter.

"This interview can be mutually beneficial," said Powell. "Frankly, it is to my benefit for this information to be published. And, of course, it makes a scoop for you. I need hardly tell you that a good many papers and magazines have called to inquire about the tests on the Pencil."

"There's a lot of interest in it."

"But the information is being withheld," said Powell darkly. "And that's because it doesn't look good for the Flying Pencil."

"That bad?"

"During the first test flight, the transmission overheated. They're working on that, but the problem has not been solved. Because it hasn't been solved, they can't fly the aircraft at what's supposed to be its cruising speed. All the tests so far have had to be low-altitude, low-speed tests. Even so—"

Clark did not look up from his pad, on which he was writing notes. "Other problems?" he asked.

"Exhaust fumes from the turbines are overheating the skin aft of the exhaust ports."

"How big a problem is that?"

Powell showed the young man a measured, pity-me smile. He shrugged. "Nobody knows. If they burn a hole in the son of a bitch . . . at over three hundred knots airspeed. Well. You can imagine. I think you said you're an engineer yourself."

"Right. I am. What's the fix for the problem of overheating the skin, do you think?"

"They're talking about installing baffles in the exhaust ports, to blow the exhaust heat away from the fuselage." Powell shrugged again. "So how hot are the baffles gonna get?"

"We've heard talk to the effect that substantial numbers of people are allergic to the epoxy-graphite material," said Clark. "The story is that the plant workers who put the Pencil together developed rashes and maybe respiratory problems. Is there any truth to that?"

"That's being investigated," said Powell. "The feds are looking. OSHA."

"Occupational Safety and Health Agency?"

"Right."

"Well, anyway. Was there an accident on one of the test flights?"

Powell shook his head. "Not really. The automatic fire extinguishers blew as Colonel Stirling was climbing through ten thousand the other morning. He had to grab for his oxygen mask. But, no; you couldn't call that an accident."

"No passengers on board?"

"No."

Clark picked up his gin and tonic, sipped, and for a moment looked at the notes he had scribbled. He was distracted for a moment by the bikini-clad Bobby, who had come to sit on the diving board and stare mischievously at the young man talking with her father.

"Are you willing to talk about the personal element?" Clark asked.

"I suppose you refer to the fact that there is no love lost between me and my . . . uh"—Powell paused to grin—"stepmother."

"That's no secret, I guess," said the reporter.

Powell rubbed his hands together before his chin. "Have you met her?" he asked.

"No."

"You'll like her," said Powell. "Hell, *I* like her. She's a striking beauty. You'll look a long time to find another girl as beautiful as Terry. And she's appealing, she's, uh, well spoken—though a little rough in her language sometimes, like a man—and she's smart, no question about it. But to be an executive officer of a big company—no. She hasn't got the education or experience."

"She owns more of the stock in Powell Industries than you do," said Clark.

"That's true. When my father died, he still owned fifty-two per cent. He left twenty-five per cent to me and twenty-five per cent to Terry. Under community-property law she could probably have taken it anyway. He left the other two per cent, incidentally, to a couple of employees who'd been with him for years. I don't think he remembered, when he wrote that will, that he'd already put ten per cent in Terry's name. I couldn't do anything about it, anyway. I mean, I couldn't make a case that she'd deceived him, used improper influence on him, or anything. So she wound up with thirty-five per cent to my twenty-five."

"How long were they married?" Clark asked.

"Five years." He snatched up his glass and swallowed some Scotch. "So I think you get the point."

The reporter nodded. "Sure. But I don't think *Aviation World* can touch on that element of the story."

"Really?" said Powell coldly. "Well, let's look at that question for a minute. If the company goes out to borrow money to continue the development of the Pencil—which it will have to do, 'cause it sure can't develop it out of cash on hand—then the banks will have questions, proper questions, about the management of Powell Industries. For the moment, the president of the company is a Las Vegas showgirl."

"A graduate of Ohio State University," said Clark.

Powell nodded. "Degree in modern languages," he said. "Speaks fluent French and German. Or so I'm told; I'm fluent only in English, myself. No industrial background."

"As a matter of interest, Mr. Powell," said Clark, "let's review your own credentials."

"Let's do," said Powell. "Harvard '69 and '71, B.S. in industrial psychology, followed by an M.B.A. I joined my father in his business in 1972 and have been with the company since then."

"Okay," said Clark, writing notes. "Impressive. You'll forgive my asking."

"Sure," said Powell. "Let me refresh your drink."

He took Clark's glass and went to the bar. Clark turned his eyes toward Bobby, who remained on the board, perching seductively in her minuscule orange bikini, playing what was for her a new and interesting game. She was a pretty child, beginning to develop. Clark forced himself to turn his eyes downward.

"Hang on here a min," said Powell. "Let me get something."

Powell departed, and Bobby dropped from the board and came to the table. "What's that you're drinking?" she asked.

"Gin and tonic," said Clark uncomfortably.

She picked up his glass and took a sip. She grimaced. "Yuchh!" she said. She walked to the bar and poured a generous shot of vodka into a glass of orange juice. "You're a newspaper reporter, huh?"

"A magazine reporter," he said.

"Any good magazine?" she asked. She sat down and drained half her glass.

"Aviation World," he said.

"Oh . . . figures. Daddy giving you the straight poop?"

"Seems to be."

The girl nodded. She lifted her glass a second time and emptied it. Then she tossed it into the pool, where it sank to the bottom. "Ol' dad gets upset, he sees me have a drink," she explained.

"You'll be lucky you don't upset yourself after what I just watched you pour down," said Clark.

She grinned. "Well, thank you very much, Chief Straight Arrow," she sneered. "Here comes Daddy with his pictures of my naked grandmother. I hope you get the charge out of them that he does."

The girl stalked away, thin little fanny twitching contemptuously. Clark was glad she was gone. He looked up at Powell, wondering what he thought the encounter might have been.

"Look here," said Powell.

He seemed not to have noticed at all that his teen-age daughter had just stalked away in some kind of huff. Maybe he was used to it. Clark focused his attention on the folder Powell had put before him.

"Playboy," said Powell. He opened a copy of the magazine and put his finger on a picture. "That's my stepmother."

Clark stared at the magazine spread. The young woman named Terry Keel had about a third of a page, pictured in a color photograph, sitting at a little study desk with a university pennant on the wall behind her head—nude but for a pair of panties, a tall, extraordinarily handsome girl, with long, shapely legs, small but flawless bare breasts, lustrous blond hair hanging around her shoulders . . . "Terry Keel," the caption said. "A language major who speaks our language, whatever the language."

"Uh . . . showgirl," said Powell, handing over a set of black-and-white photographs.

These were less impressive, publicity pictures from some Las Vegas room. The girl was unmistakable, though. In one she was entirely nude, as she would not have been allowed to appear on a Las Vegas stage. She was a natural blonde, clearly; her pubic hair was as light as the hair on her head. In other pictures she wore the kind of costumes she had worn as a showgirl: feathers, hats, little G-strings encrusted with fake pearls, with her breasts bare always. The word "statuesque" was an intolerable cliché in this context, but that was what Terry Keel was—and she was one of the few young women he had ever seen to whom the word justly applied.

"It's difficult to be unsympathetic to something like that," said Powell. "Isn't it?"

Clark drew in a deep breath. "Well . . ."

"Believe me, I'm not. Between you and me, Bob, I could go for that myself, if I weren't a married man and a father and if she were not my father's widow. Hell, man, I understand my dad. What man wouldn't have?"

Clark glanced through some other photographs in the folder. Terry Keel had been a chronic beauty-contest participant, it seemed. She would have won, he judged, if she had been allowed to shed the antediluvian one-piece swimsuits to which girls were condemned in those so-called pageants. In two pictures she appeared topless in a lounge chair beside a swimming pool. He was not sure of the significance of those. He closed the folder and pushed it across the table toward Powell.

"All I'm trying to get across," said Powell quickly, "is that Terry, while she's a fine, exceptionally beautiful young woman, is a poor kind of person to make decisions for a business corporation the size of Powell Industries."

"Your father—"

Powell flushed. "Dad . . . do you want to know something about my father?"

Clark shrugged and reached for his drink. "I came to get data about the airplane, Mr. Powell."

"You came to get information about Powell Industries," said Powell.

"Okay."

"Off the record," said Powell. "Deep Throat. Absolutely off the record. Find it out somewhere else. I'll ask for your word on that."

Clark stared for a moment at his notepad. "You have my professional word," he said solemnly.

"Dad was a cocksman," said Robert Powell. "I'm told he was hung like a horse, though I never saw it. Any woman who saw it wanted it. And he arranged for a lot of them to see it. He dropped some bastards around." Powell shrugged and grinned. "I expect any day to have some stranger walk up, grab my hand, and call me brother. Dad was a Pole. Forget Polish jokes, Bob. Poles can whack that tool of theirs into girls who haven't even been introduced yet. And that was my father's special talent."

"That and designing airplanes," Clark suggested.

"Hell, no," said Powell sharply. "He couldn't design a goddamned paper clip. But he could con people. My father was the world's greatest confidence man. He didn't design the Flying Pencil, for Christ's sake! He *promoted* it. Walter O'Connell designed it. He and others. My father was the quintessential promoter, the con man who could make anybody buy anything. You never met him, did you? He could have conned you out of your wife's panties. And sold you used chewing gum. Bob—"

"Mr. Powell. I can't publish this kind of stuff, so maybe you shouldn't tell me."

"You can get an impression," Powell went on. "The whole goddamned world thinks my father was an eccentric genius. Well, he was—but not for what the world thinks he was a genius for. He was a genius for dipping his fingers into other people's money; I mean investors' money. And for dipping his wick into strange pussy."

Clark had stopped taking notes. Powell's words were archaic—Harvardian, Clark wondered?—and emotionally charged. Clark glanced again at the *Playboy* that lay open on the table. Terry Powell was an extraordinary woman, beyond question. It was not difficult to understand this man's reaction to her.

Powell was not imperceptive. "I, uh . . . I express myself badly," he said. "I'm sorry, Bob. What I'm trying to tell you is that my father was the consummate promoter, plus an unparalleled enthusiast. He saw this idea that some engineers presented to him. He bought the idea. He sold it to Terry, among many others. And she is blind to its defects."

Clark scribbled a note of that statement.

"I'm the villain," said Powell. "I don't share my father's enthusiasm. I'm frustrating his loyal widow's effort to realize his dream. And all I want to do with you is put the whole thing in perspective so you can see the truth."

"I write for a technical publication," said Clark cautiously.

"Exactly. And you are going to get information from others besides me. And it's going to contradict what I'm telling you. What I'm trying to do is give you a background that will help you judge the information you receive."

"You are saying the Pencil will be a failure," said Clark. "And the data is being withheld."

"So they can raise the money to go on with it," said Powell grimly.

"What about Colonel Stirling?"

A sly smile spread slowly over Powell's face. He pushed the file of photographs toward Clark. "He's enamored of her already, I suspect," he chuckled. "You are yourself, almost, from looking at these pictures. What do you suppose the colonel is, after a few intimate lunches with her? Don't take my word for it. Check it out. Check it all out, Bob—everything I've told you."

It was Friday evening. Robert Powell left his swimming pool and home around five, telling his wife he had to check in at the office to be sure some information he had given the reporter was accurate and to mail him a couple of documents. He drove his Thunderbird south out of the town of Powell, into the desert.

Ten miles south, on a desert road off the highway, he came to a portable electric signboard, mounted on trailer wheels and parked at the side of the road, flashing:

THE CLOCK
DRINKS—GO-GO—PRIVATE CLUB
MEMBERSHIPS AVAILABLE

There was in fact a clock, a big round dial circled by pink neon tubes, with hands that had stopped years ago at twenty past two. It hung and glowed on the weather-beaten clapboard of a two-story roadhouse half a mile back in the desert, off the road. The lot was not paved. Four cars and two pickup trucks gathered the dust that swirled up and settled back each time a vehicle drove in or out.

The Clock was a whorehouse. The two-story building had been built for a whorehouse. What else would have been built with eight windowless upstairs rooms, each with an air conditioner set through the wall and each with a basin? For six years only, out of the last thirty, there had been no whores working at The Clock. Politics being what they were, the girls were back now. And they had a brisk trade.

Powell pushed the button, heard the buzzer sound inside, and was allowed in from the heat and dust, into the ground-floor bar.

"Ho, Robert, where ya been?" Fiona asked. She was the proprietor, though only a ten-percent owner. "Began to think ya were gettin' it somewheres else."

"That's what you'd say if I'd been in day before yesterday," he said. "For Christ's sake pour me a Scotch, with lots of fizz water and ice."

91

The room was functional—furnished with vinyl-covered chairs, a masonite-topped bar, and a refrigerator to freeze the ice. It was lighted by a pair of blackened fluorescent tubes, flickering and humming behind the bar. Fiona was a thirty-five-year-old woman with hair dyed charcoal black, a red smear of lipstick, blue jeans, a checked shirt. She poured his drink from a bottle of Cutty Sark.

She frowned. "You been in since Tony came?" she asked.

"Tony?"

"Yeah, Tony. Antonia. Somethin' special, Robert. You haven't had head till you've had it from Tony. Listen—"

"Okay, but what've you found out for me?" he asked impatiently.

"Ahh. Nothin', man. I got the word out, as ya might put it. But . . ." She shrugged. "Nothin'. So far."

A girl sauntered in. She looked as if she could hardly be eighteen years old, though Powell knew looks were deceiving among these types. Her body was womanly. She was wearing only a yellow bikini bottom and high-heeled shoes, but even with the heels she was barely tall enough to reach his chin. Her dark-brown hair hung around her shoulders and below. Her breasts were soft and pendulous and moved as she walked. Her short legs were tautly muscled.

"Tony. Meet Robert. A good man. Important man. You give him a good time."

The girl looked up at him with solemn brown eyes. Antonia. Italian? Not likely. Mexican maybe, though her features seemed to him too delicate for a southwestern Hispanic. Maybe her mother was Vietnamese.

The children of some odd unions were beginning to reach maturity in southern California.

"Fiona . . . look, this deal is important to me."

Fiona shook her head. "I gotta think you're on the wrong track, my friend."

Powell looked down at Tony. The girl was distracting. He couldn't concentrate. "Uh . . . would she have any objection to my favorite trick?" he asked Fiona.

Fiona shook her head. "The usual deal. But an extra twenty, seein' how it's Tony."

"'Kay," he said hoarsely. "All right. We can talk some more."

In the room on the second floor, he locked the girl's hands behind her back with handcuffs. Then he blindfolded her. Fiona was in the room; she would not allow one of her girls to be bound or chained unless someone from the house was present to protect her. Since the only furniture in the room was the bed and the basin, Fiona stood leaning against the wall, watching with unconcealed amusement. Powell lay on his back on the bed. The girl settled herself awkwardly, bent forward, found her balance with some difficulty, then groped for his shaft with her mouth. She sucked it in and set to work.

"There's a thousand in it for whoever brings me the word," said Powell thinly, drawing deep breaths.

"You offered that a'ready," said Fiona.

"Awright, goddamnit, make it two thousand," he whispered.

"You don't want a lie," Fiona reminded him. "You said that. You don't wanta know unless it's true. So maybe you ain't gonna find out it's true. Maybe it ain't."

Tony coughed, lost him, and had to grope for him again.

Powell had closed his eyes and was nodding rhythmically. "If so—" he whispered.

"I know," she interrupted. "If so, you'll leave it go at that."

"Just get the word around as much as you can," he grunted.

Fiona grinned. "That your old man married a hooker. You're somethin', Robert. You're damn lucky the ol' man ain't alive no more. I remember him. He'd bust your ass for this idea. I mean, he'd bust your ass for good and sure, Robert."

Powell laid his head back on the thin pillow, closed his eyes, and moaned gently.

7

"I'M NOT SURE," said Stirling. "Oh, hell, there's no problem with the aircraft. Absent a few solvable problems, the son of a bitch will fly within specifications. Marketing it . . . Terry, you've gotta understand that manufacturing and marketing are different problems. And they're called money."

"Banks," she said. "Big money."

He nodded. "Without giving up control of the company."

They sat in Dan's—the Silver Wing—lunching on small steaks, with a half carafe of red wine to be shared between them. Stirling had flown the Nimbus that morning. This was a debriefing.

"Very big money," he agreed. "It's no small deal, Terry. I sure as hell can't guarantee you the financial community will see it our way."

"Too bad Stan's not around," she said.

He nodded. "That was his strength, to sell his ideas."

"Bob didn't dare oppose him," she said.

"The Mink Bat—"

"It's a cheap shot," she said bitterly. "By modifying a few junk F-86s he makes himself look as if he's making a new business for Powell Industries. He—"

"Not quite, Terry," Stirling interrupted. "The Mink Bat may be a very marketable commodity."

"Fine. So it makes the company look viable. So he

makes a deal to sell it to some conglomerate. It's got the Cirrus, which still sells damn well. With a prospective new aircraft like the Mink Bat, he's got a stock that will sell at a premium."

"So what do you think he wants?"

"Money," she said. "An easy out. If Bob had inherited control of the company, which is what he expected all his life, he'd sell out, take his money, and settle into corpulent comfort. Bob has a simple ambition in this world: to live without working, while being an Ivy League gentleman—as he conceives of that term. His father sent him to Harvard. If he'd sent him to Ohio State, he'd have been a better man."

Stirling sipped wine. He glanced toward the bar, impatient that he was limiting himself to a glass or two of wine when he wanted a martini. "So he sells out," he said.

"He can't sell out," said Terry. "We've had some offers. Good offers. But what the buyers want is control—to take over Powell Industries and merge it into another corporation. Bob's twenty-five per cent wouldn't give a buyer control. He begged me ten months ago—and I mean, literally, he begged me—to accept an offer from a German company. It would have left us millionaires many times over." She shook her head. "I wouldn't sell, and without my stock, the German company wouldn't buy."

"Why didn't you sell?" Stirling asked. "What's wrong with being a multimillionaire?"

"Stan had died only a short time before," she said quietly. "He'd been so emphatic about the Nimbus, about what an important idea it was." She sighed, turned down the corners of her mouth. "I don't know.

Maybe I was still being romantic. Anyway, to sell out his great idea, take the money . . . Bob hated me for refusing."

"You're no romantic, Terry," said Stirling. "I've begun to understand what you want. And it doesn't have a hell of a lot to do with Stan, either."

"You wouldn't do a *damn* thing for Stan's memory," she said. "And neither would anybody else, except maybe build a monument. So let's put things in—"

"I'd like to talk about the Nimbus," said Stirling.

"So talk about the Nimbus."

"Your fins have almost eliminated the problem of overheating in the transmission. Instead of opening the intakes wider, we've added two more little intakes. The aerodynamic effect has been negligible."

"So I noticed," she said. "I read the test reports, you know."

"Okay. The baffles did not direct the hot air away from the fuselage enough to prevent skin overheating. Over the weekend the boys remounted the intake-exhaust pods, slanting them ten degrees away from the body of the airplane. This morning the decals retained their color."

"You didn't get the heat," she said.

He nodded. "It's a more expensive fix. We flew this morning with a temporary remount. For the future, we'll have to redesign and reinstall the fairings, which we'll have to do before we can go on to sustained high-speed and high-altitude testing. But it looks like that's the solution. And I'm pleased with it. It's cleaner than putting in baffles."

"Mac . . ."

"Wait. Hold off, Terry. I—"

"No. No, I want to say it. I want to propose to the board that you be elected president of the corporation."

"President? Terry, I—"

She nodded. "President," she said.

Stirling glanced around the room. He wanted to be sure no one was listening, no one could hear. "You know, look—"

"Mac," she interrupted. "I want it. Okay?"

He stared hard into her calm, steady eyes. "Why?" he asked simply.

"Don't push too hard, fly-boy," she said. She lowered her eyes, stared at the table for a moment, then met his gaze. *"To get it done, that's why.* I'm a practical bitch. Who's going to make my baby fly? Not me. Too many feathers in my background. Too many bare tits. *But Colonel McDonald Stirling* . . . that's—"

"Only if it'll fly, Terry."

"So, okay. Will it fly? I mean, money-wise. Will the Pencil fly? Or will it break us?"

"It's a damned good airplane," said Stirling.

"What would you bet on it?"

He drew a deep breath. "All right. Okay, lady. Me. I'll bet me."

"You got a deal, Mac. I'm going to nominate you for president of Powell Industries. Let's see how Bob fights that."

He flew the Mink Bat, too—to stroke Bob Powell, as he told Terry, but also out of curiosity about how the airplane would fly.

It was a piece of cake. The Mink Bat flew smoothly, leaving the runway at its designated liftoff speed, climbing hot to thirty thousand, and beginning to show a sluggish climb only above that altitude, as expected. Stirling rolled it through a series of maneuvers, everything he expected from an F-86. All systems remained within normal parameters.

Mink Bat. Somebody knew what he was doing. The name was suggestive of Foxbat, the name given the MiG-25P that was now obsolete with the Soviet Air Force but that was being offered to African, Asian, and Latin American nations as a super-fighter. So far, as Stirling had heard, the third-world pilots were destroying twenty-nine per cent of their countries' Foxbats in training, just as they did their Mirages and F-15s. Somebody's idea was right—whether it was Bob Powell's or somebody else's. Let 'em bend the Mink Bat, for a fifth of the cost. Then all you'd lose was an expendable pilot, not an expensive airplane. A lot of governments would find that idea most appealing.

He brought the Mink Bat down on the strip at Powell Industries. The crew and some engineers trotted out to hear what he'd have to say. He commended their airplane, which was what they wanted to hear.

Bob Powell himself came down to the ramp. "You like?" he asked with the ingenuous expectation of a small boy.

"Fun damned plane, Bob," said Stirling. "I didn't find a fatal defect."

Powell chuckled nervously. "And the nonfatal?" he asked.

"Oh, a little buffeting at some speeds, a little vibration. Matter of fine tuning. Comes in for landing a little nose-low. I'd fix that. A day's work, rigging, followed by a test flight. Otherwise . . ."

Powell grinned. "We hear you," he said. "Want to fly it again? Give us a week, then see what you think. Oh, is that your Porsche? The young lady said she's with you."

It was Valerie. They had driven together the fifty miles to Powell, and she had waited in the Porsche while he flew the Mink Bat. She had brought a book to read, a Louis L'Amour western, and had watched the flight only during his takeoff and landing. She would be going to work as soon as they drove back, so she was wearing one of the red T-shirts lettered DAN'S SILVER WING and a pair of blue-denim shorts.

"Boring?" he asked as he fastened his seat and shoulder belts.

"Well, I'm glad I brought something to read," she said. "Except for seeing you take off and land . . . I mean, I lost sight of you in a couple of minutes. It go okay?"

"Not bad. We'll get you back to Dan's on time, won't we?"

She checked her watch. "Sure. Plenty of time."

She had spent the night with him and had accepted his invitation to come with him to Powell this morning, to see him fly the Mink Bat. She was an accommodating girl. He liked her. He'd grown fond of her. She was peculiar, though. She had agreed to come with him this morning only if he drove to Powell in the Porsche, not if he flew over in the Bonanza. Valerie was afraid of flying.

Because they had plenty of time, he stopped at a Burger King and picked up Cokes for them. A few miles out of town, he pulled off the highway and drove a short distance into the desert, where they could sit in the mid-morning sun and drink their Cokes.

The top was off the Porsche, and though the sun was hot there was a dry breeze. A sidewinder slithered out of the low brush ahead, then put distance between itself and the car. That spooked a hare which scampered away, stirring up dust. Stirling leaned past the gear stick and brake handle and kissed Valerie. He pulled up her red shirt, exposed her breasts, and fondled them. She liked that. She laughed and pulled the shirt over her head. The sun felt good on her skin, she said. He kissed her again. They sipped their Cokes. There wasn't enough time for anything more serious, nor was the Porsche a good place for it. He told her how the Mink Bat flew. She told him something of the plot of the book she was reading. They finished their Cokes in ten minutes, then left.

"Comf'table, ain't she?" Dan asked when Stirling had taken a stool at the bar and Valerie was in the back changing out of her shorts.

Stirling nodded. "I've got a strange feeling about it, like I'm taking advantage of her. But, yeah. She's all right."

The next afternoon he took the Nimbus up to forty thousand feet. Level, it accelerated to just over three hundred knots. He held it at that speed for a little over thirty minutes, flying east over Las Vegas, over Lake Mead, then returning. He watched all his gauges, but once he was satisfied that all temperatures were within acceptable ranges, the one that most interested him was fuel consumption. If the fuel gauges were right, fuel economy was phenomenal. It was better than design expectations. When he landed and had the fuel drawn off and measured, it turned out that the gauges were, if anything, conservative. The Nimbus would fly at almost 350 miles an hour, making the same flight—say, Los Angeles to San Francisco and return—on less than half the fuel burned by a propjet at 300 and less than one-third of the fuel burned by a jet at 400.

"The son of a bitch is an *airplane!*" he shouted to Terry as he emerged from the cockpit. He trotted across the tarmac toward her and seized her hands. "It *flies*, Terry! It'll do what Stan figured!"

The next afternoon, in the board room at Powell Industries, he reported, with restrained enthusiasm, to the board.

"We've encountered the usual kinds of problems you have with an experimental aircraft," he said. "Still, I'm prepared to call the design sound—notice, I'm not just saying basically sound; I mean *sound*—and the problems so far have been corrected with minimal investment. We've got—"

"Excuse me," said Lou DiAngelo. "Am I the only one here who's looked at the current issue of *Aviation World?*"

Stirling nodded and smiled. "I wondered who would bring that up."

"Damned strong stuff," said Powell.

"You two are referring to?" asked Lola Weiss.

"An article in *Aviation World,*" said Powell. "It reports the difficulties we've had with the Nimbus. Expresses doubts we can make it fly."

"Fly in the business sense, you mean."

"Exactly," Powell agreed. "In the business sense. Raise money to complete its development, manufacture it, and market it. In view of the fact that it has . . . well, the article speaks of its 'significant shortcomings.'"

"All of which have been corrected," said Stirling. "Everything mentioned in the article has been fixed, either with a temporary patch or permanently."

"Whether they have or not," said Powell, "this article is going to hurt us in the business community. And I'd like to know who the hell leaked this information."

"I'd like to know who the hell calls it information," said Stirling. "It's no big deal, frankly. I called Ted Hammond this morning, and he—"

"Who's Ted Hammond?" asked Powell.

Stirling tapped his finger on the magazine. "This little prick Robert Clark works for my old friend Ted Hammond, editor-in-chief at *Aviation World*," he said. "There'll be a *senior* reporter out here next week, to look into the real facts about the Nimbus. In the meantime, Clark's ass is in a sling, for calling the Nimbus the Flying Pencil, if for nothing else."

"Well, he—I mean, this fellow Clark . . . he'll hide behind journalistic ethics, so-called," said Powell. "I don't think we'll ever get it out of him. I mean, who leaked this story."

Stirling shrugged. "Maybe so. But it's not going to make any difference, because a senior reporter from *Aviation World* is ready to go flying in the Nimbus. We'll get a second story. With pictures."

"And you think that will overcome the negative impression created by the current story?" asked Powell skeptically.

"When they see the fuel-consumption figures," said Stirling, "any industry reporter who knows anything is going to—"

"Will those hold up?" interrupted Richard Deering, the director from United California Bank. "You've had one flight."

"They'll hold up," said Stirling. "Even if they fall twenty per cent—which they won't—they're still tremendously impressive."

"Exactly how has this kind of fuel economy been achieved?" asked Deering.

"Weight," said Walter O'Connell, the company's vice president for engineering. "The graphite-epoxy compound gives us an airplane that's so light—yet just as strong as a conventional airplane—that it takes far less fuel to fly it."

"In theory," said DiAngelo.

"The theory's been proved, Lou," said Terry.

"The airplane," said DiAngelo with almost angry emphasis, "has had one cruising-speed, cruising-altitude test flight. Almost every other test flight has disclosed a serious problem. This one didn't. But there's a lot of proving yet to do."

"Colonel Stirling," said Lola Weiss, "do you agree that there is a lot more testing to do?"

"There certainly is," said Stirling. "It looks very good so far, but I won't deny that we have a lot of testing yet to do."

"Like what? The most important things?"

Stirling drew a deep breath. "We've got to stress the

airplane," he said. "We've got to make it perform to its limits and beyond. The engines and propeller have got to be run at speeds well beyond their operating limits, to see if they fly apart. We've got to dive the airplane and pull it out abruptly, to see if the wings fall off. We've got to freeze the airplane and wet it and overheat it in the desert sun to find out how the epoxy-graphite—"

"That's been done," O'Connell interrupted. "The material has been subjected—"

"The material, yes," said Stirling. "But not the airplane made of the material. Anyway, we've got to fly the airplane overloaded, unbalanced, with an engine out . . . we still have a lot to learn. I'm confident it will make it, but there are lots of important tests yet to run."

"You've got to set it on fire," said George Binghamton. "And you've got to hit it with an artificial lightning strike."

"So it's . . . uh, a matter of so-far-so-good, huh?" asked Lola Weiss.

"I'd agree with that," said Stirling. "So far the problems have been manageable and the fixes cheap. I can't promise you it will always be that way."

For a moment the whole board of directors fell silent and sat exchanging thoughtful glances or staring at the table. It was an oddly assorted group, Stirling reflected, not your usual corporation board of directors. He'd seen pictures of Stanley Powell working in his office, invariably in shirtsleeves, and more than that, unkempt, with hair standing on end, sometimes unshaven. His style was preserved in George Binghamton, who had worked for him for decades and would not adapt to any new order. Robert Powell sat at the table in a well-tailored, dark blue suit, and Lou DiAngelo wore a three-piece gray. The banker, Deering, dressed like a banker. At the moment he was nibbling unenthusiastically on one of the sandwiches that had been the chief item in their box lunches.

Lola Weiss had surrendered to the style so many women in business affected: white blouse, floppy bow at her throat like a hyperthyroid necktie, tailored jacket and skirt; but Terry had made no such surrender and leaned back and to one side in her chair, in a lightweight yellow cashmere sweater and a pair of faded blue jeans. Lola Weiss impressed Stirling favorably, and he wondered how she would dress if she owned thirty-five per cent of the company.

"What do you need, Terry?" asked Deering. "You don't need a resolution of the board to continue testing, do you?"

"No, I think I have enough authority as president to go on with the testing," she answered. "You gave me that authority before. I wanted you to hear the test results. And I have something else I want to bring before the board of directors."

"We don't have an agenda," said Powell.

She glanced at him and ignored his remark. "This week," she said, "for some reason I can't understand—and I guess none of you can—a highly critical article appeared in a leading trade publication. It is a damaging article. It could hurt our chances of raising capital. Fortunately for us, this time we have an ally. Because Colonel Stirling has a contract to test the Nimbus, he used one of his industry contacts and put something of his reputation on the line to get us another look and, we

hope, a better article. We are damned lucky to have a
man of his stature working with us."

"Hear, hear," said Walter O'Connell.

"Though it wasn't on the agenda, Bob," she said
wryly, with a nod toward Powell, "I have a proposal to
make to the board of directors. And if you're about to
suggest I can't raise an issue that's not on the agenda, I
checked the bylaws and have the advice of counsel—
the matter I'm about to raise can be raised at this
meeting."

"Checked with counsel," said DiAngelo. "Must be
something big!"

"It is," she said, fixing a cold stare on Louis DiAngelo. "I am prepared to tender my resignation as
president of Powell Industries, Incorporated—
provided the board sees fit to elect Colonel McDonald
Stirling president and chief executive officer. I will step
aside and hold only the office of chairman of the board
if we can secure for our chief executive a man of his
stature, experience, and reputation. I, uh . . . I offer
my resignation and move that Colonel Stirling be
elected president and chief executive officer."

Stirling's eyes were on Robert Powell. The man's
face turned white, then pink. He glanced around the
table, and Stirling could see him mentally counting
votes.

Terry needed four votes. They had discussed this
vote several times. She could count on George Binghamton's; he would go along with anything he supposed might be what Stanley Powell would have
wanted, and she had talked to him about it. Walter
O'Connell had been brought in by Stanley Powell at the
beginning of the Nimbus project, had done much of the

work on it, and resented Robert Powell's opposition to the project. Terry could count on him. So she had three votes, almost sure.

Robert Powell and Louis DiAngelo would vote no, almost for sure.

That left two swing votes: Deering, the banker, and Lola Weiss. Terry had not raised the subject with them before the meeting.

Deering, she had said to Stirling, could think of a hundred reasons for opposing anything if he were given time to ponder; but he would sometimes go along with something that looked good—and was good—when he didn't have time to consider all the possible disadvantages. And Lola. She was maybe the most objective member of the board.

Terry needed one of the swing votes. Powell needed them both.

"Under the bylaws," said DiAngelo, "you may have the right to make this motion, Terry. I think it would be foolish of us, though, to try to decide today. I move your motion be tabled to the next meeting of the board of directors."

"We don't have forever, Lou," she said. "We've put off and put off while the Nimbus has sat in a hangar corroding. Decisiveness—"

"A motion to table is not debatable, Terry," said DiAngelo. "We have to take the vote. I might suggest that Colonel Stirling wait outside, though."

"Never mind that," said Terry. "We'll vote. Those in favor of tabling my motion, so delaying again an important decision . . ."

DiAngelo raised his hand. He frowned curiously at Powell, but he was alone.

"Motion fails," said Terry briskly. "My motion is before the board. Will you accept my resignation and elect Colonel Stirling president and chief executive officer?"

"Uh, Terry," said Powell, licking his lips. "There's a lot to be decided. I mean, in terms of conditions of employment, compensation, stock options if any . . . a lot of things. But as, uh, as a matter of principle, to get the issue before the board, I . . . I, uh, second the motion."

They sat down over dinner at the Powell Country Club, a pool and tennis club with a nine-hole golf course, mostly sponsored by the company. The table once reserved for Stanley Powell, on a platform in a bay window, private in a limited sense but boldly conspicuous, was now reserved for Theresa Powell. She and Stirling sat alone there for dinner that evening. Hardly an eye in the whole dining room did not turn toward them often, trying not to be seen looking, yet concerned and curious.

As a concession to Stan's country club, Terry wore a blue silk sheath that clung fluidly to the slender curves of her long body. Candlelight flattered her; it gleamed in her hair, and it obscured the not-quite-invisible flaw in her complexion: a roughness of the skin along her cheekbones. Stirling was more conscious than he had been before that she was a beautiful young woman.

"It was simple enough," she said. "He's sharp, Mac. Let's not suppose he's not. He made a quick calculation, decided that either Deering or Lois was going to vote with us, and elected to make as graceful a concession as he could."

"He wouldn't make much of a bridge player," said Stirling. "He failed to signal his partner."

"Poor Lou," she said, grinning. "The one negative vote."

Stirling lifted his glass of champagne. "Anyway. Thanks, Terry. I hope you don't have any reason to regret it."

"Well, I hope you don't," she said. "It's not going to go as smoothly in the future."

"I'm well aware of it," he said. "I didn't take that amendment on the salary motion as a peace offering."

She had moved that his initial compensation as president of Powell Industries be $225,000 per annum. Powell, whose own salary was $210,000, had moved that Colonel Stirling be paid $300,000, and the motion had carried.

"He means to have your ass in a sling," she said.

Stirling looked around the room, aware of how eyes dropped as his glance traveled. "Well, he's got it," he said. "I'm president of a company with which I have no contract. I'm not bringing in my own management team but have to work with people I've inherited. I'm committed to manufacturing an experimental aircraft. And the first thing I've got to do is sell some banks on the idea that they should lend the company a lot of bucks."

She smiled. "Your management team is all around you," she said. "Staring at you. There aren't ten people in this dining room who don't work for you."

He glanced around again. "Jesus . . ."

"And you've got another problem, Mac."

"Which is?"

"There aren't ten people in this room who don't

entertain at least a small suspicion that you're the new president of Powell Industries because you're sleeping in Stan Powell's bed. There are some who *want* to think that, who don't want to try to explain you any other way."

He shrugged. "Well . . . anyway, I'm flattered."

Terry laughed. Her eyes met his. "So'm I," she said.

8

"UGLIEST-LOOKING AIRPLANE I ever saw, Mac," said
Jerry Goldstein.

"Can't argue with that," said Stirling.

They were inside one of the smaller hangars at
Powell Industries, where Stanley Powell had set up the
manufacturing facility to make the first prototypes of
the Nimbus. A second Nimbus had been in early stages
of construction when he died, and Stirling had now
made its completion a matter of high priority. He had
advised the board that at least four prototypes would
have to be built to complete all the test procedures the
FAA would require. One of them would be destroyed
on the ground and would never fly.

The airplane propped up in improvised cradles inside
the manufacturing hangar was nearer completion than
it might look, and at its present stage it was indeed
ugly. The graphite-epoxy composite of which it was
made was dull black. Most of the skin was not yet on,
leaving the wing spars and ribs and the fuselage string-
ers and longerons exposed like a black skeleton. Control rods and wires, some of them still dangling, ran
through the skeletal structure. The turbine engines
were in place in the rear, but the propeller had not yet
been delivered.

"I can understand the hardening of fabric to make

the skin," said Goldstein. "The concept that's difficult is that the skeleton is made of it."

Goldstein was an FAA inspector, so it was important that he understand the concept and develop confidence in it. Stirling picked up a length of wing rib—this one a rejected part, being off specs by a tiny fraction of an inch. "Bang it on the floor," he said.

Goldstein knelt and whacked the rib firmly on the concrete. It sounded as solid as metal. He banged it again, harder.

"You remember," said Stirling, "that the wings of the Harrier are made of this stuff. You know, what they call the jump jet, the one the British flew against the Mirages in the Falklands War."

"The skin . . ." Goldstein suggested.

"No, sir," said Stirling emphatically. "Skin, spars, ribs—the works. We could hardly stress a business plane the way the Harrier's wings are stressed."

Goldstein turned the rib over and over in his hands. "And this is made of fabric?"

Stirling nodded. "That rib happens to be fifty-six layers, each one cut precisely and positioned in a mold. The mold is put in an autoclave and baked under pressure. When it comes out, that's what you got—as strong as aluminum at half the weight."

"Who makes this stuff?"

"Union Carbide makes the basic fiber," said Stirling. "Look over here. They're cutting a wing panel."

Three young women were cutting a large sheet of black fabric, using ordinary shears and carefully following the marks drawn on the material.

"That's one layer," said Stirling. "That panel will

require, I think, twelve layers. They'll position that layer on top of the layers already in the mold over there. Later today, the mold will go in the autoclave. Eventually that panel will be fastened to the ribs and become a part of the wing."

"Without rivets," said Goldstein.

"Without rivets," Stirling confirmed. "Not only do we get a light airplane, we get one with absolutely smooth surfaces."

"What differences will there be between this one and the first prototype?" Goldstein asked.

"The chief one is that we're setting the pods for the engine intakes and exhausts at a new angle, ten degrees out," said Stirling. "Aside from that, we've changed the scoops that carry cooling air to the transmission. Otherwise . . ." He shrugged. "I'm going to have a different paint job put on this one. The first one was Stanley Powell's. This one's mine. I'm going to show it."

"It would be regarded as a sign of commitment," Terry said to Stirling, "if you moved to Powell."

She had telephoned late in the afternoon and asked him to meet her for dinner at the country club. He had asked her to come to Dan's instead, since he had to work late at MARC, cleaning up a few details of his departure. Terry was dressed more for the country club than for Dan's: in a pale green linen jacket and skirt, with a white silk blouse.

"What, and give up eating and drinking at Dan's?" he laughed.

"You may have to someday if you're going to be a captain of industry."

"If that's the price of being a captain of industry, fuck it," said Stirling.

Although she seemed to resist it, a smile spread over Terry's face. She shook her head. "What does motivate you, Mac?" she asked.

He drew in a deep breath. "Good food, good drink, good friends, good—"

"Shit."

"Uh . . . shit?"

"You're as motivated as any man I ever saw," she said. "You want success. Don't kid me. You think you want it on your own terms, but when the chips are down we'll see what compromises you make between your terms and your success."

"How do you define success, Terry?" he asked.

"How do *you?*"

Mac Stirling did not like the question. He did not like to think about it. It was in fact a question he had mulled over many times, alone. "I've avoided becoming a corporate whore," he said. He turned his martini between his hands, looking at the ice melting in the almost empty glass. "Or was the Air Force . . . ?"

"Anguish," said Terry. "Forgive me, Mac. None of us should be reminded of what we pay."

"So you've got a pretty good handle on what I've paid," he said. "So what have *you* paid?"

"My dues," she said. "Drop it, Mac. I don't want to talk about it."

"Okay. I don't want to talk about mine, either."

"I want to be honest with you, though. How much do you know about the way Stan died?"

Stirling drew a deep breath and shook his head. "I suppose I could say nothing."

"I could say you don't need to know," Terry said. She shook down the ice in her martini and plucked out an olive between two fingers. In this, she matched him drink for drink, and she ate her olives as he did. "If you don't know, you don't know how rational or irrational my commitment is. I'm going to tell you more about Stan than Bob will ever know."

"Only if you want to, Terry."

"What do I know about airplanes?" she asked. "I've done every goddamned thing I could to learn, but if I studied for the next twenty years I wouldn't know twenty per cent of what you know. Maybe my judgment is wrong." She sighed. "I needed another judgment on the Nimbus."

"You've got good people, Terry. Walter O'Connell. Binghamton. Bill Carey, the mechanic. Others."

"For one reason and another," she said, sipping the watery dregs of her martini, "none of them have your stature. I trust them. God, how I've relied on them since Stan died! But they couldn't break Bob's resistance—which you did in an hour."

Stirling shook his head firmly. "We didn't break anything, Terry. Bob counted the votes and saw he was on the losing side for the moment. He made a graceful concession, for tactical reasons. But he's just as much opposed to the Nimbus as ever."

"Okay," she said. "So, okay. But I want to tell you about Stan. About how he died. I think you should know."

"Heart attack," said Stirling softly.

She nodded. "Yes. His first. But he didn't go all at once. For a couple of days we thought he'd make it. It happened at the country club, during dinner. He called

116

the waiter over and very quietly told him to get the paramedics fast. And he told him, 'Man, after you call them, bring me a double brandy, and make that fast, too.' He drank the brandy—not all of it; he just sipped at it—and waited for the emergency squad. When they got there, he stood up and lay down on their cart. 'Hospital, fellows,' he said. 'Coronary unit, I think. I ain't feelin' so good.'"

"Always in control," said Stirling.

She nodded. "He wanted that brandy, he told me at the hospital, because he figured it would be weeks before he could have another drink. Anyway, he said, if he had to go out, he wanted to go with the taste of Courvoisier on his lips. Then he grinned and said he wanted to go, if he could, with his . . . Well, you know what he meant. With himself in me."

Stirling nodded.

"And for a day or so," she said, "we thought he was going to make it. He got through the first hours, the first day. Then he had another one, the second coronary, in his hospital bed. And when that happened, he knew it was over; he knew he had another day or so at most. I was there. I never left his side. Never. He had a lot of things to say to me. Nothing to say to Bob. I—" She shook her head and closed her eyes.

Mac touched her hand—the first time he had ever touched her. "You don't have to go through this, Terry."

She slammed her glass on the table, emphatically signaling Valerie to bring another drink. "Stan said Bob was a dummy, not to be trusted or relied on. He was bitter about Bob—and about his daughter, the holy sister. 'They'll try to overwhelm you, honey,' he said.

'Don't let 'em.' He told me Bob is a homosexual—which is not true, incidentally. I don't know where he got that idea. Anyway . . ."

"You don't have to—"

"Don't try to stop me, Mac. I've got this started. So . . . try to picture this. Here's this powerful man you've always relied on, lying there as white as the white sheets around him, all connected to tubes and wires. And he talked to me about the Nimbus. He told me Bob would want to drop the project. He'd want to drop it for a quick profit, so he could take his money and get out. 'Don't let him do it, honey,' he said. 'Don't let 'em gang up on you.' "

"Jesus . . ."

Terry shot an impatient glance toward the bar. "Maybe he was wrong," she said. "How good is a man's judgment at a time like that?" She let a sad smile turn her mouth and lift her brows. "What I respected most in Stan was that he *believed*. He committed himself to his dreams. But they *were* dreams sometimes, Mac, and Bob isn't completely off base when he says that Stan was sometimes wrong."

"Not a bad dream, the Nimbus," said Stirling.

"What he wanted was to change the world," she said quietly. "To him, the Nimbus wasn't just another airplane; it was a revolution in air transportation: the airplane that would move people for half the cost, that would free aviation from dependence on oil, foreign or otherwise. In the future, he said, all planes would be built like the Nimbus. He wanted to be remembered as a big man, as big as the Wright brothers. No. Wrong. He wanted to be remembered in the same class with Leonardo da Vinci."

Terry grinned and stopped.

"There are documents in the files," said Stirling, "about running the turbines on methyl alcohol—you know, alcohol fuel from grain."

"His mind never stopped. His imagination . . . One night he talked for hours about a design for an atomic-powered airliner. That was while his health was still good, and he was only sixty. But he knew it would never happen in his lifetime. In Bob's maybe. That was what made him so angry about Bob, that Bob would never turn his mind to an idea like that."

Valerie put two fresh martinis on their table. Her glance crossed Mac's face—inquiring, understanding. She could see that the conversation was anything but casual, that it had in fact become confidential, even intimate.

Terry picked up her martini, stared into it for a moment, then put it down. "Stan . . ." she whispered. "I held his hand as he died. I'd never seen anyone die before. God help me so I don't have to see it again. People don't want to believe it, but I was in love with Stan. He was thirty-three years older than I was, and that's been the subject of all kinds of jokes, all kinds of cruel speculation. You had to know Stan to understand it."

Stirling shook his head. "I didn't know him, really, but you don't have to convince me."

Terry sighed. "The point is, I *promised* him. A couple of days before he died, he asked me to promise I would do everything I could to keep the Nimbus project alive."

"I think you have," said Stirling.

She nodded. "But that's why. Because I promised. Is

that a good reason, Mac? A hysterical promise, when you've got tears in your eyes?"

He shrugged. "I can think of worse."

She picked up her martini and took a swallow. "I wanted you to know," she said. "You're making a commitment to this thing, and you need to know the origin of *my* commitment."

"Origin . . ."

Terry nodded. "I understand you. Yes, okay, *origin*. It isn't inconsistent with—"

"With the lady's ambition," said Stirling. He raised his glass and saluted her with it. "Not inconsistent. The ambition is a little easier to understand, from my point of view. But not inconsistent."

"They think I can't do it," she said. "Bob and . . . and a lot of others. I want to shove it up their—"

"Right," he interrupted. "A not unworthy motive. So . . . to you, Terry. And to the Nimbus. And to success. *Prosit!*"

When they left the Silver Wing, the moonlight was cold on the parking lot. His Porsche sat beside her Mercedes. They had eaten. They had drunk martinis and wine. They had recovered the peace she had lost when she told him about the death of Stanley Powell. They walked close to each other, their hips brushing, not for any particular reason, just because they were together and had become friends.

"Mac . . ."

"Uhmm?"

"Is anybody waiting for you?"

He glanced back toward the Silver Wing. Valerie wasn't waiting. That was how it was between them:

nothing automatic, something only when one of them asked for it. So he could shake his head, and it was an honest answer—no one was waiting for him.

"Me neither," said Terry.

He stopped short of their cars. "We could make a big mistake," he said quietly. "I mean, right now. It could be a big mistake."

"I know how to take chances," she said. "I was taught by a master. Don't you want—"

"Of course I want to."

She smiled, a little nervously. "Well . . . so do I. This isn't the first time the thought has come to me."

"No. Me neither."

"Well . . . ?"

Stirling walked decisively to the passenger side of his Porsche, opened the door, and stood aside. Terry got in.

They were silent in the car. He stared at the road. She did, too. She understood as well as he did: all the reasons not to do this, how many kinds of risk they were taking. None of that seemed so important right now. She wanted him. She wanted Mac Stirling, and he wanted her; and for this moment, this night, *that* was important. In her silence the thoughts came to her, of the mistake she could be making. She dismissed them. This was what she wanted.

They walked together into his house and went directly to the bedroom, with hardly a word. They did not need a drink; they had drunk enough at Dan's. In his bedroom, she glanced around, switched on his bedside lamp, and shot toward the switch by the door so communicative a glance that he switched off the ceiling light immediately.

She began to undress. She took off the jacket, the blouse, and the skirt. She was wearing no bra; he knew she almost never did. She was not wearing panties, either, just a garter belt of thin black straps and a pair of stockings. She kicked off her shoes and stretched out across his bed, leaving on the garter belt and stockings.

That she was exceptionally beautiful did not surprise Mac Stirling. Of course she was; she had made her living as a model and showgirl. That she was proud of her body was evident, and she had every right to be. She was slender. Her skin was smooth. Her breasts were firm and round, not pendulous. Her nipples were quite prominent: rich-colored and wrinkled. She did not trim her pubic hair, and a faint line of curly hair grew from her triangle to her navel, almost but not quite invisible. The hair stood in a curly mound between her hips, at the bottom of her belly; but it was all but absent from her pubes, leaving her dark cleft bare and cleanly defined.

He undressed.

Mac was a solid, hard-muscled man, in better condition than his fondness for steaks, wine, and martinis might have suggested. He did not tan readily, and his skin was fair in spite of frequent exposure to the desert sun.

Terry reached out and ran her fingertips over a crosshatch of faint white scars on his right hip. "Any landing you walk away from is a good landing, hmm?" she asked softly.

He glanced down. "Tan Son Nhut," he said. "Rotten damned airport. The MiGs never got me, but some kid on the ground put a rocket launcher to his skinny shoulder and took the wing off a Phantom II just as I was landing. Spectacular!"

She lifted his penis in her hand and stroked it with her middle finger. "Anyway, you saved what's important."

He lay down beside her and kissed her cheek and lips. Terry's lips were full and moist. Her eyes were heavy lidded, and her lashes were long. She wore a little eyeliner. Her hair was lightly scented from her shampoo.

"Jesus . . ." he whispered.

"Mac," she murmured. "I want *everything* from you. Know what I mean? Everything . . . not a quickie, Mac. Something good, that we'll always remember, no matter what happens. You understand?"

He frowned. "Quickie? With *you?*" He grinned and shook his head. "I can't imagine."

Mac slipped down and sucked one of her hard little nipples between his lips. She drew a noisy breath. He nibbled gently. She moaned, and he nibbled a little harder. She took his hand in hers and guided him down to her cleft. He pushed his finger into the moist place and explored everything it could reach before settling it high and beginning to stroke where he knew she was most sensitive.

"Mmm-hmm," she breathed, and she closed her eyes and smiled.

After a couple of minutes she seized his penis. "Bring it here," she whispered. "Put it in quick, do it quick, and then we've got all night for everything else."

He rolled over on top of her and shoved his shaft into her. She wrapped her legs around his back and clamped

123

their bodies together so tightly that he could only writhe and push, not hump and thrust. That was how she wanted it, and she twisted and lifted herself, pressing her belly and hips tightly to his. He was so far inside her that the whole length of his penis was gripped in her smooth wet inner flesh. She writhed. The stimulation brought him to his climax within the minute, and he broke loose inside her, pumping his fluid in a pulsing electric stream. She muttered a throaty laugh and closed her legs even tighter around him.

When he rolled off her, she rolled with him, and they lay pressed together, quiet, caressing each other's face and hair, nuzzling, kissing. After a while, he whispered the suggestion that they shower together. She took off the stockings and garter belt and went with him to the bathroom, where they clutched each other under the warm flow of water, soaping each other's bodies, sliding their hands over every part of each other. The water was a stimulant, and they were aroused to try, laughing, another penetration, standing and wet. It was awkward, and an urgency had grown on them, so they turned off the water, dried each other with big towels, and returned to the bed.

When he moved to straddle her again, she smiled, shook her head, and gestured to him to lie on his back. She surprised him. With her face to the foot of the bed, she straddled him, drew his penis into her mouth, and presented her cleft to his face. Mac pounded at the sides of his pillow to fatten it and lift his head. She let her knees slide apart to lower herself. He put his tongue to her parts that he had explored with his finger a little while before. He had little experience with this, but instinct told him to search for what was rudely called "the little man in the boat" and caress it with the tip of his tongue. When he did, she gasped.

"Oh, Mac . . . Oh, God, that's so *right!*"

"You, too," he muttered. "I . . ."

He felt her orgasmic spasms. Then his own came, and he felt her lips tighten on him as she drew out his fluid and swallowed it. Satiated and weakened, he drew her soft belly against his mouth and kissed it languidly as they settled into comfortable euphoria.

They slept fitfully, waking often to fondle each other and to kiss. Toward morning, he straddled and entered her again, and she received him happily and drowsily and went to sleep again soon after they had finished. He woke before she did in the morning, went to his kitchen, and started a pot of coffee. She woke and came in, nude, while he sat scanning the morning paper and waiting for the coffee to come down.

"I give you a hundred and forty years to quit treating me like that," she said.

It was good to see that she remained beautiful with nothing left of her style. Whatever she wore for cosmetics was gone. Her hair had been wet and fell uncombed around her neck. She sat down across the table from him, still slack from unfinished sleep.

"I'll take two hundred," he replied. "I'll need it."

"It can be arranged."

He nodded. "Yeah. It can. From this point of view, it can."

"I'm very selfish," Terry said. "I know there's somebody else . . . some little girl. But—"

"No commitment," he said.

"That you understand. But maybe . . . I don't care. But I do care."

"So do I," he said. "I'll do what I have to." He sighed. "She served our dinner at Dan's last night."

"Oh, Mac!"

"She's bright. She could see it between us. She gave me signals that she did."

Terry sighed heavily. "I can't say it would have made any difference if I'd known."

"I'll do what I have to do," he said.

"Not our worst problem, anyway," said Terry somberly.

"Right. Not our worst problem."

He got up and went to the refrigerator. Opening it, he frowned inside, looking for eggs, bacon.

"It's not just Bob," she said. "It will be the whole goddamned world—the banks, the bureaucrats, the media, even some of our own people. I mean, Lola Weiss wouldn't have voted with us if she'd suspected we—"

"Don't assume that," Mac interrupted.

"I don't assume anything," she said. "But we've bought for ourselves a new *vulnerability*. They'll use it against us. Some of them will. They'll say we're not committed to the Nimbus, we're committed to each other."

"I don't propose to—"

"Neither do I," she said instantly. "But—"

"But we'd better keep it a secret for a while."

She closed her eyes and nodded. "Not the way I want it, man. Not at all the way I want it. God no, I'm *proud*." She sighed. "But . . ."

126

Mac grinned. "We left your car all night on Dan's parking lot."

He had found eggs and now carried four of them to the counter.

She smiled. "No problem. I'll send someone from the Mercedes agency. I'll tell them it wouldn't start last night and to bring a tow truck for it. Let Dan and all the MARC people hanging around the Silver Wing see that." She laughed, then turned abruptly sober. "So here we go. Deception. A secret. Goddamnit, Mac!"

"For a while, baby," he said. "Till we get our plane on the market. Then . . . then anything, hmm? Any goddamn thing we want, you and me."

"Meantime . . . ?"

"We'll make our chances. Even if we blow it, Terry, we'll make our chances."

"For sure?" she asked.

He nodded. "For sure."

She looked out the window for a short moment, then turned her face up toward him where he stood at the counter, poised to crack eggs into a skillet. "Let's say the words, Mac. I'm ready to say them. I love you, man. I love you. Mac . . . damnit!"

"Yeah. Right. I love you too, Terry. Yeah, and . . . and like you say: *Damnit!*"

9

ROBERT POWELL SAT nervously, and in growing irritation, waiting for the chain-smoking, florid man on the opposite side of the desk to finish the telephone conversation that had interrupted their meeting. It was not a conversation, actually; the man had hardly said a word, just scowled and grunted. He had turned three-quarters away from Powell and was looking out the window, grunting, nodding, and leaving Powell to wait and to understand that he was not important enough to take priority over this call.

From time to time the building trembled and filled with a muted roar, as a big jet passed over at no more than two hundred feet, crossed the highway, and descended ponderously onto the runway of Los Angeles International Airport.

The man on the telephone was Charlie Horn. He was the top man in these noisy, smoky, littered offices, in this modest little concrete-block building half a mile from the airport. Charlie Horn. Not Charles, Charlie— on the door, even on his business cards. *Horn & Company, Investigators. Industrial Concerns A Specialty.*

"Suit yourself, friend," said Charlie Horn to the person on the other end of the telephone call. He hung up. Swinging around to face Powell, he snapped his lighter and lit a fresh cigarette. "Sorry 'bout that," he said. "You were saying?"

"I was emphasizing that everything must be kept absolutely confidential," said Powell.

"My friend," said Horn expansively, turning up the palms of his beefy hands, holding his cigarette tightly clamped in a widening grin, "absolute secrecy is my business. That's how I make a living—looking into other people's secrets but keeping my clients' secrets absolutely secure."

"You understand, then, what I have in mind? I want to know everything you can find out about the guy."

Horn's grin vanished, and he tapped his quarter-spent cigarette on the edge of a brass ashtray. "You don't really mean that, I think, Mr. Powell. You want a make on the man. I understand that. But you want the dirt, not the clean. I mean, you don't want to know what Sunday school he went to—unless he was humping the teacher."

Powell closed his eyes and sighed. "Right," he conceded.

"And the lady. You said you've had amateurs working on her case."

"I've made some . . . inquiries."

"No more," said Horn sternly. "If I'm doing it, I'm doing it. I don't want an accidental contact with anybody working the same case. I don't want to have to clean up somebody else's mess. I don't want the suspect to find out from some amateur that a make is being done on him. You follow?"

Powell nodded. "All right."

Horn took a moment to drag deeply on his cigarette. "Now, sir," he said. "Tell me who's paying the bill."

"I am," said Powell. "I hope to make it the company sooner or later, but for now I'm paying the bill. Personally."

"And you brought the check for the retainer."

"Five thousand dollars," said Powell. "There you are."

Horn picked up the check and glanced it over. "One of my office girls will drop you back at the terminal. In and out in ten minutes, hey, Mr. Powell? That's why I have this place right on the edge of the airport. You'll hear from me in a couple weeks or so."

A week after the day that Robert Powell visited Charlie Horn in the little office building just off Los Angeles International Airport, Stirling landed a Nimbus there for the first time.

The Nimbus he landed was 87SP—Eight-seven Sierra Papa—the first airplane. The second one, 88SP, was not yet ready. Stirling had ordered the plain white airplane painted with black and silver gray stripes the length of the fuselage, with the corporate symbol of Powell Industries on the vertical fin. Shorty Bellows, newly hired from MARC as a Powell Industries test pilot, flew copilot. Terry Powell and Walter O'Connell sat in the comfortable passenger compartment. Los Angeles was socked in, which was not unusual, but Stirling and Bellows lowered the Nimbus smoothly through the clouds and smog. The runway came in sight when they broke out at some four hundred feet, and the Nimbus swept almost silently onto the wet pavement.

The busy ground controller could not resist a question—"Uh, Nimbus Eight-seven Sierra Pop, say your type. Don't think we've ever seen anything like you."

"Eight-seven, Roger. This is the new biz plane from Powell Industries," Stirling replied. "We hope you see hundreds like us in the next few years."

"Good luck with that, sir. Make your next right and proceed by taxiway Gamma to the general aviation ramp. Be with us a while, so some of us curious folks can come look?"

"Three or four hours, Ground. And you're welcome to come look."

"Roger. Hold short of Beta until the One-ten crosses, then cleared to the ramp."

Shorty Bellows taxied the Nimbus while Stirling cleared its navigation radios, reset flaps, and scribbled a few notes in the log. A light rain was falling. Shorty kept the navigation lights flashing—to dramatize the approach of the airplane to the prospective buyers he expected were watching from the windows of the general aviation lounge.

Prospects were waiting—Calvin Haroldson, president of Southwest Consolidated Industrial Companies, and his chief corporate pilot, Dave Johnson. They were not reticent men, and they were airplane-experienced, so as soon as the turbines were shut off and the big rear-mounted propeller was coasting, they trotted across the rain-swept ramp toward the Nimbus. Shorty lowered the stairs, Stirling opened the door, and the two men hurried up and into the passenger cabin.

"Cal. Good of you," said Stirling. "And Dave. We've met, I'm sure, Dave, though I'm damned if I can recall where."

"Guam, believe it or not," said Johnson with a careful smile.

Stirling frowned. "Admiral . . . ?"

"Bennett. I was flying Admiral Bennett."

"Right! And we flew escort for you, to get you into Tan Son Nhut in one piece."

"Took a couple of small-arms slugs in the wing, even so," said Johnson.

"Couldn't do a damned thing about it," laughed Stirling. "The woods around the field had been napalmed thoroughly an hour before, but . . . You know how it was. Listen, gentlemen, have a seat. We thought right here aboard the Nimbus would be the best place to meet—unless you have another idea."

"Looks comfortable," said Haroldson, glancing around the blue cabin. "Do I have the honor of meeting Mrs. Powell?"

"Absolutely," said Stirling. "Mrs. Theresa Powell, Stan's widow. She's chairman of the board. And this is Walter O'Connell. He's our vice president, engineering."

Haroldson stepped into the middle of the cabin and shook hands with Terry and O'Connell. Though his hair was almost white, Haroldson was only a year older than Stirling; he was a trim, solid, vigorous-looking man with a deep tan and cold blue eyes. "I met your late husband a few times, Mrs. Powell," he said. "My much-belated sympathy. He was a fine man."

"Thank you, Mr. Haroldson. Have a seat."

The Nimbus seated six passengers in complete comfort, plus two more whose seats were not uncomfortable. Stirling had personally supervised the vacuuming of the interior of the airplane, so that not a trace remained of the litter from the constant test flying the Nimbus continued to undergo.

Haroldson took the seat Terry had suggested: one of the executive armchairs. Stirling took the other. O'Connell and Johnson sat down on Terry's left.

"I must say," said Haroldson, "this is impressive. Comfortable. Tasteful."

"Thanks, Cal," said Stirling. "But we could make a motel room more comfortable, and for a whole lot less money. What I hope will impress you is the numbers."

"If those numbers stand up, they are impressive," said Haroldson.

"If I remember correctly, you're now operating two Lears, a Citation, and . . ."

"And a Gulfstream," said Johnson.

Stirling nodded. "You set out for New York, you're going to want to fly one of those," he said. "What I'd like to sell you is the idea that if you were going to San Francisco, Denver, or Phoenix, you'd fly a Nimbus if you had one. To Chicago . . . or, say, Dallas . . . Well, I think I can make more than a good case for the Nimbus. And if I have your figures right, eighty-five per cent of your flying is within the optimum operating radius for the Nimbus, which you could fly on all those runs for half the cost. That's a mouthful, but we think we can prove it."

"Dave's got some questions," said Haroldson. "Pretty technical, some of them."

"That's why Walter has come with us," said Terry. "There's not much he doesn't know about the Nimbus."

"I'd like to walk around it," said Johnson. "Rain or no."

Stirling nodded. "You and Walter. And Shorty Bellows, if you like."

"You got ol' Shorty?" Johnson laughed.

"Been with us a couple of weeks. He flew right seat for me this morning," said Stirling. "He's logged a couple of hours in the Nimbus."

O'Connell, Johnson, and Bellows left the plane. The rain outside had slackened to a drizzle, and in raincoats they walked around it, O'Connell pointing out its features. Inside, Stirling moved to a seat beside Terry, so the two of them would face Haroldson as they talked.

"What happens if one engine fails?" Haroldson asked.

"Automatic clutch disengagement," said Stirling. "I shut one down in flight yesterday, to see how the plane flies on one engine."

"It didn't nose over, I take it," said Haroldson.

"Makes it a little sluggish," said Stirling. "We have extensive one-engine testing to do."

Haroldson ran the back of his hand across his mouth, a nervous gesture perhaps prompted by embarrassment at being unable to keep his eyes from flicking constantly across Terry's legs. She was wearing a dark blue jacket over a white blouse, with a tailored gray skirt, but the short skirts dictated by the year's new fashions would not let her sit without showing three or four inches of sleek, stockinged leg above her knees.

"So how long is it going to take to get the FAA certificate?" Haroldson asked.

"Quite a while. A year, I'd guess," said Stirling.

"And you can't deliver an airplane until when?"

"Eighteen months. Maybe two years."

Haroldson glanced out at his chief pilot running his hand along the smooth surface of the airplane's wing. "But you want orders now," he said.

"I'd like to sell you two airplanes, Cal," said Stirling.

"With some money up front," said Haroldson.

"Not uncommon in the industry," said Stirling. "Here's the deal: If you buy the standard Nimbus with the standard avionics, we'll guarantee a price of one million eight. The airplane when manufactured is going to go a little over two million; we're not sure just how much over. We'll guarantee delivery by a specified date. We ask for fifteen per cent in advance, payable on the signing of the contract. We ask for another fifteen per cent twelve months before delivery date, then twenty per cent more six months before delivery. The balance is payable on delivery."

"Does your contract include a price escalation for inflation?" Haroldson asked.

"No. We're going to bet on the economy."

"Fifteen per cent of a million eight is, uh . . ."

"Two hundred seventy thousand," said Terry.

"Two hundred seventy thousand," Haroldson agreed. "How many orders do you have?"

Stirling grinned. "Nobody has turned us down so far. Because you're the first company president I called."

"What an honor," said Haroldson dryly. "How many orders do you hope to get in, say, the next six months?"

"We'd like to get a hundred," said Terry. "Plus another hundred in the following six months."

"Fifty-four million in advance orders," said Harold-

135

son. "Ambitious. It's your best way to raise capital, though—that is, from the people who'll want to buy and fly your airplanes."

"It will cut down on what we have to borrow from the banks," said Stirling.

"Borrow instead from your customers," said Haroldson with a smile. He shrugged. "I guess it's not unusual in the aircraft industry."

"No, it's not," said Stirling.

"Where are you going to manufacture?" asked Haroldson.

"We haven't decided. Possibly overseas."

When O'Connell, Johnson, and Bellows returned, Stirling suggested they have lunch. Bellows heated prepackaged hors d'oeuvres in the microwave. Stirling offered chilled champagne from the refrigerator—or cocktails if anyone would rather. All took champagne except Bellows, who would be flying the Nimbus back to Powell.

Haroldson lifted his glass. "To your success," he said.

"Thank you, Cal," said Stirling. "I thought you'd find the Nimbus an interesting idea."

"Frankly," said Haroldson, "what interests me most is seeing how much it interests *you*. How many companies did you turn down, Mac? I mean, how many offered you jobs and got turned down before you decided to take an offer from Powell Industries?" He lifted his glass toward Terry. "Do you have special powers of persuasion, Mrs. Powell?"

"Well, I knew who I wanted," she said.

"I can't help but wonder if Stan didn't say to you: 'Get Mac Stirling. Get us Mac.' Did he?"

"She's quite capable of making her own judgments, Cal," said Stirling.

"Oh I'm sorry, Mrs. Powell," said Haroldson lightly. "I didn't mean to suggest otherwise."

"I understand," she said with a cool smile.

"Well, of course," said Haroldson. He glanced around as if looking to one of the others to bail him out of this contretemps. "Uh, at any rate, you have an interesting airplane here."

"How many can we sell you, Cal?" asked Stirling.

"Uh, well . . . regard it as entirely possible that Southwest Consolidated will buy one of your airplanes. I'll have to talk it over with Dave, and I'm sure we'll have a whole lot of questions. Certainly, certification is one of them. But it's possible. It's an impressive idea, this airplane; and if it will do what you say it will, we'd be in on the ground floor of a good thing."

"Miss D'Angostino, I believe. Miss Valerie D'Angostino? Please excuse me if I'm wrong."

She had just stepped through the door and, keys in hand, switched on the lights in the living room of her apartment. He had been sitting there in the dark, in her recliner, maybe watching her television until he heard the crunch of gravel in the driveway. Her apartment stank of his cigarette smoke. It was after two in the morning.

"Who the hell are you?" she asked fearfully.

"Take it easy," the man said. "I'm not a burglar, and I'm not a rapist. I'm a private investigator, and all I want is to ask you a question or two."

Valerie let the door stand open. "You guys come

crawling out from under every rock. You're the second one—"

"I know. The first one worked for me. My name is Charlie Horn, incidentally. Here's my card."

He lifted himself out of the chair—quick and agile for an overweight man, she thought—and came toward her, holding out his business card. As she took it, he stepped past her and closed the door.

Valerie was still frightened, but her fear was turning to anger. "How'd you get in here?" she asked.

"It's my business," he said. He locked the door.

"Yeah? Well, you're a *burglar*, mister. That's all you are in San Bernardino County: nothing but a burglar." She reached for the telephone. "I'm calling the sheriff, and you better be gone before the deputy gets here."

"Huh-uh," said Horn. He grabbed her hand and forced the telephone back into the cradle. "After we talk. Then you can call the sheriff, if that's what you want."

"So you're not a rapist, huh?" she snapped, jerking away from him. "A murderer maybe. You didn't deny you might be that."

"Valerie . . ." he said, chuckling. "C'mon. Don't flatter yourself that I'd be interested in raping you. And I sure as hell am not going to kill you. Burglar?" He shrugged. "If you decide to call the sheriff, I'll just stay and talk to him. I'll tell him you let me in. Let's see who he believes. Respected private eye—"

"Private *dick*."

"Whatever. Let's see if he believes Charlie Horn. Or if he believes Valerie D'Angostino. Can you think of any reason why a law officer might not be inclined to believe you, Valerie?"

"Private *prick*," she muttered furiously.

"Yeah. When you refused to talk to my operative, we did a little make on you. Ever see this?"

He handed her a badly reproduced copy of a criminal record sheet from the files of the Los Angeles police department. There were her front and profile mug shots, her fingerprints, and the record of her arrests and convictions. She knew about it, of course, but had never seen the ugly sheet that was on file in Sacramento and Washington as well as in Los Angeles. She took off her glasses to read it.

"Quite a record, Valerie," said Horn. He took the sheet from her. "Let's see here. Arrested, Los Angeles, March 4, 1981, possession of a controlled substance, marijuana. Sentenced ten days Sybil Brand Institute for Women, fined five hundred dollars. Arrested July 22, 1981, pandering for prostitution and possession of a controlled substance, marijuana. Pandering charge dropped, sentenced thirty days SBI, find one thousand dollars. Released SBI after twenty days, good behavior. Arrested January 12, 1982 . . . Oh boy! Possession of a controlled substance, cocaine. Possession of a stolen handgun. Possession of a forged driver's license. Conspiracy to sell a controlled substance. Convicted of conspiracy, sentenced to five years, California Institution for Women, Corona. Released on parole August 1, 1984, final release November 30, 1985. Uh . . . this is *you* I'm reading about, isn't it?"

"You son of a bitch," she muttered.

He refolded the sheet and returned it to the inside pocket of his jacket. He lit a cigarette as he spoke—"I know something else about you, Valerie. You were a registered nurse. Of course, you aren't anymore. I'm not sure you'd even be working at Dan's if he knew about this prostitution business."

"That was dropped," she said. "I was never a hooker."

"But you must have been some kind of dealer," he said. "You seem to have paid your fines without any trouble. Or someone paid them."

"I did my time," she said sullenly.

"Sure. But things have a way of comin' back, catching up with a person again, after you thought it was all over."

Valerie walked into her kitchen. From a bottle sitting by the sink she poured herself a shot of whiskey. He had followed her, and she tossed her head toward the bottle and glasses, indicating he could pour himself a drink if he wanted it. He did. Charlie Horn poured a heavy shot, neat, and tossed it back.

"Okay, Miss D'Angostino," he said in a new businesslike tone. "All I want is the simple answers to a few simple questions."

"I bet," she said. She wandered back to the living room and sat down.

"Really. My inquiry has to do with your friend Colonel McDonald John Stirling. He's quite a lover, is Colonel McDonald John Stirling. Don't tell me he isn't; I know he is. And for a while you were sleeping with him. Don't tell me you weren't; I know you were. But you aren't anymore. How come?"

Valerie smiled. "Is that all you want to know?"

"No. I want to know more than that, but I'll start with that."

"You're nuts," she said. "Big damn deal. Yeah, I

slept with the guy for a while. Then he got bored with me and stopped asking. He's not the first guy that ever did that. I guess I'm not very good."

"I'd guess you are," said Horn grimly. "What you're not very good at is covering a lie."

"What you want me to tell you, that he had weird habits? That what you're looking for, something like that? And who wants to know?"

"I want to know," snapped Horn.

"So what do you want to know? What answer would you really like? I don't imagine you much care if it's the truth or not, so just tell me what you want to know, and I'll give you that for an answer."

"You're going to get your ass in a sling, young lady," Horn growled.

"No," she said, shaking her head. "My ass has *been* in a sling, but it's not now. And I've dealt with tougher cops than you. So screw you"—she stopped to read his name from his card—"Charlie Horn."

"And I've dealt with tougher broads," he said. He stepped into the kitchen and helped himself to a second shot from her bottle. "And smarter ones."

"Ask your question and get out," she said.

"Okay, kitten," he said, smiling sarcastically. "All I want to know is, did the colonel drop you for another broad? And if so, who? That's all I want to know."

Valerie laughed. "You came all the way from L.A. to ask me that? You're not a very good liar yourself. I still want to know, what do you want for an answer? Who do you have in mind?"

"Who would it be?" he insisted.

"I figure he did drop me for another woman," said

Valerie. "But I don't know who. Nobody I know. He didn't bring her around and ask for my approval."

"You haven't even seen him with another woman?"

"He had dinner with a woman one night at Dan's, where I work. You can figure what you want out of that. It was Mrs. Stanley Powell."

"Is that who took your place?"

Valerie shrugged. "I don't know. I've seen the two of them have some drinks together and something to eat. I don't care if he's sleeping with her now. I didn't have any claim on him. I didn't like him that much. What'd you think I might do, go peek in their windows to see if—"

"Her car stayed in the Silver Wing parking lot all night one night," said Horn.

"Right. And was pulled off by a tow truck the next morning. So?"

"Goddamnit! Did they seem affectionate that night when they had drinks and dinner?"

Valerie shrugged. "No."

"Didn't hold hands? Didn't . . . ?"

"No."

"I don't believe you."

"Okay, so they held hands, kissed, he bit her earlobe, and he felt her boobs. That better?"

"This is a waste of time," he said, crushing out the cigarette he had finished, lighting another one.

"You're damned right it is. And it's time for you to leave, Charlie Horn. I'm starting to think my word would be just as good as yours if I called the sheriff. 'Cause I got you figured now. You may be a private dick, but you're a sleazy one; and I wouldn't be surprised the L.A. department's got you nailed pretty good, if ever it came to your word against somebody else's. I think you better move along, Charlie."

Horn flushed deep red. He swung on his heel and stalked to the door. For a moment he fumbled with the latch, then he swung the door open and stalked out into the night.

Valerie waited until she saw and heard his car being started and screeching away down the street. Then she picked up the telephone and dialed a number.

"Mac?"

"Uh . . . yeah. Who's . . . ?"

"Valerie. Look, a private detective from L.A. broke into my place tonight and hung around here to question me when I got home. It was all about you. And Mrs. Powell."

"Terry? Mrs. Powell? What about—?"

"They've been snooping around, Mac. He wasn't the first one. He found out about you and me. What he wanted to know is if Mrs. Powell, uh . . . well, he asked me if she'd taken my place sleeping with you. I don't know what's going on, Mac, but I figured you ought to know. The guy's name is Charlie Horn. He's a private dick from L.A."

"What'd you tell him?"

"I played him like a fish on a hook. I figured he was looking for a connection between you and Mrs. Powell. After all, what else could be so important as to bring a private dick in from L.A. to ask questions about your love life? So, when he asked me if I saw you with any other women, I said you'd had dinner at Dan's with Mrs. Powell one night. Man, did he go for that! That's what he wanted, Mac: to find out if you and Mrs. Powell are a number. I'd watch out for him if I were you. More than that, I'd watch out for whoever hired him. He's scum, Mac. Personally, I think they're all scum: private dicks. But this one's something else. And so's whoever hired him."

10

"THE WINE," SAID João Estremoz, holding up a glass and swirling it. "Is it to your taste, Mrs. Powell?"

"It is an excellent wine, Senhor Estremoz," she said. She sipped and nodded. "An excellent wine."

Estremoz smiled. "Another product of our country."

Mario Monforte laughed. "The minister must not overlook any of our products."

All day they had been attended by a delegation that sometimes reached twenty men and women. Tonight, only these two were their hosts for dinner: João Estremoz, minister of external commerce, and Mario Monforte, president of Aeromerica.

"Brazil produces many fine products," said Estremoz. "From wine to"—he grinned—"aircraft."

"We know the name Embraer, of course," said Stirling. "I've been a passenger on the Bandeirante."

"Yes," said Estremoz. "Many of them have been purchased by commuter airlines in the States."

"Plus the Centauro," said Stirling.

"Centauro?" Terry asked.

"The Centauro, Mrs. Powell," said Monforte, "is an interceptor and ground-attack military aircraft. It is for us a joint project with Italy, and the military forces of both countries use them. Embraer manufactures them here, at its facility at São José dos Campos, and Aermacchi and Aeritalia manufacture them in Italy."

"Aeromerica is not Embraer, though," she said. "I believe someone said Aeromerica is an independent company."

"Independent of Embraer," said Estremoz. "The government of Brazil owns an interest in Embraer, and it owns an interest in Aeromerica. There is no connection between Embraer and Aeromerica."

"And just to complete the understanding," said Stirling, "what is the relationship between the two companies and Banco do Brasil?"

"Banco do Brasil is our national bank," said Estremoz. "It finances many of our industrial enterprises. It will finance an agreement to establish the manufacturing facility for your Nimbus if its officers find the enterprise secure."

"I am concerned," said Stirling, "about internationally imposed restrictions on the loan capacities of Banco do Brasil. I am sure you understand and will not be offended by the question."

"Not at all," said Estremoz. "The restrictions do not apply when the bank proposes to provide financial support for an industrial enterprise that will strengthen our economy and improve the security of our foreign debt."

"And your inflation?" asked Stirling.

"We can fund your enterprise in Swiss gold francs if necessary," said Estremoz somewhat coldly. "Or in American dollars."

The two Brazilians impressed Terry as the most handsome, self-possessed businessmen she had ever seen. João Estremoz was a tall, long-headed, bald man: handsome, conspicuously self-confident, dressed in a beautifully tailored charcoal gray suit. Mario Monforte was ·younger, shorter, stockier, yet just as suave, as well dressed in dark blue, and interesting for the several heavily bejeweled rings he wore on his expressive hands.

They were the dinner guests of Monforte, in his seaside villa somewhere south of Rio de Janeiro. She supposed that somewhere in the States you could find such conspicuous yet tasteful and comfortable luxury, but she was not sure where; it was not within her experience. The house, the furnishings, the servants, the food and wine, the string trio that played in the garden outside the dining room—all were in exquisite, understated taste. She had noted, too, that armed guards patrolled the lighted grounds, as did big dogs of fierce mien.

She was not surprised, nor was Mac. Before they left California, he had spent two days with a consultant on Latin American economies, especially on the state of the inflation-ridden economy of Brazil. The two of them had spent an evening with the consultant, learning the business customs and courtesies of the country. They would not be expected, they were told, to speak Portuguese; but it would be well to remember that Portuguese, not Spanish, was the language of the majority of the population of the South American continent. Brazilians could be sensitive on that point.

They had been told, too, to expect just what they were seeing: families with vast old wealth, living serenely in a country with a huge population of bitterly impoverished citizens. Brazilian inflation was almost as dramatic as that of the Weimar Republic in Germany in the 1920's. In 1984 one United States dollar had purchased 1350 Brazilian cruzeiros; now it would buy more than 12,000. Even so, men like Monforte prospered, and the government remained firmly in control. Brazilian businessmen like Monforte, their consultant had assured them, could raise capital and could organize all the elements of a manufacturing enterprise. They could hardly do better, he had urged, than to manufacture the Nimbus in Brazil.

In the four weeks since the meeting with Calvin Haroldson, president of Southwest Consolidated Industries, Stirling had met with half a dozen more corporate officers: old friends, some of them retired Air Force officers; and he had informal commitments for the purchase of ten Nimbuses. He had to begin to plan for manufacturing. Manufacture outside the United States appealed to Stirling for a number of reasons, cheaper labor and availability of capital being the chief ones, and this was the first serious exploration of a specific possibility.

"The interest rate on financing through Banco do Brasil," said Estremoz, "will be competitive with any rate Powell Industries could obtain anywhere. The money will originate with the World Bank, you understand."

"And, of course, you will benefit substantially from the economies to be achieved through our labor rates."

"If we can take the heat," said Stirling.

"Yes," conceded Monforte. "If your labor unions and your politicians do not impose too many pressures for your having taken an American manufacturing operation out of the States."

"It's a factor we can't afford to overlook," said Terry.

"We understand," said Estremoz. "But here you will achieve important savings in labor costs. At São José dos Campos, we have built almost a whole new city for our aerospace industry. A reserve of skilled labor lives in the vicinity, and we can move more people in as they are required. Brazilians love to find work in such new industries. You will find their attitudes positive, as well."

"We have been most favorably impressed, Senhor Estremoz, Senhor Monforte," said Stirling. He had begun to feel pressured and was ready to direct the conversation into some other channel. "You have given us much to think about."

João Estremoz was skilled in subtle conversation and read Stirling perfectly. "Tomorrow," he said, "we are scheduled to show you São José dos Campos. We are, you understand, only a few kilometers from it. The drive there will not take long. Tomorrow afternoon we will fly to Brasilia, so you will have plenty of time to rest before you dine with the president and other leaders of the government."

"And allow me to suggest once more," said Monforte, "that you extend your visit a few days so that I may arrange for a brief visit to Mato Grosso. It seems a great shame for you to visit Brazil and see nothing of our famed Amazon. It is, after all, Wednesday. If you fly back to Los Angeles on Friday, you will only arrive home for the weekend." He smiled. "Weekends are for recreation. I can promise you an experience you will not soon forget."

Terry smiled at Stirling. "I have no very pressing reason to be back on Friday afternoon," she said. "Have you?"

He shook his head. "None. We accept your kind hospitality, Senhor Monforte."

"A custom," said Monforte an hour later. "Not one you are obliged to follow. Cigars, of course . . ." He smiled and shrugged.

He had just suggested that the three gentlemen step out on the terrace for a cigar and a final splash of brandy before they retired. The suggestion was so couched as to make it plain that Colonel Stirling alone was invited. It was awkward, but Stirling suspected that something significant was about to be said.

Terry covered the moment. "Please stop by my room for a moment before you go to yours," she said to Stirling. "I want to check my understanding of one or two things I heard during the day. Good night, Senhor Estremoz. Good night, Senhor Monforte. I am grateful for a most interesting day."

Monforte offered a box of Cuban cigars, and Stirling accepted one. The three men lit their cigars and walked out into the cool of the night. The sky was black and carpeted with southern-hemisphere constellations that were unfamiliar to Stirling. A million insects sang, and something sounded a deep, gravelly grunt a few yards away in the shrubbery. Probably a bullfrog, Stirling decided.

"A formidable lady, Mrs. Powell," said Monforte. "We, uh, were not quite prepared for her."

"I'm glad to hear it," said Stirling. He savored the cigar gingerly. He never smoked, except for an occasional cigar. He knew just enough about cigars to know this one was extraordinary. "She's not what anyone expects," he said.

"We assumed nothing offensive, Colonel Stirling, let us assure you."

"Oh, of course not. I understand that. But I want to say of her that the more I work with her, the more I see what an important asset she is to the corporation. She has two marvelous qualities—she is not too proud to admit her ignorance of something, and once she has admitted it, she is energetic and effective in learning about it. I wish I had more associates like her."

"She is the principal stockholder of your company, I believe," said Estremoz.

"That's right. And chairman of the board of directors. I work for her, not she for me."

"Yes . . ." said Monforte thoughtfully. "Exactly. And that is why I wanted to speak to you alone for a moment." He smiled. "Sometimes visiting businessmen who are alone away from home . . . well, you know what I mean, I am sure. I can send a young woman to your room a bit later if you wish."

"Very kind of you," said Stirling. "But I believe I will decline with thanks."

"I understand," chuckled Monforte, exchanging amused glances with Estremoz. "Well, then. We will not detain you longer than necessary, Colonel Stirling. The brandy . . . let me offer a bottle for you to take with you."

When she admitted him to her bedroom suite, she was wearing a hip-length sheer black nightgown trimmed with black lace, shoes, long dark stockings, and a frilly black silk garter belt. She had a deft sense of the erotic and when she offered him love, usually she was not entirely naked but wearing something that

151

signaled her intentions and expectations. He kissed her lightly and caressed her breasts, his hand sliding smoothly over the sheer fabric.

"What'd they want?" she asked. "Anything worth telling?"

Stirling laughed. "They wanted to offer me a girl."

"How very nice," she whispered, reaching between his legs and gently cupping his male parts in her hand. "And what did you tell them?"

"I declined with thanks," he said.

"And did they then reach the conclusion that you would be sleeping with me?" she asked.

"I think they understood. They're pretty worldly fellows, you know."

"The goddamned *assumption* again," she muttered.

"I can't help that, Terry," he said. "It's one of the disadvantages we agreed we'd have to live with."

"I'm a pretty worldly person myself, Mac," Terry said. "Even so, it's demeaning. I mean, after all, *why else* would you have a woman with you on a business trip, if not to—"

"I told them you're intelligent, shrewd, a quick study—"

"Yeah, sure," she said glumly. "And if they're peeking through a hole in one of the walls, here I am, just the way they expect: dressed like a—"

"Terry," he interrupted sternly. "You're the most *complete* woman I've ever known. You put it together: the very different things a woman can be. Like . . . cat and kitten. Both. And what's wrong with that?"

She sighed heavily. "Maybe sometimes . . . it's *tough*, Mac, sometimes."

He drew her into his arms. "I guess I'm not very

sensitive, Terry," he whispered as he held her close. "It's hard for me to think of you as needing much . . . much encouragement."

"You think I'm self-sufficient?" she asked quietly. "Are you?"

"No. I don't think you're self-sufficient. And me . . . ?" He smiled and shook his head.

"It's harder for a man to admit," she said.

"I'd say it's hard for you."

"Well, I do," she said. "I admit it. I love you, Mac. That's another way of saying it. I love you, and I need you."

"I love you too, Terry. And I need you."

They did not make love just then. They stood in each other's arms for a while, until she suggested they take advantage of the suite's huge step-down bath. They sat together for most of the next hour, in hot, swirling water, stimulated by the flow of tiny air bubbles that issued from jets and streamed around their bodies in an unceasing effervescence. They kissed and exchanged the most intimate caresses. They returned to the bedroom almost overcome by the soporific effect of the hot bath, and they made love quickly and tenderly and went to sleep.

The Aeromerica Lear jet took off from Brasilia on Friday morning, rose above clouds that extended as far as they could see in every direction, and flew northwest for more than two hours. When it landed at the airport at Manaus, the clouds were breaking and patches of sunshine lay over the green below. The little city was spread out along the river at the point where the Rio Negro joins the Amazon and from the air had the look of an ugly outpost cut in the edge of the endless jungle. When Terry and Mac and Monforte stepped out onto the tarmac, the air was hot and thick.

"God, you know where you are," Terry murmured to Mac. "It's hard to breathe."

"The equator is two hundred miles north," said Monforte. "We are in the tropical rain forest here. Fortunately, our company has an air-conditioned villa here. In the forest tomorrow, however, the heat will be oppressive."

They were taken to a restaurant near the airport for lunch, and after lunch they returned and lifted off in a small helicopter for a low-altitude run over the rivers and over some of the jungle. Even in the air, the heat and moisture pressed in against them, and the stench of rotting vegetation rose to follow them. Mac and Terry wore the clothes Monforte's company had provided— khaki shirts and pants, leather boots—and dark patches of sweat began to appear on their backs and chests. With binoculars, they scanned the river banks and the canopy of the forest, spotting flocks of thousands of birds wheeling over the dense tangle of trees and vines. The rivers themselves bore an active traffic, boats of every size and description carrying cargoes mostly, few people. Although the river banks were settled, it was plain that no settlement, even the little city of Manaus, had more than a tenuous hold on the rivers and jungle.

"Tomorrow," said Monforte loudly, straining to be heard over the roar and clatter of the helicopter, "we will go into the jungle by boat—if you believe you can endure the heat."

"We will endure it," said Terry firmly.

As they flew a few hundred feet above the trees, an

ominous change in the weather began to develop. The pilot pointed toward a wall of gray that had appeared to their right a dozen or so miles away.

"The rain," said Monforte. "We must return."

They reached the company car before the pelting tropical rain broke over the airfield. Because it fell too hard, obscuring visibility, the driver could not pull onto the road, and they sat inside the car with engine and air-conditioner running while the rain lasted. In twenty minutes or so it stopped, having flooded the airfield to a depth of several inches. The sun came out, and the field and roads began to steam. The water ran off through the drainage ditches in a wild rush to the river. The rain had not tempered the heat or reduced the humidity.

They slept in late afternoon, and in the evening they dined with Monforte and the local Aeromerica manager—simply, on pork and salad and white wine.

"Why," Stirling asked, "would an aerospace company have a branch out here?"

"Quite simple, Colonel Stirling," said Monforte. "Government policy. Our government is obsessed with the idea of developing this region. Hence the foolish Trans-Amazon Highway. It is desired to create employment here, for the Indians who are displaced by logging and mining or who are corrupted by the 'civilizing' presence of the white man in the edges of the jungle. We fly in parts and do certain engine sub-assemblies here, in a small factory employing sixty Indians. It is inefficient, of course, but the government wants it, so . . . you understand that sort of thing."

"I'm afraid we do," said Stirling.

"We fly upriver in the morning, weather permitting," said Monforte. "I suggest you sleep well tonight.

Immersion in the heat of the jungle, however comfortable we try to make you, will sap you of energy. But I promise an experience you will not forget."

They flew upriver in three small helicopters, each one capable of carrying only the pilot and two passengers. Terry and Mac flew in one, and Monforte flew in the other, bringing with him an interpreter who could talk with the Indians of the interior. The third chopper brought two armed guards. They followed the Rio Negro for some distance, then turned west on one of its tributaries and followed that for twenty or thirty miles. When they landed, it was in a jungle clearing on the bank of the stream, where the only habitation was a pair of flimsy huts and the only population twenty-five or so stark-naked Indians.

"I will tell you in all frankness," said Monforte, "that we cleared this landing space and established friendly relations with this little tribe for the express purpose of being able to bring visitors out here to see something of the real jungle. They are quite friendly. We've never had the least trouble with them."

Two of the Indian men were tattooed. Most of the rest, men and women, were smeared with red paint. They wore nothing, not even loincloths, not even beads. They were short, heavy-bellied, of a medium dark color. They stood staring at the helicopters, neither curious or frightened, looking if anything a little sullen, even a little hostile. Some of them carried bows and a few crude arrows. The interpreter strode boldly toward them, extending toward them a small white cloth bag—tobacco, Terry judged. One of the men reached for it and took it. They palavered for some time, while the party of whites stood in the meager shade of the helicopters, sweated, and watched warily.

"We've had no problems with any of them," said Monforte.

"Even so, you've brought guns," said Stirling dryly.

"Even so, I'm going to give you one too, Colonel," said Monforte. "Not because I'm concerned about the Indians. Because one never knows exactly what one might encounter. You observe I will carry a pistol myself."

He handed Stirling a belt and holster and a heavy .357-magnum revolver.

"One hell of a cannon," Stirling observed, hefting the oversized pistol.

The interpreter returned. "It is well," he said. "They will provide two canoes, each to carry three of us. They say they know where great caimans are to be seen, and one man says he saw a monstrous anaconda only yesterday." He smiled. "They are lying, I imagine. They would promise to show us monkeys studded with diamonds if it would assure our hiring them as boatmen. But I think we will not be disappointed, even if we see no anacondas or caimans."

They loaded into two dugout canoes, Mac and Terry and Monforte in one, the interpreter and two guards armed with rifles in the other. Four Indian men, two kneeling in the bow and two in the stern of each canoe, would paddle. The whites sat in the middle.

"Don't dangle your fingers in the water," said Monforte. "No one has lost a finger to piranha in five years, but a woman once did."

The two canoes kept within a few yards of each other as the Indians began to paddle. For the most part, all

157

they did was keep the bow pointed downstream, letting the swift current carry them, saving their energy for the hard work of paddling back upstream later. Even so, their naked brown bodies streamed sweat.

The river was maybe fifty yards wide, and they took the canoe out nearly to the middle of it, into the relentless sunshine, but out from under the overhanging branches from which a snake might drop. The water was smooth except for a slight wind riffle and the swirls and eddies where the current rushed over a submerged rock or fallen tree. It was green and looked alive.

The forest to each side was dark. Hardly a shaft of sunlight penetrated the canopy of leaves. It, too, was alive: with chirping, tweeting, whistling, grunting, growling, slithering. All of this life was invisible from the river, except for birds that flitted through the trees, thousands of insects that wheeled through the air, and an occasional monkey swinging from one limb to another.

The stench was overpowering. "Everything grows fast, dies fast, rots fast, and sustains the next oncoming life," Monforte explained.

Terry put her eyes to her binoculars often but only for seconds at a time. She had a sense of the life pressing in around her and was reluctant to blind herself to what might be within arm's length. Her clothes were wet now, and stank, but she was fascinated—as was Mac, who more boldly surveyed the trees with his binoculars.

Just then, one of the rifle-carrying guards in the other canoe shouted something. Monforte lifted his binoculars and peered ahead, then put them down and pointed to a snake draped over a root at the edge of the water a little downstream. Terry put up her binoculars, looked, and chilled at the sight of the archetypal hideous viper. It was maybe eight feet long, as thick as a man's arm, yellowish brown on top, with a darker pattern, and yellowish white on the bottom. Its head was extended over the water toward them, and its mouth was open, exhibiting long curved fangs.

"That's a bushmaster," said Monforte. "You hardly ever see one this close to the river. It's the most dangerous thing in the jungle."

The Indians turned the canoes toward the middle of the river, to put more distance between themselves and the reptile that plainly terrified them. The ones in the bow let fly a dozen arrows at it. Their arrows struck the roots around the bushmaster, but none of them hit it. It did not retreat. It lifted its head, opened its mouth wider, threatened.

"They are not afraid of man," said Monforte. "They are not afraid of anything. That is what makes them so dangerous. You happen on another snake, say a fer-de-lance, which is even more poisonous, it will retreat if it can. You happen on a bushmaster, it will attack. And pursue."

The Indians in the two canoes were muttering among themselves, some calling back and forth between the canoes. They were disturbed, apparently, to see a bushmaster so near their village. They began to gesticu-late, and Stirling noticed that one of them was in animated conversation with the interpreter.

The interpreter spoke in Portuguese to Monforte. Monforte nodded, and the Indians in the second canoe turned it and began to paddle laboriously back up-stream toward where the bushmaster remained coiled around the root.

"They want my men with rifles to return and kill the snake," said Monforte. "They say it is a menace to their people and that the white men should use their guns to relieve them of that menace."

In a minute or two the second canoe was out of sight. The long, narrow dugout carrying Mac and Terry and Monforte swung in closer to the bank, so they could see whatever was to be seen in the edge of the jungle. They saw a few small, rough-eyed caimans, looking like alligators, but none of the great caimans that some-times grew twenty feet long. For an instant Terry thought she saw a jaguar prowling through the undergrowth—but she saw it so briefly she could not be sure.

They began to hear the sound of a motor. It was distant at first, then it became recognizable as the sound of an outboard bringing a boat upstream. The Indians glanced nervously at each other and paddled closer to the river bank. They were afraid that the wake from a speeding boat would tip the canoe and throw everyone into water that probably was not, yet might be, alive with piranha.

"If they are civilized, they will slow down," said Monforte. "Some think it sport to overturn Indian canoes. Of course, when they see *us* they—"

The boat came around the bend in the river. It was a rugged, mud-smeared skiff, some twelve feet long. It carried three men and a varied load of bales, hides, and what looked like junk. The three men were bearded, dressed in dirty white clothes with tattered straw hats—

except for one, who wore a stained undersized gray felt fedora. One sat in the back, gripping the tiller of the outboard motor. Two sat in the front. Now, as they approached the canoe, the two in the front reached for double-barreled shotguns, and one of them stood up. The man in the rear throttled back and steered the boat toward the canoe.

The boat drew close, to within ten feet, and abruptly the man in the front leveled his shotgun on the canoe. *"No se mueva!"* he yelled.

"¿Qué quiere usted decir?" asked Monforte.

The boat swung around parallel with the canoe, and the man in the middle aimed his shotgun, too, at Monforte and Stirling.

"It's a robbery," muttered Monforte. "Be careful. This kind are dangerous."

The three men in the boat grinned and nodded. Their grins exposed stained teeth, some missing, and whitish gums. Their tattered white clothes were wet with sweat, and filthy. Terry could smell them across the ten feet between the boats and thought them the ugliest, most frightening men she had ever seen.

"Necesitamos el dinero, señores." This was Spanish, not Portuguese. *"Y . . . pistolas. Sí. Esas pistolas. Pronto."*

"They want our money and our guns," said Monforte.

The man running the outboard turned to move closer to the canoe, then cut his throttle to allow the boat to drift backward as the canoe drifted forward.

The man in the middle rose and held his shotgun in folded arms. *"¿Cómo se llama?"* he asked, nodding toward Terry.

161

She shuddered, horrified by the very fact that he had noticed her.

"What's that? What's he asking?" Stirling grunted.

"He wants to know her name," said Monforte.

"Tell him it's none of his business."

"They're dangerous, Colonel Stirling. They are quite capable of killing us."

"*Es una muchacha bonita,*" the man laughed. "*La amo! Eh, señorita! Muéstreme sus tetas!*"

"He wants you to show him your—"

"I understand him," Terry mumbled, her voice weak and breaking. "For God's sake—"

"For God's sake, let him see them, Mrs. Powell!" Monforte pleaded.

"Terry . . ." said Stirling grimly. "We need to distract them."

Slowly, glancing back and forth between Stirling and the men in the boat, Terry unbuttoned her shirt. The three men stared, chortling, licking their lips. Her hands trembled as she pulled the shirt back and uncovered her breasts. She watched for the man in the bow to lower his shotgun, even a little; but he didn't; it remained pointed squarely at Stirling.

"*Blancas!*" giggled the man in the bow of the skiff. "*Blancas . . .*" He grinned. Then his grin faded, and he gestured with the muzzle of his shotgun. "*Señorita,*" he growled. "*Ven tu!*"

"He's ordering her to come with them," whispered Monforte hoarsely.

"Jesus Christ . . ." Terry moaned. She dropped to her knees in the middle of the canoe. "Don't—don't let them . . ."

The boat edged closer to the canoe, until they were

almost touching. The man in front repeated his gesture with the muzzle of the shotgun, and his face had now turned grim, angry. *"Señorita,"* he muttered. *"Pronto."*

A shot echoed across the water, followed instantly by another. It was Monforte's guards, shooting at the bushmaster. The three men in the skiff swung around toward the sound of the shots.

Stirling jerked the .357 magnum from its holster. Leveling it quickly in both hands, he shot the man in the bow of the skiff. The huge bullet, with the immense shocking power of the magnum, exploded the man's chest. Flesh and bone and blood flew from his back, and he was thrown from the boat and into the water. Stirling shoved the muzzle of the pistol past Monforte and fired at the man in the middle. The shot hit that one's shoulder and literally tore off his arm, leaving it hanging by a tangle of ruptured tendons. As the man fell screaming among the bundles and junk in the middle part of the skiff, Monforte fired a shot at the man in the rear, who by now was raising the muzzle of his shotgun. Monforte missed him, but the shot distracted him and slowed him, and Stirling's third shot punched through his belly, bursting him and throwing him backward over his outboard and into the river.

The Indians were on their feet, loosing arrows into the wounded man in the middle of the boat. In a moment he was pierced by six arrows and ceased to scream. Two of the Indians scrambled onto the boat, lifted him, and heaved him overboard.

As Terry clutched her shirt and covered herself, she saw the greenish water of the river begin to churn just beyond the boat. Something attracted by the smell of blood had come to feed on the bodies. The crack of a splash sounded across the water. A big caiman had launched itself from the bank. It was followed by three more.

The Indians in the rear of the canoe began to paddle, to move away from the activity in the water. The two in the boat fumbled for a moment with the outboard, then took charge of it and headed the boat upstream, passing the canoe. They waved and grinned as they went by.

The second canoe rounded the bend, its Indians paddling furiously. The interpreter yelled at the Indians in the powered boat, but they only grinned and waved. As the canoes neared, the Indians exchanged news. They began to laugh with delight. They had had a good day, earning money from these white men who were riding in their canoes, killing a bushmaster, and capturing a fine outboard-powered boat. Suddenly they were rich.

That was how Monforte explained it. "Unless you have a different idea, Colonel Stirling, Mrs. Powell, I don't propose to make any report to any officials. The matter is closed as far as I am concerned. My employees will follow my instructions in that regard."

"The Indians?" Terry asked.

"They couldn't be happier. Likely enough, those men had abused them. Anyway, they have their boat and their motor, and they will joy-ride up and down the river until the gasoline runs out, then throw the motor overboard and paddle the boat like a fine big canoe."

"You promised us an experience we wouldn't forget," said Terry.

11

"WHY'D IT HAVE to happen when you were out of the country?" asked Shorty Bellows disconsolately. "If, Christ Almighty, you'd been here—"

"What difference would that have made?" Stirling asked with a quick shrug. "It would have happened just the same."

"But the TV reporters, and the cameras . . ." Shorty persisted. "Shit! Maybe you could have handled them some way, made them understand."

Stirling looked out across the ramp to the runway. The second Nimbus, 88SP, sat there on its side, the right wing broken off and bent back, the fuselage streaked with smoke stains, dried foam distorting its clean lines. A rope fence had been put up around it, and three emergency trucks sat around it.

"Brake froze," said Bellows. "Fast-taxi test. Of course we had no idea of taking off. We were just taxiing on the runway, bringing it up just short of takeoff speed, hitting the brakes, trying everything. Standard test procedure. FAA requirement. So, okay, a brake froze. That's one of the things we were out there to find out: if a brake would freeze under that kind of abuse. And it did. With the right wheel stopped and skidding, naturally the left swung around, the right strut got stressed and twisted and collapsed. She went down on the right wing, ruptured a fuel cell, and fire

165

broke out. We hit it with halon, and by the time the equipment arrived, it was down to a smolder. But—"

"But the news people decided to make a big deal of it," Stirling finished his thought.

"Illiterate idiots . . ."

"What'd the FAA inspector think?" Stirling asked.

"Didn't say a word," said Bellows. "Just shrugged. But the goddamned L.A. television stations were out here in an hour, shooting film of the Nimbus that 'crashed on takeoff.' Hell, Mac, those TV reporters don't know an airplane from an asshole. You should have seen how they reported it."

Stirling reached out and clapped a firm hand on the test pilot's shoulder. "What'd you expect?" he asked. "When did you ever see a TV report—on any subject whatever—that was even halfway accurate? Can't get excited about that. One of the facts of life, Shorty."

Shorty Bellows sighed loudly and turned his eyes toward the crippled Nimbus. "Can't do us any good," he said.

Stirling turned to stare at the airplane. "I'm taking that son of a bitch into the air the day after tomorrow," he said. "In front of every television camera we can get somebody to bring out here."

He issued the statement to the news media before he spoke with the production staff: Nimbus 88SP would fly on Thursday; the brake failure had been routine, caused by stressing the brakes beyond their capacity as part of routine tests. The airplane would be repaired and ready to go within forty-eight hours.

"You're asking a lot, Mac," said Jerry Goldstein.

"I'm going to fly it myself, Jerry," said Stirling.

"Nobody but me. Over the goddamned desert. If it falls out of the sky, it lands on the rattlesnakes."

Goldstein shook his head. "If Colonel McDonald John Stirling is killed in the crash of an airplane I approved for a certificate of airworthiness without a thorough inspection beforehand—"

"All that's wrong with the bastard is the right-wheel brake," argued Stirling. "Everything else is standard. You've inspected it all before."

"Got to inspect it all over again," Goldstein insisted. "You've gotta understand my point."

"Okay. How long will it take you to do it?"

"Well . . . hell, man. I mean, usually we'd want two days."

"I'll give you six hours," said Stirling.

Goldstein sighed loudly. "Okay, Mac. Give me four."

"Four hours," Stirling agreed. "The aircraft will be ready for you and your boys at ten hundred hours Thursday. I'm gonna have news assholes here at fourteen hundred, and I'm gonna fly the son of a bitch."

"*If* we clear it," said Goldstein. "I can't let you kill yourself, Mac."

Stirling jabbed his hand forward for a handshake. "You got a deal, Jerry," he said.

An hour later, Robert Powell was in his office.

"Goddamn, I admire the way you move when you move," said Powell. "You're going to put Eight-eight Sierra Pop in the air Thursday afternoon, and I have no doubt of it."

"I have no doubt of it," said Stirling. "It was a piece of good luck, really, that the brake failed and spun her around and snapped her wing Saturday afternoon. Piece of good luck that the news guys caught up on it. Best possible kind of publicity for us. We're gonna put the son of a bitch in the air Thursday afternoon, and I'm gonna give them a flying show with it. Only one thing, Bob. I'd have liked to have the plane off the runway and back in for the necessary work yesterday. I understand it sat there on your orders."

"It was my judgment," said Powell smoothly, "that you ought to see it exactly as it was. Otherwise . . . I mean, there are those who would try to conceal the exact dimensions of the incident from you."

"So. Okay. But the shop could have used an extra twenty-four hours. It would have been a good idea to have the aircraft examined thoroughly at least, to see what had to be replaced. We're damned lucky. No major structural component was broken."

"Oh, that's good," said Powell. "So it'll fly Thursday, then. I can't say how glad I am to hear it."

"We've got a winner, Bob," said Stirling. "It's going to work."

Powell walked to Stirling's office window, from which he could see the service vehicles now carefully moving the Nimbus toward the hangar. "I'd like to ask you something, Mac," he said. He stood at the window in his dark blue suit and his blue-striped white shirt, with his hands thrust into his trouser pockets. "Since you've called a big press conference, why couldn't we show off the Mink Bat, too? It's a Powell product, after all. Isn't it important for the Mink Bat to have good press coverage?"

"Not this time, Bob," said Stirling. "If we weren't trying to overcome some bad publicity we got, then maybe, sure. But not this time. We have to focus all the attention on the Nimbus this time. Let's think about an intro for the Mink Bat sometime soon. Right now . . . you understand."

"Oh, sure," said Powell. "Sure. Understood entirely."

"Know me this time, Laker?" Terry asked the security guard on duty outside Hangar One.

"Yes, ma'am," said the young security guard. It was four A.M. Thursday. He looked at his clipboard, making absolutely sure. "Yes, ma'am. You're allowed in. Just about nobody else. Colonel Stirling—"

"I know, Laker," she said. "I know. And thanks."

She walked into the hangar. Both Nimbuses were there, 87SP sitting to one side, 88SP in the center, propped up, a wing off. The lights blazed down on a small crew working on 88SP. Mac Stirling stood beside the autoclave, nervously tapping his foot and glancing repeatedly at his watch. He had not shaved in thirty-six hours. Nor had he slept. And he looked it.

"Mac . . . If we can't do it, we—"

"Can't do it," he interrupted. "And that's the deal. We can't. When the airplane spun around, it wrenched the main wing spar loose from the principal structural components of the fuselage. It's not difficult to fix, and it's not expensive, but you can't do it in two days. We've had to cut and lay out a new main spar: seventy-two layers of the cloth, which are now in the autoclave being baked under pressure. Of course, that's not all. I mean, we don't manufacture the fuel cells; we buy them; and the replacement for the one that ruptured is scheduled to be delivered at eight hundred hours. Plus skin panels damaged by the fire. I—"

"Mac, for God's sake! If you can't, you can't."

"That fuckin' Bob!" growled Stirling. "The time that idiot wasted . . . anyway, the news cameras wouldn't have been here if—"

"Mac! You've gotta get some sleep. C'mon, face it. We'll make it. Some other—"

"You bring any good coffee?" Stirling asked. "This instant stuff is . . ." He grimaced. "God, instant coffee! The very best of it tastes like something somebody swallowed and coughed up again."

"I brought you real coffee, Mac. And breakfast. Sit down. C'mon. In the airplane."

They climbed into the first Nimbus, 87SP, and sat down in the passenger cabin, at the little table. Terry unpacked a thermos of coffee and a box of pastries. Stirling leaned back and closed his eyes.

"Damage was far worse than I thought," he said. "I blew it when I called the news people in here this afternoon. We can't be ready. Can't. C-A-N-T, can't."

"So. We can't. I love you just the same, Mac. We've got that straight between us, haven't we?"

He nodded. "Straight." He closed his eyes and rubbed them with his fists. "God, yes, Terry. Whatever happens . . ."

She hadn't slept much either. She was conspicuously tired, dressed in jeans and a sweat shirt. She sipped coffee, and the hand that held the cup trembled faintly.

"You call Jerry?"

"He'll be here. Or so he said. There's enough coffee for him."

Stirling munched on a Danish and drank two cups of

black coffee, without saying much. The light was dim inside the airplane, only what came in through the windows from the overhead fluorescents in the hangar. He leaned back in his seat and drifted in and out of fitful sleep.

"Sir. Mrs. Powell. There's a man here—"

"Is his name Goldstein?" Terry asked the guard.

"That's it," said Laker.

"You remember how I was going to fire you?" she asked the young man. "You remember? Well, there's a promotion instead if you forget you ever heard of Goldstein. Right?"

Laker grinned. "Actually, I think he said his name is McNamara. Anyway, that's the way I've got it written down. Okay? Let him in?"

"Bring him in here."

Jerry Goldstein entered the cabin and took the seat to which Terry pointed. Stirling was awake, inhaling the steam off still another cup of strong black coffee. He rotated his shoulders and stretched his legs.

The FAA inspector tipped his head to one side. "Won't be ready, huh?" he asked.

Stirling shook his head.

"Well I'm sorry, Mac. Mrs. Powell, I . . . I understand how important this is. I can, uh, postpone as long as you want. Could you be ready by, say, one o'clock?"

"One tomorrow," sighed Stirling. "For sure. For damned sure. Just not any time today."

"Too late for your news conference," said Goldstein solemnly.

"Right," conceded Stirling. He hunched and flexed his shoulders. "Uh, Jerry . . . off the record. Okay?"

"With caution," said Goldstein.

"You weren't here this morning. No one knows you're here. Suppose the TV news shows run film of Eight-eight Sierra Pop flying this afternoon. Suppose—"

"You said it couldn't be ready today."

"It can't. And it won't. I'm not going to fly an uncertificated aircraft. On the other hand, unless someone came to you and specifically asked—"

"If anyone specifically asks, I'll have to say we did not inspect Eight-eight Sierra Pop and clear it to fly today," said Goldstein.

"And if nobody specifically asks?"

"I owe no obligation to call the television stations and tell them the airplane they saw flying as Eight-eight Sierra Pop was not—"

"Don't say it, Jerry!" Stirling interrupted. "You never even thought of it. You inspect Eight-eight tomorrow or the next day. You alone, instead of a bunch of guys—"

"Mac. If anyone else asked for this—"

"If it were anybody but you, Jerry," said Stirling.

Goldstein looked at Terry. "You figure this?" he asked. "I'll tell you why, Mrs. Powell. Mac and I've been through a lot of shit together. This bastard saved my ass when I made a boo-boo once, and I—"

"Never mind, Jerry," said Stirling. "Old history."

"If this deal creates more shit, we'll both swear we lied to you," Terry said. "The security guard who let you in thinks your name is McNamara. At least that's what he wrote on his sheet."

"We're not going to fly an uncertificated airplane," Stirling said. "This flight is nothing but a media stunt. It's absolutely inconsequential except—"

"Except in the grand arena of public opinion," said Goldstein. "So, okay. I don't know you people. I don't even want a cup of coffee from you. I think you been shat on. Otherwise . . ."

"Thanks, Jerry," said Stirling. "I can't say we'll try to return the favor sometime. We can't say anything like that. But thanks."

"If it hits the fan," said Terry. She shook her head. "We never saw you."

At fourteen hundred hours—two P.M.—an airplane marked 88SP was towed out of the hangar. Stirling was at the controls. In the view of a score of television cameras and a hundred reporters from the print and electronic media, he started the engines and taxied the Nimbus across the ramp and out the long taxiway. He paused at the distant end of the runway only long enough to run up his engines and check his instruments, then came roaring down the runway and lifted off just in front of the cameras.

On the evening news, the NBC affiliate in Los Angeles described how Mrs. Theresa Powell stood beside her car on the ramp, watching her president and chief executive officer flying a public demonstration of her late husband's last great project. The reporter made sure also that the camera lingered on her chic short-skirted pink dress; and a full minute of the coverage showed her following the flight through big binoculars.

Colonel Stirling climbed fast, impressively, until the Nimbus was almost out of sight, then turned and swept into a four-hundred-mile-an-hour flyby over the Powell Industries airport. Reporters noted that the airplane was quieter than most bizjets, yet had ample power for a dramatic climb after it passed by.

Mr. Robert Powell, son of the late Stanley Powell, stood beside Mrs. Theresa Powell and proudly watched the impressive performance of his father's airplane—according to the news stories. Reporters asked him how it had been possible to repair so quickly the airplane that had spun on the runway and broken off a wing only five days before. Robert Powell responded that the damage had been minor, actually, and that anyway, it was easy and cheap to make new parts and repair the Nimbus.

When Colonel Stirling landed, he taxied to the big doors of Hangar One. They opened, and a tractor immediately pulled the airplane inside. The doors were closed, and Mrs. Powell explained that the interior of the new airplane was not quite ready for inspection by the news media. They were welcome to come back again, to inspect it at their leisure, and—once it was certificated for passengers—to fly in it.

Mac strode across Hangar One. Carey, the mechanic who had first shown him 87SP, stood waiting for him, grinning. "Okay, Carey," said Mac. "Soon as everybody's out of here . . . repaint 'em."

Stirling had to accept changes. He had lived a defined life for many years; now he was compelled to change his ways and live another life entirely.

He purchased a condominium in Powell—in a complex about mid-distance between the homes of Terry Powell and Robert Powell, and he joined the country club. He had been content with his little house, but the hundred-mile-a-day commute had become a burden.

The presidency of Powell Industries enforced other changes. More often now he found himself sitting at a desk, in a white shirt and tie and a dark blue suit, attending meetings, talking endlessly on the telephone, reading memos and reports, or standing at his office window looking at the flight line and wishing he were out there climbing into a cockpit, about to fly.

He was accustomed to a public life. A fighter pilot, then a test pilot, an officer in the United States Air Force, attaining finally the rank of bird colonel: it had not been a private way of living. But this was different. In the past, something notorious had almost invariably been followed by months, even years, of obscurity. As president of Powell, he was under constant scrutiny, if not by the news media—which in fact were only occasionally interested in him or Powell Industries— then certainly by the officers and employees of the corporation, who watched his face for expression, listened intently to his voice for inflection, searching, constantly searching, for some hint as to how he might use his power for or against them. This was a new kind of public life, much harder to take.

He liked to walk across the shop floor, particularly in Hangar One, where parts for the third Nimbus were now being laid out and baked in the autoclave. The old people, like Bill Carey, who had been with Stan Powell and was so good an aircraft mechanic that he could find a job anywhere, easily, would grin at him and shake his hand and trade inside jokes. Newer people, the intense young designers for example, viewed him with suspicion. What was the president of the company doing in their shop?

He did not, therefore, look forward to the Powell

Industries country club reception and dinner. It was set for a Saturday night. ("Kind of corporate shit I detest," Stirling had remarked to Terry.)

It was not black tie, thank God. The party gathered at about four, to swim in the pool, then to move to a buffet, finally to sit down to the Southern California simulacrum of a luau.

"A real pleasure, Colonel Stirling," said Ruth Powell, Robert's wife. She looked up into his face through her eyeglasses. "We've heard so much about you."

Stirling looked down into the flat, earnest face of the five-foot-one, leathery-tanned, hard-bodied, graying woman; and he smiled at her. "Why thank you, Mrs. Powell. Let me compliment you on your dress. I understand you made it, from the ground up, so to speak."

Her quick smile was genuine. " 'So to speak.' Exactly, Colonel Stirling. It's an affectation, of course. Flax. I spin the thread, weave the cloth, make the garment. The sort of thing a woman does when she has nothing much better to do."

He could not reply in kind to that, not yet. He limited himself for the moment to smiling blandly. "Call me Mac, will you please?" he said. "I was a colonel only a short time, and I can't get used to being called—"

"Mac," she said. "And call me Ruth. It *is* a pleasure to meet you."

"Aren't you going in the water?" he asked.

She grinned and spoke quietly to him behind her hand. "I'm afraid I haven't a swimsuit," she said, laughing. "At home I never wear one—in our pool, I mean—and I . . . well, I'd hardly dare jump in nude, would I?"

"You do, I'll be in the same way, five seconds later."

"I think we don't dare, Mac," she chuckled happily. "But when you come to our house, we will. And only Bob will lie in his floating chair in his boxers."

Terry came to his side moments later. "Bowdoin," she said. "Her father owns a railroad. Or Rhode Island. Or something. I forget which. Something with 'road' or 'Rhode' in it. Stan loved her. Bob resented that, too."

"I don't really have to make a speech, do I?" Mac asked.

"Oh, you do, you do. Everyone's waiting for it. Serious drinking can't begin until you do."

"Then I'd better do it soon," he said. "Mine can't begin either, until I do."

Someone banged a spoon on one of the tables. Stirling stood uncomfortably in front of the bar table. He was still dressed in jeans and a white golf shirt, having been unwilling to strip to his swimming trunks until the speech was over. He put his sunglasses aside.

"Uh, ladies and gentlemen. I'm, uh, little experienced at making speeches. I don't much like to make them. I like it a whole lot less to have to listen to them." (Appreciative quiet laughter.) "Especially on an occasion like this, when we've got together to have a good time. I'll keep it short."

A few souls, maybe ones who had already visited the bar two or three times, applauded. Stirling nodded at them and smiled.

"I've met most of you. All of you, I hope—except a

few of the wives and husbands who don't come around the office. I know all of you are interested in what the company's doing, what our prospects are, what our risks. After all, we're all committed to this company. We've put a lot in it."

Pausing for the spatter of applause, he turned to Terry and whispered, "Am I saying this? I can't believe it."

"Okay. In brief. We delivered 161 Colts to dealers in the first half of the year. That's a thirteen per cent increase over last year, but I need hardly tell you it's small compared to deliveries of competing Cessnas, Pipers, and Beeches in the small-plane market, and the Colt represents only twenty-six per cent of revenues. Our leader is, of course, the Cirrus. We delivered seventy-four units in the first half, an increase of eighteen per cent; and the Cirrus represents seventy per cent of our revenues. Stanley Powell understood that Powell Industries could not depend that much on the Cirrus in the decade of the nineties, and that is why he developed the Nimbus. I share Mrs. Powell's often-stated conviction that the Nimbus is our future.

"We have two prototypes flying, and the third is being put together. We are talking to the governments and to private companies in Brazil, the United Kingdom, and in Italy about the possibility of assembling the aircraft in one of those countries—from parts manufactured principally here. Testing continues. We have suffered no major setbacks. There seems to be no obstacle to FAA certification within a reasonable period of time.

"The good news is that we now have fourteen orders

for the Nimbus. I'm talking about signed contracts with money up front. The sale of two units to Southwest Consolidated was announced to you earlier. We have sold twelve units since. That means that we have almost fourteen million dollars up-front cash in the bank. When we go out looking for major financing, which we are going to have to do, those orders are going to look awfully good.

"In fact, Mrs. Powell and I are flying to New York Monday. We have scheduled meetings with two major banks, and on Thursday we are guests at a luncheon of the National Association of Securities Analysts. Besides that, we'll be talking to officers of some big corporations, the kind that might buy whole fleets of Nimbuses. It's going to be a busy week, and we hope to come back with several kinds of good news."

They took a two-bedroom suite at the Waldorf, set up a handsome model of the Nimbus on the marble-top coffee table, and Monday evening offered cocktails and hors d'oeuvres to a small delegation of reporters from the financial and aviation press. The next morning they drove in a rented car to Stamford, Connecticut, where they met first with officers of Xerox Corporation, then in the afternoon with officers of GTE. Their meetings with bankers began on Wednesday.

Their first meeting was with Manufacturers Hanover, and they sat down in mid-morning in a windowless conference room, where paintings of former officers of the bank stared down from walnut-paneled walls. Two people met with them: Durward Wilson, a vice president, and Joan Schmidt, an assistant vice president.

"You picked an odd time, didn't you, to start selling a fuel-efficient airplane?" asked Wilson. "I mean, right now oil is a glut on the market."

"We're still not going back to fifty-cents-a-gallon jet fuel," said Stirling. "Far from it. Anyway, the Nimbus offers economy first when a company buys it, then again when it operates it."

"How do you hope to fund your manufacturing and sales programs, Colonel Stirling?"

"I'm hoping to receive advice on that, Mr. Wilson," said Stirling. "My own idea is a bond offering: a mortgage on the company."

"Well, the company's credit is obviously good for something," said Wilson. "On the other hand, you will wind up paying a premium in the credit market if you can't convince the investment community that your new project is sound. Your prospective bondholders aren't interested in liquidating Powell Industries."

"That's one reason we're here: to convince investors that the project is sound," said Terry.

"One of the problems that we in the financial community see," said Schmidt, "is with the management of Powell Industries. I have to be frank. I'm a securities analyst, and when I look at your executive roster, I don't see the varied talents needed to manage a major industrial corporation. You're a pilot and aeronautical engineer, Colonel Stirling—and very good, we understand—but you have no management background."

"Spoken like a true M.B.A.," said Terry.

"As a matter of fact, Mrs. Schmidt is an M.B.A., from Harvard," said Wilson.

"I have two or three masters of business administration in the office," said Stirling. He grinned at Schmidt. "I suppose I could hire more if it would impress you."

"Not quite the point, is it, Colonel?" she responded. "Anyway, I'll be one of the analysts at the luncheon tomorrow. You'll find I'm not the only one who's going to raise the issue."

Stirling grinned. "I'll think of an answer between now and then," he said.

But he woke at six A.M., nauseated, stomach cramping, with a severe headache. Shortly, he began to vomit. From six until ten, he was hardly able to leave the bathroom. Terry called for a doctor, who came, examined Mac, and assured them that he was suffering from nothing more serious than food poisoning, probably from last night's dinner, and would recover in a day or so, with rest and a bland diet.

"I'll call the New York Society of Securities Analysts," she said when the doctor had left. "I'll explain, apologize, tell them we hope to meet with them another time."

Mac lay on his back, pale, gleaming with perspiration. "Don't even think of it," he muttered. "You have to go . . ." He shook his head. "Don't even think of it," he muttered weakly. *"You've gotta go."*

"I couldn't! I couldn't possibly."

"Terry . . . I'm too weak to argue. *Go,* for Christ's sake! It took me months to set this up. The speech I was going to give is in my briefcase."

"But the *questions!*"

"Answer what you can. You know the answers to most of them. What you can't answer, you can't. And that's the key: Answer what you can with the facts, and admit you don't know when you don't. You've got to go, Terry. You've *got* to."

Joan Schmidt, Terry discovered, was seated beside her at lunch. "We . . . uh, well, we *could* have postponed," she said. "If Colonel—"

"I have his speech," said Terry.

"But the questions . . . you'll be asked lots of questions."

"Yes, I hope so," said Terry.

She feigned calmness she did not feel. Mac had helped her choose a dress for this meeting: a dark blue silk sheath, with an attached scarf that draped across her shoulders—skirt fashionably short, décolletage covered by the scarf. She wore a single piece of jewelry, a gold chain bracelet. Schmidt, who wore a charcoal gray pin-stripe suit, with white blouse and a floppy bow at her throat, complimented her on her dress.

The luncheons of the National Society of Securities Analysts were attended by specialists, who came expecting to get specific answers to specific questions about the companies whose officers were invited to speak. Transcripts of the questions and answers were published and distributed to all the members. The members present for this luncheon were the ones especially interested in the aircraft-manufacturing industry.

Terry was introduced, stood at the podium, and read the speech Mac would have given, adding to it nothing but an explanation as to why he was not there. When she finished, she was applauded; and Joan Schmidt rose to recognize members for questions.

"Mrs. Powell," said a balding, bespectacled man who rose at a table toward the rear of the room. "What license and type rating will be required for a pilot to fly the Nimbus?"

"Multi-engine, centerline thrust," said Terry. "As you know, that's not so difficult a rating to get as the kind a pilot has to have to fly a business jet."

"Another question, if you don't mind. At the operating altitudes for this airplane, passengers are going to need oxygen in case of depressurization. What provision are you making?"

"Drop-out units, the same as on airliners," she answered. "Capacity, uh, twenty-two cubic feet. Plenty of oxygen until the airplane can descend to an altitude where it's not needed."

Another man rose. "How will the aircraft be de-iced, Mrs. Powell?"

"Pneumatically on the wings," she said. "Electrically on the propeller and windshields."

"Mrs. Powell," said a young woman sitting at the table immediately in front of the rostrum. "You hope to sell economy. But if the insurance rates established for the airplane are too reflective of its radically new and somewhat experimental nature, they may cut heavily into your economy. What are you doing about that?"

"At the moment we haven't done anything about it," said Terry. "But we expect to invite representatives of the insurance industry to take the Nimbus apart from one end to the other and to fly it extensively, to satisfy themselves about its safety and reliability. We're not quite to that point yet. We will be shortly."

Before the questions shifted to management and

finance, they asked a dozen more questions about engineering and performance. She confessed her inability to answer one of those questions. The rest she answered with quick, succinct statements. She was surprised, not so much that she knew the answers, but that the questions were, after all, not so very difficult.

"I'm sorry Colonel Stirling is not here," said Joan Schmidt. "I asked him a question yesterday that I suppose other members of the Society would like to hear answered. I'll put it to you, Mrs. Powell. The president of Powell Industries is a former Air Force pilot and test pilot, with some experience as an aeronautical engineer. Some of us find your management strengths a little mysterious. Who manages Powell Industries? And how?"

Terry nodded and smiled at Schmidt. "*I* recruited Colonel Stirling for Powell Industries," she said. "I wanted him because I thought the company needed a strong guiding hand, which it hadn't really had since the death of my late husband. And I think Colonel Stirling has met every expectation. Our feeling is that aeronautical engineers ought to be able to manufacture airplanes and that people with a decent education and a modicum of intelligence ought to be able to manage a business. You have to work at it, that's all."

Schmidt smiled. "All you have to do is work hard, eh, Mrs. Powell?"

Terry turned toward her—moving the microphone over so that what she said to Joan Schmidt would be heard by the others. "That's exactly right, Joan," she said. "You weren't born a securities analyst, and you didn't learn to be one at Harvard. You work at it. You read everything that comes to your desk. You ask questions and listen to the answers. You study, and you think. And if you're motivated enough to do that and keep it up, you can analyze securities or manage investment portfolios or . . . or build airplanes." She turned again to the audience and shrugged. "Or tend bar, for that matter."

A ripple of laughter swept up from the tables, followed by loud applause.

Later that night, Mac and Terry lay together in bed, both of them tired and thought-filled, as they often were these past couple of months. He was still weak but was no longer nauseated and had eaten a bowl of soup. They were propped up against pillows, their attention less than half fixed on a movie showing on the bedroom television set. More of their attention was on each other, and still some of it was dominated by the thousand things that demanded it.

Terry wore black high-heeled slippers, with dark stockings, a black garter belt, and a yellow silk blouse unbuttoned. She had pulled his erect penis out through the fly of his blue Jockey shorts, and she fondled it as they watched Lord Vader use the dark side of the force to strike down an incompetent space admiral. Mac caressed the insides of her thighs, now and then pressing his fingers into her cleft and stroking her moist parts.

"I love you, Mac," she whispered.

He nuzzled her neck. "I want to marry you," he said.

"Soon," she whispered.

"We're kidding ourselves if we think people don't know about us, Terry."

"I don't know," she said. "We've talked it out

before, Mac. If everybody knows about us . . ." She shrugged. "Maybe it really won't make any difference, but I think our first judgment was right. We don't want people asking: Does he believe in the Nimbus because he believes in the Nimbus or because he sleeps with Terry Powell?"

"He believes in Terry," said Mac. He withdrew his hand from between her legs and pushed himself up on the pillows. "Whether you and I sleep together or not—"

"Nobody'd believe it," she interrupted. "Just like nobody'd believe you and I could talk business when we're in bed together."

He grinned. "And I'm not going to, more than another minute," he said, slipping his hand up under the yellow silk of her blouse and gently rubbing her breasts. "But I'm going to say this one more time: that you're a *partner*, Terry, and would be to any man who had the brains to appreciate you."

"Partner . . ." she mused. "I like that. Am I, really?"

He nodded. "You know you are. Lady, you had a *triumph* today. You and I are partners in every sense of the word. And one of these days we're going to make the whole fuckin' world know it."

She laughed, deep in her throat. "You suppose the iron ladies give head? I mean, prime ministers and company presidents and—do you suppose Joan Schmidt . . ."

"Why not?" He bent down to kiss her between her legs, thrusting his tongue inside her, found her clitoris, and massaged it with the wet tip of his tongue. She

186

moaned with pleasure. After a minute, he looked up, smiling. "You suppose the iron men don't do that?"

"Yes. That's what I do suppose," she said.

"Well then, they're not so damned smart."

Terry rolled away from him. She rose on her knees on the bed and pulled off the yellow silk blouse, pulling back her shoulders and thrusting out her breasts, proudly showing herself to him. Then she bent over him and drew his hard phallus into her mouth. She began to work on him, up and down, slipping her tight lips back and forth over his shaft. In only a moment he came, and she swallowed the gushing fluid and kept on sucking and licking until he was limp.

Both of them supposed they would make love again that night, but they went to sleep with the lights on, without even switching off the television.

"WHEN *HE* HIT town! Jesus, man . . ." The bartender shook his head and smiled reminiscently. "Seriously, though, he was a great guy."

"So I've always heard," said Charlie Horn. He lifted his glass and sipped bourbon. "Spend a lot of time in here?"

"Here. Everywhere," said the bartender, a white-haired florid man, probably sixty-five years old, wearing a red vest with black stripes, a white shirt with red sleeve garters. "Spent a lot of time in Vegas."

"A friend of mine knew him," said Horn. He had picked up a discarded convention badge—National Association of Ceramic Pipe Manufacturers—and had put his own name in it. For the benefit of this bartender he was playing weary conventioneer. His cigarette pack lay on the bar, and he smoked as they talked. "Supplied some tile for his plant in Powell, California. Figure that? Guy got his own town, named after him."

"Well, Mr. Stanley Powell was the man to deserve it," said the bartender earnestly.

The little bar was dimly lighted, mostly by the red neon tubing that bordered the mirror. Two bare-breasted girls, wearing short red satin skirts, net stockings, and high-heeled black shoes, carried drinks to the customers at the tables.

"Yeah, he went everyplace," the bartender continued. "I can honestly say, though, this was one of his favorite places."

"Quite a cocksman, my friend says. Says no girl was safe within ten feet of him."

The bartender nodded. "He enjoyed the ladies, that's for sure."

"He pay for 'em?"

The bartender's face clouded. "I wouldn't hardly think so. Why would he? Every girl in town knew him, wanted to go out with him. He didn't have to pay for it."

"Yeah, I guess so," said Horn, smiling, nodding, trying to repair the damage. "Anyway . . . God, he sure married a beautiful one."

"Terry Keel," said the bartender. "Never forget 'er. No, sir. I'll never forget her."

"You knew her, too?"

"No, not really," said the bartender regretfully. "You know, man in my position can't afford to go for the show at The Sands, and she never came in here. But . . ." He smiled, shook his head. "Wish she had."

"Not just your ordinary showgirl," Horn suggested.

"No. Nothin' ordinary about Terry Keel. She was in Vegas . . . le's see, 'bout four years it must have been. Nothin' ordinary about her."

"I'm curious," said Horn, "if you never saw her . . . y' know what I mean? How'd you know how great she was?"

The old bartender's face widened in a happy smile. "Some things y' just know," he said. "Everybody knew."

"That's what I hear," said Horn unhappily.

"Nobody ever spoke a bad word about her," said the bartender.

Horn raised his glass as if in toast to Terry Keel. "Kind of a legend," he said. "Hey, listen, I was gonna ask you if you knew a girl who might be interested in a little fun. God, is it possible there might be a girl in town who was a friend of Terry Keel, who might be available and . . . y' understand?"

"I can think of a couple," said the bartender. "'Course, you know, they work till awful late, and afterward they're . . . well, against what people think, most of 'em go home and go to bed."

Charlie Horn put a twenty-dollar bill on the bar. "If you can give me a couple names, I'll take my chances," he said.

The bartender slapped his hand quietly but firmly over the bill. "I guess I can think of a third one, now that you mention it. Look for Shelley Rosenkranz—known around here as Sheila Rose."

Two hours later, Horn sat on a banquette in one of the side rooms at Caesar's. He had bought dinner and wine for Shelley Rosenkranz—Sheila Rose—a dancer in the line at the current show at The Sands. It was her night off.

"You never saw Terry? Hey! Six feet. Body that'd light your fire. Cute. Smart. She came roarin' in here with a university education, a spread of pictures in *Playboy,* modeling experience, a portfolio of pictures. The Sands was lucky to get her. That's how she saw it, and that's how they saw it. Y' ever see the show?" Charlie Horn nodded.

"The girl that fronts for the showgirls, the one that's head of the line . . . y' know? That was Terry Keel. Lead dancer. Showin' a pair of tits that'd have tempted Christ when Satan couldn't. Man!"

"If she was that good, why'd she hang around here?" Horn asked. "She could have—"

"Hey! Why do any of us? 'Cause we have a good time here."

Horn looked down, a little disconsolately, into a plate of lobster chunks, bits of crabmeat, and scallops, beginning to stink already in a sauce of wine and herbs. He picked up his glass of cold white wine. None of this was to his taste, and it had cost Robert Powell a small fortune.

"And she had a good time?" he asked.

"What ya drivin' at?"

"Nothing special. Like I told you, Powell Industries has applied for a big loan, she's the principal stockholder and an officer, and we're doing a little check on all the officers."

Shelley Rosenkranz shrugged. "So tell your bank to lend the money," she said. "You're gonna find out nothin' bad about Terry."

He ordered them fresh drinks, Scotch for her, bourbon for himself. For half an hour he dropped the subject of Terry Keel, while he encouraged Shelley Rosenkranz to drink three Scotches. She was a beautiful young woman; she had to be to do what she did for a living. She was tall. Her body was generously proportioned but taut. She used makeup to conform her features to the convention for Las Vegas showgirls, also to try to cover the evidence of her age, which he guessed at thirty-five or more.

"Well," he said, pushing his glass away as if he regarded the dinner as over and the interview as finished. "I guess you've told me about all you know about Theresa Powell."

"Terry? Yeah. She was a great gal."

Horn covered a yawn with his hand. "Where'd she live, Shelley?"

"While she was here? Different places. Why?"

"Standard procedure," he said. "I'm supposed to list her former addresses. You know . . . horsecrap stuff."

Shelley grinned. "I don't know where all she lived. She lived one *good* place. You know The Starfire? The new place?"

He nodded.

"Well, she lived in the penthouse the last year or so she was in Vegas. You know who Vince Strozzi is? She was Vince's girl. That is, she was until Stanley Powell grabbed her."

"I think I've heard the name . . ." Horn said tentatively, frowning as if trying to remember where he had perhaps heard of Vincent Strozzi. Inwardly, he was elated. She lived with Vince Strozzi? Bingo! "Strozzi, you say?"

Shelley nodded. "That Stanley Powell must have had some kind of guts, movin' in on Vince Strozzi."

"Yeah, if we're thinking of the same guy."

"We're thinking of the same guy," she said.

"And Terry lived with . . ."

"Listen, the guy liked her. She looked good. Hey, why shouldn't she? She was single."

"Right," said Horn. "Why not?"

* * *

He awoke. Maybe it was because the sun was up. Maybe it was because he had heard something. He resolved immediately not to drink bourbon anymore; he'd switch to Scotch, which they said didn't give you a headache the next morning. He remembered . . . Shelley. Sheila. He reached. She wasn't there. She got up. She . . . goddamn! He grabbed for his billfold. It was there, but . . . shit! Hey, what . . . ? Two guys.

"What is this?" He scrambled up and reached for the Smith & Wesson he had stuck under the edge of the mattress before he went to sleep—an old habit. He pulled it and aimed it at the two guys sitting in chairs watching him. "Awright. Who you guys? What is this?"

"Now we know," said one of them. They were both big men, but this one was the bigger of the two. They wore open-collared, bright-colored shirts and pastel-colored slacks. "He's unfriendly."

"You better believe it," growled Horn. He pulled back the hammer on the revolver. "And you better start talkin'."

"We came to hear *you* talk, Charlie," the man said. "We got a couple of questions. Just a couple, that's all. So relax."

"What the shit . . . ?" Horn muttered. *"You—"*

"You might want to check over your weapon there, Charlie. Might find it's not loaded. You do sleep sound when you're sleepin' one off."

Charlie Horn turned up the revolver and looked. "Shit . . ."

"You don't need it, Charlie," the man said. "It's you that's unfriendly, not us."

Horn tossed the useless pistol to the center of the bed. "Okay," he said. "You're in charge."

The man who was doing the talking turned down the corners of his mouth and shook his head. "No, nothin' like that, Charlie. I mean, you've got the only gun in the room. We just came up for a friendly talk."

Horn shook a cigarette out of an almost-empty pack and snapped his lighter to light it. "How'd you get in?"

The man shrugged. "Sheila let us in."

"She called you."

"Uhm-hmm. Seems you've been asking questions about Mr. Strozzi. Taken a big interest in him. And, of course, you're a private dick from L.A. I'm sure you can understand that Mr. Strozzi is curious to know why you're so curious about him."

"I'm checking up on somebody else, just came across his name, that's all."

"Terry Keel."

"Right."

"You want to ask Mr. Strozzi about Terry Keel? Directly?"

"Uh, no. Not . . . necessary."

"Well. I've got a word of advice for you, Charlie. If you want to know anything about Mr. Strozzi, including about him and Terry Keel, the way to find out is ask Mr. Strozzi directly; don't go snoopin' around. Y' understand? It makes Mr. Strozzi nervous to have guys snoopin'. I mean, you can understand that. Right?"

Charlie Horn nodded.

"Good. You got a standing invitation. Come see Mr.

Strozzi anytime. Anytime you got any more questions. Okay, Charlie?"

"Right," said Horn. "Sure. Right."

"I didn't want to tell you on the telephone," said Charlie Horn to Robert Powell. "I would have stopped to see you on my way back to L.A., but of course your instructions are not to come near you. So . . . anyway, it's worth your flying in to hear this."

They sat in Horn's office just off Los Angeles International Airport, and once again Powell was distracted by the landing of big jets that swooped over the roof of the office building and settled onto the runway not far from Horn's window. Horn crushed a cigarette in his ashtray and immediately lit another.

"Was she a hooker?" Powell asked.

Horn laughed. "Yeah. The Mona Lisa's a picture, Mount Everest's a mountain, and Terry Keel was a hooker."

"Meaning what?" asked Powell irritably.

"You ever hear of Vincent Strozzi?"

Powell shook his head.

"Well, you ought to've. He could buy and sell Powell Industries out of pocket change. His grandfather was Giorgio Strozzi, who was a boss on the Jersey waterfront back when it was rough and tough. When the old man went to the penitentiary—and he died there, I might tell you—his son, Vincent's father, took over. That was Joe Strozzi. Remember the Appalachin Meeting? Joe Strozzi was there. He had an accident later—got a bullet through his head in a Paterson, New Jersey hospital room, where he was supposed to be recovering from a heart attack. And that brings us to Vince Strozzi. It's a regular dynasty."

"Which has what to do with Terry?"

"She lived with him. She was his girl. In Vegas."

"A hood? A Mafia hood?" Powell asked, a grin spreading across his face.

"You've gotta be careful about that, Mr. Powell," said Horn. "That's what Giorgio was, for sure. Joe . . . Sure, but in a different way. I mean, you know, that kind of thing has changed a lot."

"Oh, sure. So he gets shot in his hospital room."

"Vincent Strozzi," said Horn carefully, flipping open a small notepad and checking his notes, "was educated at Rutgers and New York University. He's a lawyer, believe it or not. He was already living in Vegas when his father was killed. He doesn't own a hotel or casino, but he owns pieces of lots of things. There's no Strozzi Family anymore, as such. He—"

"Is he a Mafioso or isn't he?" Powell demanded.

"Sure he is. Absolutely. But not a hood. He's never been arrested. He's smart, smooth, handsome, a sharp dresser . . . a clever man. The new kind."

"She lived with him?"

"The story is that she lived in his penthouse on top of The Starfire Hotel. That's where she was living when your father met her. She was cohabiting, as we say, with Vincent Strozzi."

"You can prove it?"

Horn lifted his chin high. "Well . . . that's a problem. I was visited by a couple of muscle boys and told to quit asking questions about Mr. Strozzi. I've got to quit. But I can send other men, that Strozzi's guys don't know, to follow up, try to find out exactly what the story is. Only thing, uh, Mr. Powell, it's going to cost more money."

"Figures," said Powell glumly. "But all right. I want *solid* information. I don't want egg on my face when—"

"Right," said Horn. "Understood."

Terry was sitting in Stirling's office at Powell Industries when his secretary interrupted their conversation to tell her there was a call on her line that seemed rather important and to ask if she would like to take it in the president's office.

"Who is it, Lois?"

"A Mr. Vincent Strozzi."

"Transfer it in here."

She gestured to Mac to pick up his telephone and listen, while she picked up the one on the low table before his couch.

"Mrs. Powell? Theresa? It's Vince Strozzi. How are you?"

"Well, I'm fine, Vince. How long has it been?"

"Six years, a little more. Too long, huh?"

"Well, I did get your flowers and letter when Stan died. It was kind of you, Vince."

"I would have come to the funeral, Theresa. To pay my respects. I wasn't sure if you'd want me to come, though."

"I'd have been glad to see you."

"You know how it is. I tend to generate a certain kind of publicity. Anyway . . . I'm afraid I have a reason for this call—other than just friendship, to say hello, and all. Something's going on, Theresa. Affects you. I want you to know."

"You have a problem, Vince?"

"I'm afraid it's you who has the problem. There was a private detective in town day before yesterday, asking questions about you. He found out about us and asked about the relationship. A couple of friends of mine called on him and suggested he direct any inquiries about my business specifically to me—which he did not choose to do. He went on back to Los Angeles. I don't know why he's asking, but I thought you should know."

"I appreciate the call. Who is the guy? Do you know?"

"Yes, his name is Charlie Horn. He has a little private-investigator office just off Los Angeles International Airport. He's strictly a small-time operator, with no very good reputation."

"Charlie Horn. You run into him before, Vince?"

"No. But I made inquiry before I called you."

"Well . . . well, thanks, Vince. I'm not sure what I should do. If anything. What should I do, Vince?"

"You want my advice?"

"Sure."

"Okay. Do nothing, Theresa. Absolutely nothing. After all, what can the man find out? Whatever you do, don't confront him. That would only be playing into his hands. You know I've had experience. If you need a lawyer with special expertise in handling these matters, let me know."

"Okay, Vince. And thanks again."

"Come over to Las Vegas sometime, Theresa. For a nice evening. Like old times."

"Vince, I'll do it. And I'll be grateful."

Mac waited until she had moved to the window and was looking sadly, maybe angrily, out at the flight line. Then he asked her who Vincent Strozzi was.

She sighed. "A friend of mine." She turned her back to the window. "You haven't asked me, but I don't suppose you thought Stan Powell was the first man in my life. I was twenty-six when I married Stan. And Vince—"

"Vincent Strozzi? The head of the Strozzi—"

"Mafia family. Yes. Yes and no, actually. It's not the same anymore; it's not the old deal. Vince has nothing to do with the old business."

"What's he do for a living, then?" Mac asked.

"I'm going to tell you what he doesn't do," she said. "I know a lot more about that aspect of it. He has nothing to do with narcotics. Nothing to do with prostitution. Nothing to do with loan-sharking or strong-arm collections. It's a different world—"

"As he explained it to you," Mac interrupted.

"You want to listen?" she asked. "You want to hear? Or you want to tell me?"

"Sorry, honey. Go ahead."

"I had some experience with this kind of stuff," she said. "Theresa Kielce, Polack from Pittsburgh. My dad worked in the Jones & Laughlin mill. So did my grandfather. So did my brothers. My dad got hurt in 1966, when I was eleven. He was put out on the street, with what the company provided, what workmen's compensation provided, plus Social Security. We were okay. I mean, we didn't starve. But how you suppose my dad made enough to send me to Ohio State?"

"Terry . . ."

"No. Don't stop me. How you suppose? I'll tell you. He was a numbers runner. Now we got state lotteries, and it's all become highly respectable, and you can hear the numbers called on television. I'll tell you something else. If our numbers book had taken off the top the percentage the state lotteries take, the operators would have been found in a gutter some morning with their heads bashed in. You got a better deal from illegal numbers than anybody's ever got from a state lottery. Anyway, my father made his living that way—auspices of the family that ran things in western Pennsylvania. I should have been scared of a man like Vince Strozzi? Forget it. I'd known his kind all my life. Except that he was the biggest one I'd ever met. He couldn't kid me, Mac. I knew his kind. What I saw around him was very familiar."

"You're telling me he's just a big numbers banker."

"No. He sells labor peace, which the Strozzis always did. He's no loan shark, but he can arrange big financing, out of money that comes from sources we wouldn't want to talk about. He's got the usual stuff: trucking, hotel services, a piece of the big gambling action. You know, c'mon. Fencing. Money laundering. But I'm telling you for sure: no narcotics, no whores, no rough stuff."

"Respectable businessman," said Mac.

"Don't play holy man with me, Mac. Who had the numbers switched on two airplanes so we could show the world how fast we can repair a Nimbus? Who got an FAA inspector to overlook it? Small-time, big-time . . . shit."

"All right," said Mac. "I don't give a damn, really. But what's this private dick going to find out?"

"He's going to find out that before I met Stanley Powell, I lived in Vince Strozzi's penthouse in Las Vegas," she said. "What's that make me? A gun moll?"

"How'd you make the break with Strozzi?"

She shrugged. "Why not? Stan wanted to marry me, make me a partner—at first a very junior partner—in his life and business. Vince was married. There was no chance of being any kind of partner with him. Anyway, listen, I made a good salary all the time I lived in Vince's penthouse; I wasn't his property; I had dates; I lived my own life. When Stan . . . well, he went to Vince and said, 'Hey, I want to marry Theresa.' Vince gave us a nice wedding present, the silver that you've eaten with at my house. Some people were surprised. Nobody who knew Vince Strozzi was surprised. Nobody who knew Theresa Kielce was surprised."

Mac sighed. "It's not a personal question, Terry," he said. "I don't care—well, really I can't say I don't care. I do. I care about everything that concerns you. But . . . what can this man Charlie Horn come up with? In the business sense. What's the downside risk?"

Terry turned once more to the window and looked down toward the flight line, where a Nimbus was sitting with its propeller turning, ready for a test flight by Shorty Bellows. "For about a year I lived with— No. Let's say it straight: I *slept* with a man who is reputed to be a mover and shaker in organized crime. The telephone call you just heard is my first contact with him since Stan and I were married, except that he sent flowers to Stan's funeral." She shrugged. "What can anybody make of that?"

"Uh . . . how do I say this? What was the emotional content of your relationship with Vincent Strozzi?"

She smiled bitterly. "Is that a business-type question?"

"Personal."

"I never said I was an angel, did I? Are you? If you

are, I don't want to know you. No, I wasn't in love with Vince. And he wasn't with me. We got from each other what you'd suppose. He gave me a month's trip to Europe: Paris, Rome, London. I lived like a goddamned *queen*, Mac. Me, Theresa Kielce, showgirl, daughter of a Polack steelworker. I . . . I learned something. Don't ask me what. If you don't know, I won't tell you."

"Okay," said Mac. "Forget it."

"How much damage?"

"Maybe none."

"But the rules are changed."

"The rules were changed the night Charlie Horn went to see Valerie," said Mac.

"Charlie Horn . . ." Terry mused. "The son of a bitch. He *has* to be working for Bob."

Mac nodded. "Well, we don't know for sure. But it's a reasonable assumption."

"I want his ass, Mac," said Terry.

"We're going to have it. Bet on it, hon. We're going to have his ass and good."

13

"WHAT YOU THINK, Shorty?" Stirling asked Bellows as they stood beside Nimbus 88SP, the second prototype, on the ramp at the Powell Industries airfield.

Bellows shrugged. "I've flown worse."

But both of them knew this was different. This morning they were going to put stress loads on the Nimbus; and with this airplane, if a wing fell off you couldn't eject as you could from a jet fighter; you would have to make your way to the exit door in the passenger cabin, maybe in an airplane tumbling crazily, spinning, maybe breaking up. They wore parachutes, but those would be of no value if they couldn't get out.

"Well, we'll go at it in easy stages. It's a one-man job, you know. You don't have to go."

"I'll go," said Bellows.

They climbed to ten thousand feet. Nimbus 88SP was equipped with the cooling fins and the canted intake-exhaust ports that blew the hot exhaust away from the skin. The propeller on this one was a little different, too; the blades were a little longer and a little thinner; they developed as much power with a little less strain on the transmission and turbos. The plane was a bit quieter, a bit smoother.

The air was clear at ten thousand, above a murky overcast lying low over southern California. They were in touch with air traffic control, which had been made aware that they were going to do some stalls and spins.

"Center, this is Eight-eight Sierra Papa."

"Go ahead, Sierra Pop."

"Level at ten. Ready to enter stall-spin series."

"Uh, Roger, Sierra Pop. Uh, turn to one-six-zero. Maintain one-six-zero for three minutes before entering your series. We have a United 727 at twelve, descending. He's at your nine o'clock position and five miles. Will advise when clear."

"Okay. We don't have the 727. Turning right to one-six-zero."

"Eight-eight Sierra Pop, the 727 is now at your six o'clock position and descending through ten. No longer a factor. Suggest you enter your stalls at nine-zero degrees."

"Eight-eight Sierra Pop. That puts the sun in my eyes, sir. How about three-six-zero?"

"Uh, correct, Sierra Pop. Sorry. Turn to three-six zero. You are clear of traffic. We will advise."

"Eight-eight Sierra Pop, Roger."

In spite of the altitude and the assurance by Center, Stirling flew the Nimbus through clearing turns before entering his first stall-spin. He banked and turned ninety degrees to the right, to give Bellows a good look out the right side; then he turned ninety to the left to have a look to the left himself. Reestablished on three hundred sixty degrees—due north—he cut the throttles and raised the nose to bleed off speed. The Nimbus lost airspeed rapidly, slowing from three hundred knots to a hundred twenty.

"Shorty?"

Bellows nodded.

Stirling advanced the throttles to climb power, extended the flaps to takeoff setting, and lifted the nose sharply. The idea was to climb too steep, losing airspeed until the Nimbus stalled. They needed to know how the airplane would react when some day a pilot climbed too steeply out of an airport. When it stalled, how much altitude would he lose before he could recover? What was the best tactic for recovery? And, of course, was the Nimbus strong enough to stand a spin?

On approach to landing, with full landing flaps down, the Nimbus would stall at eighty knots. It was designed to stall at one hundred with the flaps at takeoff setting. Stirling glanced at the airspeed indicator. One hundred ten and no sign of the stall, no buffeting, no signal from the stall horn.

"One-zero-five," said Bellows, a little tense. He had flown airplanes into intentional stalls a thousand times, in pilot training and later in testing; but, no matter, he never got used to it. His fists were clenched tight. "One-zero-zero."

The buffeting began. The Nimbus shook, giving its own warning, apart from the stall-warning horn, that it was running out of airspeed. Air was burbling over the wings, not giving efficient lift.

Stirling had taken it this far before. He was glad to feel the buffeting. It was good that the Nimbus would not break over without warning its pilots.

He, too, was tense. It was always just possible that a new airplane would go into an uncontrollable spin or would tumble; and unlike a fighter, a business plane was not designed to take much of that. He was confident of the Nimbus, but this was going to stress it.

Stirling glanced at Shorty, then put the struggling plane into a gentle right turn. This was how a takeoff stall was likely to occur, while the airplane was climbing and turning toward a new course. It was also what would generate a spin.

The stall horn shrieked.

"Here she goes," Bellows grunted. "Nine-zero knots. Altitude ten four sixty-five."

The nose broke over, down and sharply to the right, as the Nimbus went into a spin. The horizon whirled around them as the airplane turned nose-down, tail-up and spun sickeningly toward the top of the overcast.

Stirling's mouth was dry, but he was grimly in control. He pulled back the throttles and jammed down the left rudder. The spin slowed. The Nimbus completed a rotation and a half, then stabilized in a straight dive. He eased the yoke back. The nose came up. He advanced the throttles to cruise setting. The airplane was back on straight and level flight. He retracted the flaps.

"Ten one thirty," said Bellows. "She lost three hundred thirty-five feet. Not bad at all."

Stirling grinned. "It's an airplane!" he said exuberantly.

"A pilot with any smarts at all could pull out of a climb stall with spin," said Bellows.

"Right. So all we have to do now is stall-spin her a dozen more times. You want to take this one?"

"There's no question, Mr. Powell," said the sober, intense young man. "Once you were able to give us the name of the motel where they would be staying, it was somewhat expensive but really a pretty simple matter to install the bug. We paid—"

"I don't want to know who you paid," said Powell. "You did it. Good enough. You're absolutely sure—"

"That it's them. We are absolutely sure. We have photographs, too." The young man, who until now had seemed incapable of smiling, smiled at last, though only faintly. "I suppose you understand. This is our specialty. I've done it fifty times. Would you like to see the pictures?"

Powell nodded, and the young man handed him a manila envelope. The pictures were nothing exciting: only three enlargements of telephoto shots, showing Stirling and Terry entering a motel room in Santa Monica. It was the motel to which Powell had referred Horn, the motel where they stayed during their two-day visit to Los Angeles to meet with representatives of United California Bank. They had been careful. They had taken two rooms, and the room register showed them as occupying separate, not even adjoining, rooms. The pictures showed, however, that they had at least entered one of the rooms together.

"We had to bug two rooms," the young man explained, once more dead serious. "Since we didn't know which one—"

"All right. You have the tapes with you. Let's hear what you've got."

This meeting was in a motel room in Barstow. Charlie Horn's young operative had driven out from Los Angeles to meet here with Robert Powell. He had brought a recorder-player as well as the tapes, and now, in a morning-bright room overlooking the swimming pool, he snapped the tape cartridge into the player and pressed the button for high-speed advance.

"You may want to listen to it all," he said. "But let's get to the good part first."

The voices sounded hollow, echoing—the recorded voices of two people talking some distance from the microphone. Without other evidence, it would have been impossible to identify them as the voices of Mac Stirling and Terry Powell.

—You know what?

—What?

—People who manage places like this ought to be condemned by law to sleep a certain number of nights a year in their own beds.

—Well . . . I wasn't planning on sleeping much.

—Speak for yourself, lover. The old man's gonna have to get in an hour or two of shut-eye this night. Look. We gotta be bright-eyed and bushy-tailed tomorrow.

—Yes *sir*, Colonel. I don't vouch for the bright-eyed, but I know one guy's gonna be bushy-tailed.

—You bitch.

—Well, look at you! You don't *look* reluctant.

—When was I ever reluctant?

—Uh . . . well, after four times you get a little troublesome.

—That's not reluctant. That's—

—Worn out. I gotta keep in mind you're older than I am.

—I'll be able, long as I've got teeth.

—Teeth? Well . . . my li'l nippies are real fond of your teeth. But—

—There are more important things.

208

—Than nippies or teeth. Now, on the other hand, *my* teeth—

—Hey! Jesus! Easy there.

—God, yes. I wouldn't want to disable it.

—No, for God's sake. Don't disable it, hon. Whatever you do.

The young man pressed in the STOP button. "Okay? It goes on. They stopped talking, I need hardly tell you. But there's something better a little later. I mean, *I* think it's more significant. I imagine you will, too."

He advanced the tape.

—Oh, Jesus, Mac! You got it figured out yet that I love you?

—I'd be damn upset if you didn't.

—Mac . . .

—Terry?

—I love you. I don't want anything else.

—Me neither.

—Pour me just a sip of that, just a little. I mean, I . . . loving you has gotten to be more important than anything else. Whatever happens—

—Whatever happens, baby. For sure.

—I couldn't bear it if—

—Don't worry. I love you, Terry. I couldn't love you any more. I don't know how I could.

—It doesn't make anything easier.

—When did that tough Polack broad Theresa Kielce ever go for what's easy?

—My old man will kill me when he finds out I'm sleeping with a New England Congregationalist shithook. And plan to marry him. I mean, you gotta join the church, lover.

—Fuck that.

209

—No, fuck this. C'mon.

"And so on," said Charlie Horn's young man. He popped the tape from the machine. "They're going to get married. That's going to make a difference, isn't it? Shacking up's one thing, but—"

"Right," said Powell. "She sold him to our board and she's selling him to the banks as a worthy successor to my father—because of his experience and competence as an aeronautical engineer. I figured from the beginning that what she really wanted was a cock. Now, on top of that, she's fallen heavy for him, gonna *marry* him. You're damn right it's going to make a difference. The next time she tries to sell him—"

"Here are the tapes, Mr. Powell. You can listen all the way through. Those are the parts I judged most interesting."

"What about the business?" asked Powell. "They say anything about the company, about the business?"

"Not really. Some comment about their having made a good presentation to the bankers. Nothing I thought very important. You may find something useful."

"Vincent Strozzi . . ." said Powell.

The young man shook his head firmly. "No. They don't mention him."

"I wish you could find out something for me about—"

"No thank you, Mr. Powell. That's out of my line. It's out of Charlie's, too, if he'd admit it. You couldn't afford what I'd have to be paid to risk winding up face down in a ditch along some desert highway between here and Vegas."

"Look—"

"It's not just that *you* couldn't afford it, Mr. Powell. The Rockefellers combined couldn't afford it. No way. You got what you paid for. Tapes and pictures. That's my line. That's as far as I go. I appreciate your business. You need me again, I can do the like again. But mess around with the Strozzi operation? No way. And if you'll take a word of advice, you'll stay clear of it yourself."

"Theresa." He pronounced her name in the old-world way he always had—Tear-*ay*-sah—and with the same gracious solemnity with which he had habitually greeted her. He turned her hand over and kissed her palm.

"Vince," she said. "It's good. It's been too long."

He was a little grayer than he had been before, but except for that, he was the same man she had known six and seven years ago—tall, slender, well tailored, his handsome face marred by a tic that caused his right eye to twitch every few seconds in the semblance of a quick blink. He covered it—not entirely successfully—with green-tinted, airman-shaped spectacles. His smile was still open and friendly, and he retained his habit of fixing his gaze almost unmoving on her eyes whenever he was talking to her.

"Sit down, Theresa," he said. "A little lunch will be brought up."

They sat down at a small table set for two, with heavy white linen, china, and silver. A single red rose stood in a crystal bud vase in the center. The big window by the table overlooked the hotel swimming pool, twelve floors below, and beyond that the desert and the distant mountains. She had sat at that table many times before—for lunches, candlelight dinners, breakfasts . . .

"Vince . . ." She did not know how to begin, what to say.

He was about Mac's age, maybe two or three years older. He was what he was entitled to be, a self-confident man who had won his battles against a variety of enemies and established for himself a niche in which he was secure and comfortable.

"You've done well, Theresa," he said. "I've watched."

"Oh hell, Vince . . ."

"Don't protest. You have done very well. Oh . . . first . . . I have something for you. A little gift." He paused to shrug. "Maybe for you it will be a reminder."

He reached behind him and took from the floor a package wrapped in brown paper. He handed it to her, and she unwrapped it. It was a framed painting by LeRoy Neiman. In the brilliant colors that characterized Neiman, she stood at the footlights, backed by a dozen dancers, receiving the applause of the diners and drinkers at The Sands. She was, of course, all but naked. Her G-string was a patch of white between her hips. The feathers of her headdress were more patches of white. She stood triumphant, hands stretched up and out, proudly showing her bare breasts, stomach, belly, hips, nates, legs. She was, as LeRoy Neiman had seen her, the epitome of the Las Vegas showgirl.

She had a serigraph made from this painting, which Neiman had autographed and sent her. But she had never seen the original. She could only guess what Vince had paid for it.

"'A little gift . . .'" She shook her head and smiled warmly at him. "Vince . . . you're too much."

"At whatever you do . . ." he said. "You're the best at whatever you do. When you were here, a showgirl, you were the best. And now—"

"Thanks, Vince, but it's not that simple."

"Lots of them who could have moved on are still here," he said.

"Maybe they didn't have my advantages," she said.

Vincent Strozzi nodded at the painting. "Even there," he said. "Even on the stage, wearing feathers, you were different." He smiled and shrugged. "Scores of them would like to come up to this penthouse. Few of them do. *You* did. You stayed. The only one. No ordinary showgirl."

"You and Stan were no ordinary men."

Strozzi laughed. "Let's stop exchanging reminiscent compliments," he said. "You have done well since you left Las Vegas. The Polack found a wife and a partner."

"And the Guinea has a wife and no partner," she said.

"Exactly." He frowned and nodded. "While you, fortunate soul, have a new partner. I've checked up on your new partner, Theresa."

"So what have you found out that I ought to know?"

"McDonald John Stirling is the many times great-grandson of a couple who came to this country before 1700. His father is a member of the Sons of the American Revolution. Many of those people scorn people like us. I see no evidence that your Mac does, but I suggest you think about the possibility."

Terry laughed. "I have seen no sign of the possibility, Vince."

Strozzi shrugged. "He's a white Anglo-Saxon Protestant. Good schools. Two good marriages. Respectable military career. Honorable retirement while still a young man—"

"Vince . . ." she interrupted softly.

"You love him," said Strozzi.

Terry nodded. "Dumb maybe. But I do." She lowered her chin, shook her head. "How do you explain something like that?"

"You loved the Polack," he said. "That wasn't bad judgment."

"If that hadn't worked out, I could have come back to Las Vegas maybe," she said. "I can't come back now."

"No. You're no showgirl now."

She frowned. "Everything used to be so simple."

"You were ambitious. And you are still."

"I am. That's true, Vince. I am."

"So what do you want?"

She looked away from him, out the window. "Stan called me a partner," she said quietly. "Mac Stirling calls me a partner. And—"

"And Stan's son Robert calls you—"

"A bimbo."

Strozzi shrugged. "You have his inheritance. Most of it. How do you expect him—"

"Others think the same," she said. "Nobody's got the guts to say it, but Bob Powell's not the only one who thinks I'm a floozy."

"And you care."

"I can't help it."

Strozzi picked up the bud vase and sniffed at the rose. "A certain sensitivity—"

She interrupted. "That's why the airplane is so important. I want to show how I can take a project that Stan left unfinished and finish it myself, make it successful. I wish I could have done it without Mac Stirling, frankly. But I couldn't. I'm not an engineer, and my reputation . . ." She shrugged. "So I brought in Mac. You understand, I had staff engineers, including one very good one—O'Connell, that Stan hired from Lockheed—but I needed a man with a reputation in the industry, a man with some stature and a certain aura of glamour about him. I resent it, too, to be entirely honest. I mean, I resent it that I had to turn over operational control to Mac Stirling. I still resent it, even if I have fallen in love with him. Do you understand, Vince?"

"Perfectly," said Strozzi. "Why not?"

"Incidentally, I didn't fall in love with him until after he was president of Powell Industries. There's a rumor that I gave the presidency of the company to the man I was sleeping with. I—"

"You don't have to explain, Theresa. In fact, I wish you wouldn't. Explanation is graceless. Protest is worse. Do as you wish. You are in charge."

"If they gang up against me, I won't be in charge. I mean if they vote with Bob. And that is what Charlie Horn is for: to build a case against me that Bob can give to the stockholders and the board."

"Theresa," said Strozzi frowning. "What can he find out about you? Is there anything I don't know?"

She shook her head. "No."

"Then what you call the case against you will be that you have been a nude model and a Las Vegas showgirl, also that you lived for a time with a man who is reputed to be a—How do they say? What is the stylish name now?—a *capo di capi* of *La Cosa Nostra.*"

"An adventuress who bewitched an older man and influenced him to give her more of his worldly goods than he gave his son."

Strozzi snorted. "Enough, Theresa! This is an excess of sensitivity. This is self-pity."

For an instant her eyes hardened with anger; then she slackened, and in a moment a small, amused smile softened her face.

Strozzi, too, smiled. He beamed on her. "One of my companies," he said, "is in the venture-capital business. You understand what I mean. We are in the business of finding sound and productive investments to which the accumulated capital of some of our other companies can be prudently committed. I suspect that the amount needed to fund the production of your aircraft would not strain our capital resources unduly." He grinned. "You understand."

"I'd have a problem with Mac," she said soberly.

"Yes. And I would have a problem with you," he said. "I think you would rather not be financed by me, unless you couldn't find the money anywhere else. I want you to know, though, that it is available."

"I'm grateful, Vince."

"Now, as to Charlie Horn. I could arrange to have him discouraged from further inquiry. But . . ." He shrugged. "Your stepson would just hire someone else. I would not worry about him. Unless, Theresa, there is something more."

"No, Vince. There is nothing."

"Then we may have our lunch served." He raised a finger and signaled a man who had stood at a distance throughout their conversation. "So tell me then, Theresa, what does one of these airplanes of yours cost? I have occasion from time to time to fly here and there in private planes, and some of my associates travel constantly. Maybe we should have one of your airplanes. Also, I am thinking about the officers of one of our unions, who are always traveling. Can you really recommend one of your new airplanes?"

14

"EIGHT-EIGHT SIERRA POP. Eight-eight Sierra Pop. Acknowledge."

"Eight-eight, roger."

"You're trailing smoke, sir. Yellowish smoke."

"Eight-eight, roger. Request emergency clearance."

"Cleared to runway three-zero, sir—or one-five-zero, your choice. Emergency equipment will be standing by."

"We'll take three-zero. Coming around on a left turn."

"Understood, sir. Understood. Uh, Citation Nine-seven Yalta Quebec, extend your downwind. Bonanza Four-eight-zero-zero, break off your approach, return to Fox Hollow and stand by on standard pattern. All traffic, enter holds ten miles or more out, pending emergency landing. Eight-eight, cleared to land. We see your gear coming down, sir."

This should have been a routine flight. All they were doing—he and Shorty Bellows—was calibrating test instruments. They had flown from Powell to Phoenix, spent an hour on the airport, and had just taken off for their return.

Stirling eased the Nimbus around. Too steep a bank, too slow a turn in these circumstances could be fatal.

"Transmission," said Shorty Bellows. "Temp still

within normal range but going up. Oil pressure gone. I mean gone. Zero. We're throwing oil. That's what he sees, not smoke."

"Uh, tower, we think we're spewing oil, not smoke."

"Eight-eight, could be. Can't tell from here. Emergency equipment in place."

"Thank you, sir. We're still developing power, expect more or less normal landing."

"Roger, Eight-eight. Best of luck, sir."

Stirling flew as narrow a circle as he dared, to return to the runway minutes after what had seemed a normal takeoff. The Nimbus was now parallel to the runway, flying a course two hundred ten degrees, at altitude approximately one thousand feet above the surface of the runway. They could have made a downwind landing, but that was always dangerous—better to fly a standard pattern, if he could, make the one-eighty-degree turn, and come down to the runway with the wind at his tail. For the moment the transmission was still transmitting power to the propeller, and a return to runway three-zero (thirty degrees) seemed possible.

"Temp climbing like mad," said Bellows. "Less than a minute, she's going to seize up."

"I'm going to let her seize up," said Stirling grimly. "I'm going to keep power as long as I can, then let her seize up."

"That's going to burn up everything."

"Right now what I'm worried about is burning up *us*, old buddy."

"You could turn in while we still have power and put her on the runway halfway down. She doesn't need the whole length."

"I'll turn when she seizes up," said Stirling. "Let's put down landing flaps."

"Flaps going down," said Bellows, his left hand holding down the switch.

Although he had not yet reached a point abeam the end of the runway, Stirling turned into his base-leg course, one-twenty degrees. He pulled back the throttles and let the Nimbus begin to sink.

"Son of a bitch . . ." grunted Bellows as the overheated transmission locked with a grinding crash that shook the Nimbus. "I'll feather the prop."

"Power gone," said Stirling into the microphone. "We'll be coming down mid-runway at best."

"Roger, sir. Equipment moving into place."

With no thrust from the propeller, the Nimbus quickly lost speed, and Stirling had no choice but to lower the nose and regain maneuvering airspeed by gliding, giving up altitude for speed.

"Hang in there, Shorty," he said. He was surprised at the thinness of his voice. He licked his lips. "I think we'll make it."

"You'll make it, Mac," said Bellows weakly.

"Cut the master switch," said Stirling.

With electrical power cut off, the Nimbus was without radio communication. Without engine power, it was a glider, and Stirling flew it like a glider: watching his airspeed, looking for a touchdown spot on the runway. He was sweating. His hands were tight and rigid on the yoke.

He had one more turn to make, from base leg to the runway heading. This was dangerous: to turn ninety degrees without power and at minimal airspeed. A spin-stall now was certain death. He eased the Nimbus around gently. He was only four hundred feet above the runway.

"Out of the arc, Mac!"

Bellows was telling him his airspeed was too low. Stirling shoved the yoke forward.

"In the arc," Bellows muttered.

Putting the nose down had cost altitude again. They were now only two hundred feet above the pavement. And the turn was not complete. Stirling could see the red and yellow emergency equipment, with a score of flashing red lights, lining up beside the runway, ready to chase him when he touched down. He lowered the left wing and completed the turn. One hundred feet altitude.

The Nimbus was lined up on the runway now, but more than half of it was behind. Stirling raised the nose to increase the sink rate. The plane responded and sank rapidly.

The last minute always seems like an hour and a half. He put his left wing down again to compensate for a left crosswind, and the Nimbus obediently held the course toward his touchdown spot two-thirds of the way down the runway.

"It's a sweet-flying son of a bitch," Stirling remarked to Bellows.

"Always is," said Bellows tensely. "But look at those goddamn fences out there."

Shorty was talking about the high chain-link fence beyond the end of the runway, beyond which lay a highway bordered with ditches.

Stirling raised the nose some more, pulling back steadily on the yoke. What he'd learned as a kid—hold 'er off, don't let her land, hold 'er off, hold 'er. The

221

Nimbus flew just above the runway, wheels five feet above, then three feet, then touched with a gentle screech.

He held the nose up. The airplane sped down the runway nose-high, bleeding off speed. He didn't touch the brakes yet; holding up the nose and opposing the wings to the air was far more effective braking than he could get from the wheel brakes. The Nimbus slowed but still rushed toward the fences. Only when the speed was no longer great enough to hold the nosewheel off the pavement did he jam down on the pedals as hard as he could.

"Shit!" yelled Shorty as the Nimbus bumped off the end of the runway pavement and skidded across the grass.

It ran up the slight incline toward the fence forty yards away, then slammed into the chain-link at twenty miles an hour, just enough speed to collapse its nose and drag down a hundred feet of fence.

The equipment—foam trucks, ambulance, tanker—rushed up to surround the Nimbus. Stirling gave the drivers a thumbs-up signal from the window before they began to submerge his airplane in foam.

Walter O'Connell, vice president, engineering, tossed two vinyl wafers in the center of the conference-room table. His face was flushed.

"I don't give a damn what anybody says," he growled. "Look at those sons-a-bitches! They didn't rupture. Cut! Cut, by Christ! Somebody poked a sharp tool through both of them."

The board of directors was hearing his report for the

first time, but Terry had heard it before. "What's the word for that, Walt?" she asked.

"*Sabotage,*" he snapped angrily. "Somebody set out to destroy the airplane and murder Mac and Shorty, who were flying it."

Robert Powell picked up the two vinyl discs from the table and examined them intently. "These are—"

"Seals," said O'Connell. "Seals off the body of the transmission. The lubricant—oil, mostly—is in the gear box under high pressure, and it's hot. When those damaged seals popped, as they were bound to do once the temperature and pressure rose, the lubricant spewed out into the hull, was sucked through the vents into the propeller arc, and was shot into the air behind the airplane. It looked like smoke, which was what the tower thought it was, but it was atomized lubricant."

"How did those seals hang in as long as they did?" asked Lola Weiss. "I mean, they'd already taken off, flown to Phoenix, taken off again—"

"We made a low-power takeoff out of the Powell airstrip," said Stirling. "That didn't blow the sabotaged seals. But when we made a full-power takeoff . . . Pop! Both of them."

"Who could have done it?" asked Deering, the banker.

The members of the board of directors shot glances at one another. Louis DiAngelo finally spoke. "We've had labor troubles," he said quietly. "We've got a new labor problem, now that the rumor is around that the Nimbus may be manufactured outside the United States. There are people angry enough—"

"It seems to me," said Robert Powell, interrupting

DiAngelo, "that we have no choice but to increase security around the entire manufacturing and testing operation. It is outrageous to think that we should be faced with a deliberate attempt to destroy one of our airplanes, with the test pilots on board. It is *outrageous.*"

"To say the least," said Lola Weiss. "So what do we do about security?"

"I've had a few contacts," said Powell, "with a detective agency in Los Angeles that specializes in industrial security. It may be that—"

"Called what?" Stirling interrupted.

"Uh, well . . . called Horn & Company," said Powell. "Uh, this man, named Charlie Horn, has solved problems of this kind for a number of companies. It's his specialty."

Stirling exchanged the briefest, most subtle of glances with Terry. "You, uh . . . you recommend this Horn agency, Bob?"

"Well, uh—I'm not sure how far I'd go about recommending it. I'm not an expert on that kind of thing. But I understand that Horn & Company has a good reputation and has done some good work for other—"

"You know this Horn?" Stirling asked. "Want to make the contact for us?"

"Well, I . . . I suppose I can."

"Why don't you do that, Bob? Get us a bid from Horn & Company. See what they'd charge to investigate this matter and put a tight security ring around the company until we get the saboteurs identified and stopped."

"Does the board . . . ?"

"So moved," said O'Connell quickly.

"Without objection, it is authorized," said Terry. "Hearing no objection . . . Bob, can you give us a report day after tomorrow?"

"You worked for Stanley Powell, didn't you?" Stirling said to the uniformed security guard at Hangar One.

"Yes, sir. Malloy's the name, Colonel Stirling. Jim Malloy. I came to work for Powell in 1972."

"He was a great man, wasn't he?"

"Mr. Powell? Oh, yes. One of the best."

Stirling nodded. He had a paper cup of coffee in one hand, a doughnut in the other. The sun had just risen, and the morning was red and wet. He had brought a bag of doughnuts, and he offered one to Malloy, who accepted gratefully. The guard was a small, bespectacled, gray man. His uniform hung loose.

"Mrs. Powell is trying to carry on with everything Mr. Powell wanted to do," said Stirling. "It hasn't been easy for her."

"Yes, I know," said Malloy.

"Now, on top of everything else, somebody intentionally damaged the second Nimbus, and we almost lost it."

Malloy shook his head. "I can't understand that. I'll tell you one thing for sure—nobody broke in here when *I* was on duty."

Stirling grinned. "I wasn't asking that, Jim. I know they didn't. And I don't think they got past Laker, either."

Malloy drew a deep breath, paused and seemed to

ponder, then nodded as if he had decided something. "Y' know," he said, "it wasn't necessarily somebody that broke in. Or got in without authorization."

"Now you're talking," said Stirling.

"Well, I mean, it could have been—"

"Somebody who was authorized to be in the hangar," Stirling interrupted. He nodded. "We're thinking the same thing."

"Somethin' else, too," said Malloy. "It had to be somebody who knew something about the airplane. You know, somebody didn't just *happen* to damage the seals that would make the gear box lose oil during the takeoff. Somebody had to know what they were doin'."

Stirling nodded. "Have you heard about the new security people that are coming in?"

Malloy shook his head.

"A Los Angeles detective agency. Specialists in industrial security. Hot shots."

Malloy frowned. "I see."

"I'd appreciate it if you'd do something for me, Jim," Stirling said, taking a sip of hot black coffee.

"Why, sure."

"They're going to be giving orders. That's okay. They're temporary. Don't argue with them. Just do what they say. But—" He handed Malloy a small white card. "That's my home phone number. Call me anytime. If they make any changes that don't seem right to you, let me know. Anything funny. Okay?"

"Why, sure. 'Course. I mean, I'll be glad to."

"I know you understand what's going on, Jim. I don't have to explain it."

"You don't have to draw a picture for me, Colonel

Stirling," said Jim Malloy, nodding. "I've had my ideas 'bout what's going on. Just didn't seem like it was my place to talk about it."

Stirling pointed to the card in the guard's hand. "Call me anytime," he said again. "Anything you want to talk about."

Terry was in the hangar shortly after eight. She took Bill Carey, the mechanic, aside for a private conversation.

"There's something I've been counting on, Bill," she said.

"Yeah?" He fixed a quizzical stare on her. "Uh—"

"Which side you'll be on when the shit hits the fan. Which it may be about to. You follow me?"

Carey nodded. "I know what you're talking about," he said. "When Stan died, I wasn't sure I wanted to stay with this company. I couldn't imagine you—" He grinned. "Well, I guess I don't have to say. And as far as Bob Powell is concerned . . ." He shook his head. "I don't have to say that, either."

"You have any idea who tampered with the airplane? Or how?"

"You can bet I've been thinking about nothing much else for the last few days."

"And no idea?"

He shook his head. "No idea."

She handed him a card. "That's Mac's home phone number. And you know mine; it's in the book. You want a private conversation, give one of us a call. If anybody hassles you—"

"I got you. And thanks."

* * *

Jerry Goldstein sat across Stirling's desk. He had brought the report of the emergency landing of 88SP.

"I don't know, Mac. I can't imagine it. All I know is, we had this call from Senator Meredith's office, asking for a copy of the emergency-landing report on Eight-eight Sierra Papa; and the next day Joe got a call from the senator personally. Obviously, there's something behind it."

"Now, the senator said . . . let me get it exactly straight."

"Senator Meredith told Joe there was good reason to think you are trying to cover your problems with the Nimbus by claiming somebody's out to do you in. The senator said we should take the story of tampering with a big grain of salt."

"You saw the seals," said Stirling flatly.

"As I told Joe. You understand, *I'm* not questioning your position that the plane was sabotaged. Neither is Joe Tully, for that matter. But, for some odd reason, we're getting flack from a United States Senator about it."

"So what happens next, Jerry?"

"Joe sent the senator a letter, telling him that I had personally inspected the seals and found irrefutable evidence that they had been gouged with a sharp instrument, which could not have happened in the normal operation of the aircraft. And that's it. We haven't heard any more about it."

Stirling sighed loudly. "Wonderful. Now we've got a friend on Capitol Hill."

"Senator Garth Meredith is a protectionist, Mac. He gets frothing mad when he hears about another industry proposing to do some of its manufacturing overseas.

The word's around that you are seriously considering manufacturing the Nimbus in Brazil. That would be enough to set him off."

"That's not what set him off," said Stirling bluntly. *"Somebody* set him off. Somebody who wants to screw up the certification process."

"The tests—"

"The tests are going okay when I don't have to worry about somebody having tampered with the airplane before I take off."

"Off the record, Mac," said Goldstein earnestly. "The tests *are* going well. All the flying tests are producing entirely acceptable results. When you get the third prototype ready for static tests—"

"It'll be ready in two weeks, Jerry."

Goldstein smiled. "In two months we'll reduce it to junk," he said. "Then we'll have the data—"

"Let me tell you something, Jerry," said Stirling. "This is off the record, too, and it certainly isn't meant to influence you, to urge you to go faster—but I want you to know I've got firm orders for forty Nimbuses. It's not certificated, and we don't even know where we're going to manufacture it; but people who know airplanes and have seen the test results so far—"

"I'd buy one myself if I could afford it," Goldstein laughed.

"So would I," said Stirling. "But, listen, I appreciate what you've told me—about Senator Meredith, I mean. Looks like I've got a political problem on top of everything else. *Marvelous!"*

Ruth Powell glared angrily at him, but she could not speak. She lay naked on her stomach, drawn up into a strained and awkward posture, arms behind her back, left wrist handcuffed to her right ankle, right wrist to her left ankle. She was gagged with a soft red rubber ball that was pressed between her lips and teeth by a strap that passed through the ball and buckled behind her neck. She grunted at Powell and glared at him from behind her eyeglasses.

"Well . . . you see her every week. You tell her," Powell said into the telephone. "I know, Mary. I know. That's what I want to do, but I've got to—"

He glanced at Ruth as he listened to the voice that had interrupted him. His eyes ran up and down over her tanned, wiry little body. She had nice tits for a little woman, he thought. Always had. He glanced down at his erection. She was turning gray, but she still made him hard.

"All right, Mary. I'm in the middle of a fight. That's the word for it: a fight. What? Of course. Control of the business. The chippy still has more stock than I do, and—Well, there wasn't much I could do about it. And now she's brought in a retired air force colonel, and she's sleeping with him. She—"

He put a finger to his mouth, telling Ruth her grunting was interfering with his telephone call. He knew she was all right. She knew how to be emphatic enough if she wasn't.

"Well, I'm sorry, Mary, but that's how it was. Our father had no morals whatever, no sense of decency. I know Mother—Well, there wasn't much I could do about that, either. So when you see Mother, tell her maybe we're about to get satisfaction at last. These people are going to be tripped up by their own—Huh?"

Ruth twisted her shoulders and moaned. He frowned

at her. He certainly didn't want his sister to hear anything that sounded like—

"I'll keep that in mind, Mary. Always. You know I do. Your prayers and Mother's are a source of great comfort to me. I feel their power. And God bless you too, Sister. And thank you for calling. Yes. Good night."

He put down the telephone and reached immediately for the little buckle behind Ruth's neck. He released the strap, and she spat out the ball.

"You bastard!"

He raised his chin indignantly. "What's the problem?"

She sighed and again twisted her shoulders. "I wanted the ball out. For a minute I thought I was gonna throw up. You know that's the second time you've done that: taken a long-winded phone call while I was . . . hey, y' know! C'mon, man. It's no time to ignore me."

"It was my sister."

"I figured that out. Sister Maria Immaculata. What'd she want?"

"She wants me to come visit my mother." He sighed. "I suppose I should. Want to go to Boston with me?"

Ruth shook her head. "I can't stand listening to the three of you talk about your father."

"We have every reason for the way we feel about him," said Powell. "I more than my mother and sister. Mother's all right. She lives okay. And Mary . . . well, she chose the Church. But me . . . me, he screwed."

Ruth flexed her strained shoulders yet again. "It's difficult to think of a man with all you've got as screwed," she said.

"One chippy after another," snapped Powell. "I

know you don't like my mother; you think she isn't good enough for you and doesn't have your brains; but my mother was a good wife to him: a good homemaker, faithful . . . He'd have left her poor if he'd dared. Then he married that Lana. I'm lucky there was anything left to inherit. If she hadn't slurped up half a bottle of brandy and set out in the night to drive an impromptu Five Hundred, she'd have gotten her hands on *all* the stock in the company, plus his patents and everything else."

"Well, Terry—"

"Another one! I mean, for Christ's sake, a naked showgirl, right off a Las Vegas stage? Out drinking one night, he—"

"I know, Bob. I know how he met her. But there's no point in your hating her."

Powell shook his head. "I don't hate her," he said. "I just want what's mine. The company should have been *mine*, Ruth. *I* should be the president, not my father's last chippy, then her lover. I—"

"I know. You've said it ten thousand times. That's not how your father wanted it, unfortunately."

"I don't care how he wanted it. I educated myself to take over, came to work for the son of a bitch, and took his shit around the office for fifteen years. Sure, he used to say I wasn't shaping up to take over. So, she *did?*"

"I think you better unlock these things, Bob. I'm not sure I'm feeling like what we started out to do."

He put his hand to her crotch. "It made you wet," he sneered. "You like it as much as ever."

"It's the only thing that gives you an erection," she said.

"Even so, dear . . . if you didn't love it, we wouldn't do it."

"All right," she grunted, pulling on her cuffs, straining, grimacing. "So I like it. But right now I don't like it. I want loose, Bob."

He took the key from the bedside table, inserted it in the cuff on her right wrist, and pulled the handcuff loose. She took the key then and loosed herself from the rest of her chains.

As she released herself and then reached for a cotton nightgown, he watched her sullenly. His erection was failing. "Am I supposed to go to bed horny?" he asked.

"I didn't think you *were* horny," she said. "You seemed to be all filled up with something else."

"You want to give me a lecture on not hating my father, not being resentful toward Terry? I've had one of those already."

"It's despicable of you to keep telling your poor innocent sister how much you value her prayers," said Ruth.

"What? I *do* value them. It's something you couldn't understand. Prayers . . ."

Ruth stood and shoved her feet into a pair of mules. "You want a drink? I'm going to the kitchen for a minute."

"I'm faithful, Ruth," Powell insisted. "I pray. I really do. I confess my sins, and I repent them."

"Is it a sin," she asked him blandly, "to conspire to damage your own company?"

"What's that supposed to mean?"

She smiled in tolerant amusement as he went to his closet and pulled out a robe. Being undressed when she was clothed made him acutely uncomfortable.

She adjusted her glasses. "You want the Nimbus to fail," she said.

"It's a bad project."

"No it isn't. And you know it isn't. Your father was a genius. Whatever else he was—"

"A flawed genius."

"Okay, a flawed genius. But the Nimbus was a brilliant idea."

"So you too are suddenly an amateur aircraft engineer? I'm surrounded with them."

She stood in the doorway, on her way out of their bedroom. In her loose, faded cotton nightgown and oversized mules, she was a faintly ludicrous figure, yet a strong little woman. "If it weren't for your father's genius—and what he left you, even though we don't have all of it—plus what I have from my family, what would you be, Bob? Do you really think you have the ability to be the produce department manager in a supermarket?"

"Goddamn you!"

She nodded. "And goddamn anybody who tells you the truth—which is what your father did, which is why you hated him." She paused, sighed. "You'd rather have the Nimbus fail, which might make you the president of a sadly reduced Powell Industries, than see it achieve a major success under someone else's leadership. I've seen you take that attitude before, Bob. Your father saw it, too, and you might have had more respect from him if he hadn't."

"Ruth, for God's sake . . ." Powell pleaded.

"You know what he wanted for you?" she asked. "He wanted you to live comfortably. He liked your marriage because he knew that, even if he led the company into a disaster, you'd have the wherewithal to live comfortably."

"That's all he thought I was good for."

"What else did you show him? You're lazy. You lie. You cheat. And you are a stinking cesspool of self-pity."

"And what are you, then, Ruth?" Powell whispered hoarsely.

"I'm an ugly little woman who accepted the only respectable marriage she could get and tried to make the best of it. I'm the mother of two kids who show some promise, which inspires me to hang in. And I'm still a little bit in love with you."

"Jesus Christ . . ." muttered Powell.

"Why kid ourselves?" she asked.

"I thought maybe I had your support in—"

"Destroying the company rather than let somebody else run it?" She shook her head. "No, Bob, you've never had my support for that."

"I'm not going to destroy it. I . . . I've got my own project."

"The Mink Bat? Yes, wonderful. It's cobbled together out of junk parts, to make a flying Saturday-Night-Special for little countries. Anyway, it's not your project. You're not an engineer, and you couldn't have done even that. Your father—"

"What do you want of me, Ruth?"

"Accept what you are. Accept what you've got. We can live very nicely, bringing up our kids. You can—"

"You've always had your knife out for my balls."

She snorted. "If I wanted your balls, I'd bite them

off. You give me plenty of opportunity, since that kind of thing is all you want from me anymore."

"Well . . ." He sighed. "Okay. We're gonna see. You're married to the man who ought to be president of his family's company, and that's what I'm going to be. You'll see, Ruth. You'll by God see."

Stirling was in bed with Terry. He was exhausted from a long and difficult day, during which he had never gotten into the air but had had to send Shorty up alone to put the Nimbus through some engine-out tests, while he remained in the office and contended with balky materials suppliers, objections by lawyers to the terms of a new company insurance contract, the proposal of a design engineer to change the dimensions of a hydraulic cylinder in the nose gear of the Nimbus, and a receptionist's claim that she was the victim of racial discrimination—plus the problem brought to him by Jerry Goldstein. He had left the office while three telephone calls, which he had described as urgent to the secretaries who received them, were still not returned.

Food and drink had had little appeal to him when he got home. He had nibbled only a little of the Chinese food Terry had brought and had drunk only a glass of white wine. She had insisted he lie quietly on his back on the bed and let her stimulate him gently with her lips and tongue. He had reached one climax, and she was stimulating him toward another when the telephone rang.

"Stirling here. Oh, sure. Put the senator on. Hi, Barry! Hey, it's good of you to call. Huh? We—Damn right. Absolutely. It's going to revolutionize general aviation, Barry. Listen, you get out here, and I'll put you in the left seat. You fly it once and—Right. For sure. Okay. Well the problem I needed to tell you about originates with Senator Meredith. I know he's a friend of yours. I know the guy's well meaning, but I have an idea somebody's been feeding him—Sure. You can bet I will. Okay . . ."

THE CONFERENCE WAS at poolside, at the country club in Powell. It was Saturday morning, and although no one had asked them to, the wives of Powell Industries employees were urging their children to play quietly and keep to the shallow end of the pool so as not to disturb Mrs. Powell, Colonel Stirling, and Walter O'Connell. Those three were intent on a small file of papers spread on a round table under an umbrella—Mrs. Powell in a blue bikini, the two men in swimming trunks.

"I don't see why not," said O'Connell. "I'll be damned if I see why not."

"Well, it's not radical," said Stirling. "It's been done before."

"Are you two absolutely certain," Terry asked, "that *anything* is necessary? In the absence of sabotage, after all—"

"I don't want to risk my life, or the lives of any of the hundreds of thousands of passengers we hope will be flying in the Nimbus in the next ten years, on two little vinyl disks," said Stirling. "Sure, those two were tampered with; but it is entirely possible that one of them will break someday—and it would only take one, not both—and we'll lose all the lubricant out of the gear box, just as happened to me and Shorty. Your oil blows out, your transmission seizes up, and—"

"And you're without power," said O'Connell. "Over the Phoenix runways, that's one thing. Forty thousand feet over the Rocky Mountains in instrument-flying conditions, it's one hell of a different thing."

"It's unlikely," said Terry.

"We don't deal in what's likely or unlikely," said Mac. "We have to deal in possibilities. Whether failure is likely or not is beside the point. Whether it's possible is the point."

"I'm not arguing against a fix," said Terry. "I'm just asking for an explanation."

"It's a brilliant idea," said O'Connell. "I—"

"Not so brilliant," said Mac. "But I think it will work."

"Tell me again," said Terry.

"Okay," said Mac. "We load the gears and shafts with a heavy coat of wax. There's a wax that's been developed for this kind of thing. It melts only at high temperatures. If you lose your oil and the temperature in your gear box goes up, the wax melts. It becomes a sort of grease that will lubricate the transmission temporarily, until you can get the Nimbus down and safely onto a runway. It gives you twenty or thirty minutes. And that would normally be enough."

"Tell me one more time that it's not a brilliant idea," said O'Connell. "It's the kind of off-the-wall idea that Stanley Powell used to come up with."

"It's going to take a lot of testing," said Mac. "But I've gone over the specifications for this wax, and I don't see any reason why it won't work. What's more, the cost will be absolutely minimal. I propose to coat one of the new transmissions with the wax, run it without oil, and see what happens. If it works as we expect, we'll put it in the new transmission that's being installed in Eight-eight Sierra Pop next week."

"I'm for it, one hundred per cent," said O'Connell.

"Settled," said Terry.

"I appreciate your coming in," said Valerie. "It's a little hard for me to get away."

"Glad to come," said Terry. She glanced around Dan's Silver Wing. "This place has happy memories for me."

Valerie nodded. "Where's Mac?" she asked. "We haven't seen him for a month."

"Well, he's been awfully busy," said Terry. "But right now he's in London, talking to the British government about the prospect of manufacturing the Nimbus in Scotland."

"Instead of Brazil?"

"It's a possibility. Everybody seems to think the Brazil thing is settled. It isn't."

Terry sat at the bar. She had come in mid-afternoon, as Valerie had suggested, so they could talk during the hours of slow business. There was only a few years' difference in their ages, and as Terry sat in her tight blue jeans and a sweat shirt, facing Valerie, who was dressed very much the same, they looked like friends, maybe even sisters.

"I called because this guy Charlie Horn is around again," said Valerie quietly, so that the man nursing a beer at the other end of the bar could not hear. "Not in person, actually. He has another man working the case. I tried to call Mac, but when they said Mac was away for a couple of weeks I decided I'd better call you."

240

"Charlie Horn is working for Powell Industries now," said Terry.

"So I heard," said Valerie. "I couldn't believe it."

"He's a specialist in industrial security," said Terry.

"You believe that, you'll believe anything," said Valerie.

"Do you know anything about him that Mac or I don't know?"

"Maybe. I don't know what you know. But I can tell you, he's real sleaze."

"How do you know this other man is working for Horn?" Terry asked.

"He's the one who was here and asked me questions, a week before Charlie Horn broke into my house."

"What's he doing?" Terry asked. "Talking to people?"

Valerie nodded. "To the test pilots from MARC. I don't know what he's asking, exactly. The only question I've heard was, how much did Mac Stirling drink? And did he drink when he was flying?"

"Have they bothered you again?" asked Terry.

"Charlie Horn has called me twice. That's all. Wanted to talk about whether—I'm sorry. What he wants to know is whether Mac's any good. I mean, you know . . . whether he's good in bed. I told him to go to hell. Then he offered me five hundred bucks for a taped interview on the subject."

"I'm not sure I want to tell Mac that," said Terry. "I don't know how far he'd go. I'll tell you one thing, though—Mac's not going to stand for your being harassed. Neither am I, for that matter."

"Don't stick your necks out for me," said Valerie. "I can take the heat."

"You don't have to."

"Don't stick your necks out, Mrs. Powell," said Valerie firmly. "Let me take care of myself, and don't get yourselves embarrassed. I'm going to tell you something Mac doesn't know, that I don't want him to know unless you have to tell him to keep him from doing something dumb that makes trouble for you. Okay? Charlie Horn knows this. It's no big secret. But I've got a criminal record. I did some big time in the slammer. Don't stick your necks out to save my reputation. I haven't got any."

Terry reached across the bar and put her hand on Valerie's. "You've got credit with us, Valerie," she said. "We'll be looking out for you, the same as you've looked out for us. Partners. Friends. Understand? And call me Terry. Mrs. Powell makes me feel old."

"I appreciate your receiving me, Mrs. Pendleton," said Thomas Litton. "You understand, we have no wish to revive unpleasant memories. It's strictly a matter of—"

"Duty," she said dryly.

"Well, yes. Certainly. A matter of duty."

"A security clearance," she said. "Strange. I would have supposed Mac Stirling had every kind of security clearance a man could have."

"Government types," said Litton. "This is an industry clearance. It's not entirely different, and we do have access to much of the government information; but we try to verify what we have heard, using independent sources."

"If I called Mac and checked your credentials . . ."

"He would tell you he never heard of me. Anyway, I hope he would."

"Since I have nothing much to tell you, what's the difference?"

"Some of the questions are personal," said Litton.

"I don't have to answer them," she said. "What is more, I am under no obligation to tell you the truth."

Litton smiled. He was a smooth young man, experienced, shrewd. He was employed by Dayton Industrial & Financial Security Services—DIFSS—of Boston. He was a graduate of The College of New Rochelle, but he dressed and spoke as if he were fourth-generation Ivy League: a practiced and effective deceit.

Priscilla Pendleton—Bunny to her closest friends—sat in the living room of her home in Darien, Connecticut, dressed in white blouse, gray cashmere sweater, plaid skirt, Topsider deck shoes. Her light brownish blond hair was frosted to give it highlights. Her features were regular, but unmemorable; she was a handsome woman in a conventional sense. It was mid-afternoon, and she was sipping her first Scotch of the day—Glenfiddich, on the rocks. The children were home from school and were romping in the grove behind the house. It would be eight before her husband was home, showered, and ready to sit down at table; and she had four hours to be ready for him.

"It is my understanding," said Litton, "that your divorce was essentially friendly, that you and Colonel Stirling simply came to an agreement to disagree."

"He was Captain Stirling then," she said. "And I have nothing negative to say about him."

"How did he handle his liquor?"

"Like a professional officer," she said acerbically. "And he swore like one. He drank. Damned right he did. But I never saw him fail to do his duty, either domestic or military, because of what he'd poured down the night before. He was a pro. In every sense, he was a pro."

"He has a reputation today for . . . How shall I say?"

"Try bed hopping," she suggested. "Polite term. And you want to know if he did it during our marriage? Sure, probably. I never knew for certain. But we weren't divorced over that."

"You were divorced because . . . ?"

"Career conflict," she said. "I called him a little boy. All he could think about was flying his airplanes. And the wife of a fly-boy lives in cinder-block houses in the vicinity of air bases." She shrugged and cast a glance around the comfortable, antique-furnished room. "It wasn't for me, huh?"

Litton smiled. "No. I can see that." He looked down at a notepad, from which he pretended to read. "He has a certain reputation today for wanting, uh, kinky sex."

Priscilla Pendleton laughed. "What's kinky?" she asked.

"Oral?" ventured Litton. "It's said of him that—"

"Grow up!" she laughed.

Litton pretended to laugh with her. "He won people's loyalty, didn't he?"

"Like mine," she said bluntly, her smile fading. "What do you want, Tom? I met Mac when his prep school and mine shared a dance. He was handsome, personable . . . I dreamed about him for months, years. When he showed up again, I was overwhelmed. But he'd chosen a career that didn't suit me. I was romantic. I thought I could adapt myself to his choices or influence him to give up his for mine." She shook her head. "We all have choices to make in this world, value judgments . . . I made mine. He made his. And there is nothing you can do about it. It has nothing to do with his security clearance or whatever it is you are investigating."

Litton frowned, considered. "You have nothing negative to say about the man," he suggested.

"Nothing I would tell you," she said.

"Jack Fuckin' Armstrong, the All-American fly-boy," said Robert Clark. "I mean, write a fuckin' article pointing out the defects in his big airplane project—and get it straight in the ass, go to hell, don't, whatever you do, write anything that suggests anything wrong with Saint McDonald John Stirling."

"Okay," said Charlie Horn. "You based your article on what Robert Powell told you. We know that. We know you got in trouble with your editor over it. We know you've been doing some independent work, trying to come up with facts that will justify you and restore your standing at your magazine. What have you found out?"

Clark, unsteady but not aware that he was unsteady, lifted his glass of VO and tossed it back. "I been lookin' around," he muttered.

"Sure. I know you have. The question is, have you found out anything?"

"Yep. I found out something. Something that ain't gonna be published in *Aviation World,* no way."

"So it doesn't do you any good," suggested Horn. "But maybe you can get back at Jack Armstrong, just a little, if—"

"If I tell you," said Clark. He shook his head. "Nope. Gonna publish it a different way. Article for *National Enquirer* maybe."

"Under your own name?" asked Horn.

"No. Hell, no. Not and work for *Aviation World* anymore. Under a different name, what you call a pseudonym."

"What would you get paid for an article like that, Bob—assuming they buy it?"

"Couple thou," Clark mumbled.

"Is it finished? Ready to go?"

"Yeah. Just gotta figure out how to submit it—I mean, you know, get it to the right editor."

"And you'll get two thousand maybe."

"Plus my satisfaction."

"I'll give you three thousand for it," said Horn. "On condition that I also get all your notes."

Clark squinted skeptically at Horn. "Cash," he said.

Powell ruffled the typewritten sheets with his thumb, then began to read. "This better be worth . . ." he grunted.

Charlie Horn grinned. "Just read it," he said.

Retired Air Force Colonel McDonald John Stirling carefully nurtures an image of All-American Boy Scout, the image he seems to think he needs in his present job as chief executive of Powell Industries. The truth is rather different. In fact, Colonel Stirling may be exactly the appropriate successor to the late Stanley Powell (Stanislaus Pawel Bierniacz), who reveled in his reputation as two-fisted drinker, lover, and bed-hopper. Colonel Stirling, we learn by careful inquiry, has been all of these in his day and may even have earned the presidency of the late Stanley's company by his ability to fill ol' Stan's bed as well as his office.

A Leap to Safety

Another Air Force colonel guffawed when told how Colonel Stirling was nurturing a new image. Among his memories of the man he calls "Mac" Stirling is a vivid picture of "Mac" leaping—drunk and naked—from a motel window into a swimming pool, only a step ahead of an irate husband who had come to the motel to confront his wife and her fly-boy lover. A check of Phoenix police and court records confirms that "Major M. J. Stirling, USAF" was fined $200 and costs for "drunk and disorderly conduct." A further charge of public indecency was dropped. This happened twelve years ago, when, incidentally, "Mac" was still married to his second wife.

The Dawn Patrol

A more serious incident involved First Lieutenant Stirling and an aborted ground-support mission in Vietnam. Although Lieutenant Stirling was cleared of charges by an Air Force board of inquiry, the veteran pilot who tells the story recalls that Stirling's rear-seat weapons operator was compelled to take over control of an F-4 and return to Phan Rang airfield when he observed that Lieutenant Stirling was flying erratically and endangering the airplane and others flying nearby in tight formation. The charge against Lieutenant Stirling was that he had come to the airfield drunk but had nevertheless attempted to fly the dawn mission. The board of inquiry found only that he had attempted to fly when he was ill. His commanding officer insisted nevertheless that thereafter he be carefully checked for signs of intoxication before he was allowed to take off on any mission.

Chairlady of the Board

The chairman of the board of directors of Powell Industries, and the woman who got Colonel Stirling his job, is Mrs. Theresa Powell, widow of the late Stanley. Before her marriage to Stanley Powell, she was Terry Keel, a topless dancer in a Las Vegas nightclub, sometime nude model, once portrayed bare-breasted in *Playboy* magazine. The charming Terry lived and worked in Las Vegas for about four years, before she married Powell in 1981. In the late '70's, Lieutenant Colonel McDonald John Stirling was a frequent visitor to Las Vegas, where he is still remembered for spectacular high jinks. Did he and Terry Keel get together during one of those wild visits? When she sought him out and sold him to her board of directors was she selling a man whose qualities as well as qualifications she had already sampled, in Vegas?

Whether or not that might be true, certainly she learned to appreciate the manly qualities of her new company president very shortly after he took over her late husband's office. He had hardly settled in before the other officers of the company noticed the intimate nature of the friendship between the chairlady and the new president. Hardly a business trip could be taken by either of them alone. Wherever they went, they went as a pair—including a romantic flight to Brazil, ostensibly to look at a plant site.

Bed and Board

That the president and the chairlady of the board share a bed is notorious to anyone who knows them. They are at little pains to conceal it, except as much as they can from the bankers and others who might be reluctant to invest in a company whose chief officers are engaged in funny business as well as the airplane business. Their business judgments are called into question. Does Colonel Stirling really believe in the Nimbus—or has he undertaken to promote the radical and highly controversial airplane because it is something Mrs. Powell wants? Has she won him to her side in the controversy over the Nimbus by citing facts and figures—or by using an entirely different sort of figure in the old-fashioned way?

"Rough damn stuff," Powell grunted. "What do you propose to do with it, Charlie?"

Charlie Horn reached across Powell's desk for the typescript. "Get it published," he said. "It's no good if it's not published."

"Who's going to publish it?"

Horn smiled and raised his chin. "Part of my business," he said. "I can always get stuff like that published."

"But who's going to publish it?" Powell persisted.

Horn tapped the sheets with his finger. "This is going to be seen beside every cash register in every supermarket in the country," he said. "It won't be the front-page story. Mac and Terry are no rock stars. But it'll be published."

"What if they sue for libel? It'll get back to us."

"Journalists protect their sources," said Horn. "Anyway, I've gone over Clark's notes. The facts in there stand up. As for speculation . . . well, speculation isn't libel."

"The part about flying drunk in Vietnam bothers me."

"It says he was cleared. It's an accurate report. He was charged with flying drunk and was cleared. The truth is, there was a cover-up; but Clark couldn't prove that and didn't say it."

"Whose name is going to appear on the article?"

"Not Clark's, of course. One of the staff reporters for the paper that publishes it. He'll use Clark's script and notes and maybe change it a little to conform to the paper's style."

Powell shrugged. "Three thousand bucks . . ."

"You'll get it back," Horn laughed. "Or a good part of it, anyway. After all, the paper is going to pay for the article."

Powell nodded. "Okay. Let's have some timing on it, so maybe we can coordinate the publication of the article with whatever else we might want to do."

"Who has flown it?" Litton asked.

The man on the chaise longue shrugged. He pushed down his sunglasses and focused appraising eyes on Litton. "Three pilots, far as I know," he said. "Mac Stirling, Shorty Bellows, and Cal Hennis. And Hennis only flew it once."

"Just three?"

"That's the story," the man said. He let the sunglasses fall back down over his eyes and looked away from Litton, more interested in the bikini-clad girls splashing in the clear water of the pool. "Just the three of them."

"Who's Hennis?"

"Test pilot. Flies for MARC. Stirling had him fly one of the tests while the Nimbus was at MARC. The rest of 'em he either flew himself or had Bellows fly."

"Anything significant in that?" Litton asked.

"Might be. I'm not sure."

The man on the chaise longue was Marty Dodge, himself a test pilot for Powell Industries, for the Mojave Aeronautical Research Center, and sometimes for Bell Aircraft. He had complained at the bar in Dan's Silver Wing three nights ago that Mac Stirling had never let him fly his pet airplane. One of Dan's waitresses had earned herself fifty dollars by telephoning Charlie Horn. Because Litton was an East Coast private investigator, only temporarily working under contract for Horn & Company and unlikely to be recognized in the Mojave Desert, Charlie Horn chose him to make the contact with Marty Dodge and meet with him. He had offered Dodge a steak dinner in return for an interview and had suggested they take their before-dinner drinks at poolside at his motel.

"You understand my interest?" Litton asked.

"Not for sure, no. Just what is your interest?"

"If the Nimbus is as good as Colonel Stirling is touting it to be, my company is going to lose sales to it. I'm trying to find out just how good it really is."

Dodge grinned, dropped his chin, and peered quizzically at Litton over the tops of his sunglasses. "Just a casual interest," he said sarcastically.

"If you're asking if the answers are worth something, they are," said Litton bluntly. "That is, if you have good information."

"Like that the damn thing won't fly?"

"Like that the damn thing won't fly," Litton agreed.

Dodge grunted and shifted on the chaise longue. He and Litton had changed into swimming trunks in Litton's room before coming out to the side of the pool; and both of them were white and beginning to turn pink in the relentless desert sun. Dodge was drinking Scotch over ice and was sweating heavily. "Trouble is," he said, "the damn thing *does* fly. Not only that, it flies damn well."

"Do you have any sense that they are coddling it through the tests to make it look better than it really is?"

"Sure they are," said Dodge. "Who wouldn't?"

"Are you telling me they're cheating? Is that what you're telling me?"

"That all depends on what we mean by cheating," said Dodge. "If you mean like cheating at cards, lying and like, then no; I don't figure they're cheating. But—"

"How about covering up negative test results?" asked Litton.

Dodge turned on his side and looked at Litton. "How much do you know about airplanes?" he asked. "Not much, if I judge right. Look. I can give you information. You'll have to attach your own descriptive words. I mean, if you want to call something cheating or coddling or whatever, that's up to you."

"But you . . . want money for the information," said Litton cautiously.

Dodge shrugged and turned back toward the bikini girls. "You want the information," he said. "You're asking me to break a confidence. Why should I do that for free?"

"All right. How much?"

Dodge turned his head, showing Litton a grin. "Tell you what," he said. "You're paying for the drinks. You're paying for dinner. After dinner we can go out to a place I know in the desert where a man can have a mighty good time. You pay out there. Deal?"

"I like the way you do business," said Litton.

"Okay," said Dodge. He finished his drink and lay on his back. "There've been some problems nobody seems to want to talk about. You know, Stirling is one hell of a pilot, and one day he had to be—or damage his prototype. What happened, he was flying—alone on that flight—and the Nimbus lost all electrical power. He was left with enough in the batteries to talk to the tower and tell them his predicament, but he—"

"Engine ignition?" Litton asked.

"No. That doesn't work off the alternators and batteries. That's an independent electrical system in any airplane. But he was left without navigation instruments, without autopilot, without lights, and—most important—without the power to lower his landing gear. Of course, there's a backup system that works with a hand crank, and Stirling cranked away at it for all the time it took to work the wheels down by hand. When he was finished, his indicators showed that the two main wheels were down but the nose wheel wasn't.

If he'd tried to land that way, he'd have had major damage."

"Okay, so—"

"So, you've gotta give it to the guy; he's a hell of a pilot. He did two fly-bys of the tower, with them looking at him; and the tower operators confirmed that his nose gear wasn't down. It was hanging down, but only halfway down. So he came around a third time, brought her down over the runway, eased her down, and banged his main gear on the pavement. The jolt shook the nose-gear assembly into its extended position, and it locked. He flew around once more and came in for a perfect landing."

"Hell, that's a *success* story," Litton objected.

"For Stirling it was. Not for the Nimbus. After all, he'd had an electrical failure followed by a mechanical failure. Not so good. Not encouraging. The electrical problem was a failure, easily remedied. Nothing had to be redesigned. But the nose-gear failure was a design problem. They had to redesign the nose-gear-extension mechanism. What's more, Stirling insisted on a second backup system. Now there's a tank of compressed air above each landing gear. If all else fails, the pilot can release the air and force the wheels down with that."

"But they solved the problem," said Litton.

"You want to hear about one they haven't solved? De-icing. Originally, the designers figured that because the hot engine exhaust is discharged into the propeller arc, they wouldn't need to de-ice the propeller. Wrong." He shook his head. "It didn't work out that way. At high altitudes the propeller blades gradually developed a load of frost, which slowly accumulated and became a load of ice. Naturally, it didn't accumulate on all the blades at a uniform rate, so pretty soon one blade was heavier than the others. It doesn't take much of that kind of imbalance to set up a fatal vibration. Twice they had to throttle back to idling speed and come down to an altitude where the ice would melt off the prop. That's okay maybe over the Mojave Desert, but you wouldn't shed any ice coming down over Minnesota in February."

"So what did they do about it?" asked Litton.

"At first Mac figured maybe they could solve the problem by coating the propeller blades with a lubricant, stuff like Teflon. Maybe then the frost wouldn't accumulate; maybe it'd fly off. But that didn't work. During one high-altitude flight a chunk of ice flew off one blade and hit the next. Bang! Stirling and Bellows thought they'd broken off a blade—or even busted a drive shaft. They got a scare out of that one."

"So what are they doing about it?" Litton asked insistently.

"Well, it means they're going to have to install a de-icing propeller and the electrical equipment to power it, which is going to cost them weight—and weight in the tail, where they don't want it. The Nimbus tends to be tail-heavy at best. So . . . New prop. New tests. It's going to change their fuel-consumption estimates, too."

"They're talking about putting the plane in production before much longer," said Litton.

"No way!" Dodge laughed. "Certification is still a long way off. And they've got problems."

"Any other problems?"

"Well, there's always the problem of efficiency. Every modification eats into it. They've been flying sealed-tank tests, to see how much fuel it really burns. I don't know what they're getting for figures."

"Can you find out?"

"Maybe."

"Could you get me the exact figures for a thousand dollars cash?"

"Can always try," said Dodge.

16

DAMNIT! NIGHT WAS supposed to bring a man some relief from the heat. Jim Malloy had given up a good job in Detroit fifteen years ago to come to California and take a job guarding the hangars for Mr. Stanley Powell. He'd cursed his job back in Detroit, where some nights your feet froze from walking on solid ice, and his wife had promised they would love California. Well, damnit, he didn't like it. Eight hours after sunset it was supposed to be cool and pleasant. Some nights, actually, the desert got downright chilly, but tonight the wind didn't blow, and heat still rose off the earth, trapped under a low layer of cloud that was unusual; and if he hadn't learned better, he might have thought it felt like rain. The nights were long, but he volunteered for them. It was better than the daytime, when the sun really sat down on you and baked you brown. He was sixty-three years old, and his wife reminded him that the cold would be bad for him. Well, maybe, but it would be better than being burned to death by the white-hot sun that burned up and dried up everything.

And now, tonight, damn! There it went again! They were doing some kind of tests on the power train of the Nimbus and were running the engines up to their highest possible speed, way beyond operating speed. The idea was to see how much they could take, as

Malloy understood it; and they ran these tests in the middle of the night because nobody could stand to be in the hangar while they were going on—besides which, they said it was dangerous in there, that something might fly apart.

They were using the new airplane, the black one that hadn't been painted yet. It had no radios or any of that kind of thing installed, just the engines and transmission and propeller; and they had it shackled to the hangar floor. Colonel Stirling was in the cockpit, pushing in the throttles and watching the engine instruments, and Mr. O'Connell and a bunch of other engineering types were huddled around another set of special instruments, in a cluster behind a wall of sandbags, monitoring the output from the special sensors attached to various parts of the power train. Also there were two observers in there: men from the Federal Aviation Agency.

The airplane seemed to scream, like a live thing being tortured. In fact, that's what they called what they were doing: torture tests. It was a torture to a man's ears, even outside the hangar. They had come out and handed him a set of the kind of earguards they were all wearing—like fat earphones that you wore over your head. He pushed his into place and still he could hear the shriek of the spinning turbines and the roar of the propeller.

He wondered how long it would go on. This was the third night he'd had to endure this unearthly noise.

Walter O'Connell came into Stirling's office carrying a file folder. "Here's the word," he said. "It's pretty good, too. It's not bad at all."

"Gonna satisfy Jerry Goldstein?" asked Stirling.

"No reason why it shouldn't. Everything's well within limits."

Stirling grinned. "For a while there I thought we were going to throw a prop blade through the hangar roof."

"We were in no danger of throwing one. We did destroy one, though."

"Uh-oh."

"Yep. Hairline cracks. Too much centrifugal force. More than it could take. But what the hell? Two-and-a-half times redline speed? Of course we burned up the turbines, and we have cracks in the gears. Everything's been taken down. Some of the stuff has been X-rayed, and the rest of it will be. At one-point-five times redline everything held. We got the first part failure at two times redline. It was a good test, Mac. Jerry Goldstein didn't say anything, of course, but it was obvious that the machine met specifications."

"Just one prop blade?"

"Well, we're sending the others for X-ray and the other tests. They could have microscopic cracks. This one's got cracks you can eyeball if you look closely enough."

"Be sure it's smeared with yellow paint, Walt. I sure wouldn't want it accidentally installed on one of the planes."

"Already done, boss," said O'Connell.

"There's no point in crying, there's no point in raising hell, there's not even any point in trying to find out who did it," said Terry. "Hell, I *know* who did it. At least I know who motivated it."

Stirling sat beside her on her bed, frowning over the week's edition of *American Defiant*—"The Independent Newspaper for People Who Want to Know What They Don't Want You to Know." It was a tabloid, printed in red and black. The front-page headlines were—

—"Elvis Lives! In Mountain Retreat, Composing, Writing! p. 2."

—"Famous Psychic Has Seen 1991 L.A. Quake! What Will Happen! p. 5."

—"'Had No Choice,' Says Sandy. 'It was kill or be killed!' p. 8."

—"Flying Pencil? Nude Showgirl, 'Colonel Mac,' Fly High. p. 13."

On page thirteen there were three large photographs, badly printed and fuzzy. The largest was of Terry, strutting, with a broad smile, on the stage at The Sands. Two black rectangles censored the photograph: one across her breasts, one across her hips, concealing the fact that she had not been entirely nude but had been wearing a sequined G-string. The second photograph was of Mac; it was a mug shot, from the Phoenix police department, taken the night he had been arrested after his precipitate departure from a motel room window. The third photograph was of the Nimbus on the day its gear failed in the high-speed taxi tests—sitting crippled, down on one broken wing.

The story was the one Horn had bought from Clark, supplemented to include an aside to the effect that "the notorious Miss Keel, prior to her marriage to Stanley Powell, had shacked up for more than a year in the Las Vegas penthouse of a reputed Mafia kingpin."

Mac slapped the newspaper. "If this is all their ammunition, it doesn't amount to a hell of a lot," he said. "I'm not going to say I don't care. What I really don't care about is anyone who would deny the value of the Nimbus because of anything that's in this story."

"But we've got cancellations," said Terry.

"Two airplanes," said Mac.

"And how many inquiries?"

"Three inquiries. Plus a dozen calls confirming orders and expressing sympathy and support."

Terry grabbed up the newspaper. "It's got the mark of Bob Powell all over it," she said. "His style."

"We've had one more call," said Mac. "Senator Meredith's office. Staff prick. Wanted a copy of whatever release we are issuing in response to this garbage."

"And you told him?"

"There will be no release, no response."

"What about the call from the *Los Angeles Times?*" she asked.

"And half a dozen others from real newspapers," he said. "I told them to do their own investigative reporting, that we will cooperate."

"What do we do about *us,* Mac?"

"From now on," he said, "if anybody wants to know what my relationship with Terry Powell is, I'm gonna say I'm in love with her and I sleep with her and I'm proud of it. I want that—" He pointed at the LeRoy Neiman painting she had hung in her bedroom. "—in my office. On the wall facing my desk. Where I can see it every time I look up."

Terry reached for his hand. "No more secret, huh?"

"No more secret," he said. "We love each other.

261

We're going to be married. That comes first. Then the Nimbus. We're going to go on and get it certificated, and—"

"Mac . . ."

"We might lose part of our support on the board of directors. I mean, if we lose one or two votes—"

Mac slapped the newspaper. "When the stockholders elected you president and when they accepted your recommendation that I succeed you as president, they knew everything this story says about you."

"They didn't know about Vince Strozzi."

"And they don't know it now," said Mac firmly. "They're smart enough to sort out the facts from the innuendo. All they've found out from this story, really, is that I was once arrested for jumping out a window in a Phoenix motel—plus that I was cleared of charges of combat flying while shnocked. *Cleared*. Some smart-ass rear-echelon cowboys busted ass to make that charge stick, and they couldn't make it stick. As witness the fact that I made it from first lieutenant to bird colonel *after* the incident."

"So what do we do about the story?"

"Pretend to laugh," he said.

"I'm not laughing."

"Neither am I. I said *pretend* to laugh."

"No one had to show us this," said Mario Monforte. He had handed the *American Defiant* to João Estremoz to pass on to Dr. Carla Olivera. "There was no obligation."

"I should distinctly have preferred not to show it to you," said Lola Weiss. "But Terry Powell asked me to

262

bring you a copy. They suppose someone would show it to you sooner or later, and they'd rather you received it from them."

"I am a public servant, a politician if you will, and quite accustomed to the intemperate, inaccurate attacks of the press. But I can understand how distressing this has to be to Colonel Stirling and Mrs. Powell."

"Actually," said Lola Weiss, "they don't seem particularly upset by it. Mac is in Vancouver, talking to the manufacturer of the gear box. Terry is in Washington with the legislative counsel of our industry trade association, helping prepare the case against restrictive legislation that might prevent our company from manufacturing the Nimbus in Brazil. Terry called me from Washington, told me to buy a copy of the *Defiant*, and show it to you. If they are distressed, they've shown little sign of it."

Dr. Carla Perfecta Olivera, counselor for international commerce of the Brazilian Mission to the United Nations, tossed the newspaper to a nearby chair. The slangy journalism of the tabloid challenged even her fluent, practiced English; even so, she turned up her nose at it and shook her head.

It was at Terry's suggestion that Lola Weiss was in New York, meeting with João Estremoz. They had come to the States for discussions with several companies, and had had no definite appointment with Mac Stirling or Terry Powell. When they telephoned from Miami to say they were on their way to Washington and New York, Mac and Terry had found it very difficult to take time out for a trip to New York to discuss the prospects of the joint venture with Aeromerica. In any event, Stirling did not want to be pressed by the Brazilians until he had finished his talks with the British.

Terry had urged Lola go to New York to meet with Estremoz and Monforte. Lola Weiss was a director of the company. She was a knowledgeable business consultant. She made a good appearance. She was not in Robert Powell's pocket.

"Ah, good," said Estremoz. "I developed a genuine affection for those two people, as I said before. This kind of thing—" he pointed at the newspaper "—can be most hurtful, and I should not want two such people to be hurt."

"I had occasion to see in Colonel Stirling a man unlikely to be distressed by much of anything," said Monforte dryly.

"Your government is not impressed with this sort of thing," Lola said.

"No, dear Lola, not at all," said Estremoz. "We are, after all . . . would I offend you with the term 'men of the world'?"

"Joe . . ." she laughed.

She called him Joe; it was easier for her than João. This was her third day in New York, the third evening she was having dinner with João Estremoz, and the second night she would sleep with him in his suite in the Waldorf. He was staying over a day longer than he had intended, as was she. He'd had no appointments today. They had taken the Circle Line cruise around Manhattan, had visited the Museum of Modern Art, and had viewed the city from the top of the Empire State Building—things she had never done before, though she was born and reared in Queens. Every bit of it was surprising, most of all that she was anxious to have dinner, to be finished with it, so they could go to their room and to the big bed there. After all, it might be for the last time.

She was realistic. Tomorrow Joe would fly back to Rio de Janeiro, and she would fly back to Los Angeles. Probably they would never see each other again. He was forty-eight, married, and a minister of his government. She was thirty-seven, unmarried, and—as she had come to suppose—not likely ever to marry.

The four of them—she with Joe, Dr. Olivera with Monforte—were having dinner here in the suite. The waiters had left a few minutes ago, leaving the wheeled serving tables with hot ovens beneath, the wine, still more bottles of wine and champagne in silver ice buckets. While she and Dr. Olivera had changed in the bedroom, the two men had lit all the candles and extinguished all other light. The curtains were open; the city was on display below.

Never before in her life had Lola sat at dinner with her cream-white, freckled, red-nippled breasts exposed —even to one man, let alone to two men and another woman. Joe had bought her a nightgown this afternoon. The long white skirt was of sheer nylon, falling from her waist to her ankles in long sharp pleats that whispered when she walked and played a game of hide and show as the shadowy white lines swished around her hips and legs. A design of lace circled her hips and partially concealed her pubic hair but not at all her buns. Sheer nylon lay in filmy white drapes around her shoulders and upper arms. Her generously proportioned, pendulous breasts were dramatically bare. She was conscious of them as the most erotic thing about her—for she could not think of herself as beautiful and had always been awkward about attracting the attention of men. Joe had whispered in her ear that the candlelight gleamed on what he softly called her titties. No one had ever called them by that affectionate term before; she liked it; and her eyes constantly wandered downward to catch a glimpse of that candlelight gleam.

Carla—which is what Dr. Olivera had invited Lola to call her—was also elegantly exposed, in a long black silk skirt, double split from her ankles to her hips, while from her hips up she was naked. She was a tall woman, very thin and bony, with loose-swinging little breasts and wrinkly brown nipples. She carried her head high and her back straight, and from her calm, heavy-lidded eyes she projected an air of condescension. She had not appeared until this dinner, and Lola wondered if she slept with Monforte in his own suite on the floor below, or if she had appeared for the dinner only.

The two men were dressed in well-tailored double-breasted suits, blue and gray. They smoked cigars. They had toasted the women in champagne. It was, Joe had assured Lola, a splendid Latin evening, the sort of thing to be enjoyed, a memory to be savored. He would, he had whispered in her ear, never forget it.

Monforte had dismissed the waiters before the women came from the bedroom, and now he knelt and took hot dishes of food from the warming ovens. Estremoz opened the wine. They would dine on lobster, scallops, flakes of sole, and shreds of crab, stirred together in a piquant white sauce—together with some fresh vegetables lightly steamed in butter. Dr. Olivera —Carla—spooned servings onto their plates. Estremoz poured white bordeaux.

"I should like," said Estremoz, "to propose a toast. To the success of Powell Industries and its marvelous new airplane."

"And to a partnership," said Lola as she lifted her glass. "I hope we can form one."

"Indeed," said Estremoz. "And, my very dear Lola, I am going to suggest in a moment that we say no more of business this evening. But I feel obligated to send back to California, for the attention of our good friends Colonel Stirling and Mrs. Powell, a bit of interesting information that Senhor Monforte picked up this afternoon."

He turned to Monforte, who smiled thinly and nodded.

"He conferred today with the New York officers of Banco do Brasil. Not about the funding of a project, you understand, since that is not yet close enough to agreement for us to be arranging money for it. But he did inquire of Powell Industries. What is the word in the New York financial community?"

"They've seen the *Defiant,* I suppose," said Lola. Since the talk had turned again to business and she was speaking in her wonted businesslike tone, she was suddenly far more self-conscious that she was half naked. Involuntarily, she dropped her eyes to her bare breasts. "And they—"

"They didn't mention it," said Monforte. "Bankers don't read scandal sheets. It will take a while for the story to get through to them."

"The only negative word about Powell Industries and its airplane," said Estremoz smoothly, "is that its fuel consumption has been greatly underestimated. Problems with propeller icing and certain other problems have added weight to the aircraft and reduced its efficiency. When the verified test figures are finally released—so the story goes—the Nimbus will not achieve enough fuel-cost savings to justify acceptance of its lower speed."

"Joe—"

"*Please,*" he interrupted. "Don't defend it. Don't be disturbed." He bent over her and kissed her lightly on one of her nipples. "We don't accept this talk. We are only reporting what the talk *is.*"

"Would you like to do the company a favor, Joe?" Lola asked.

"Of course."

"What we need to know is *where* this kind of talk comes from. I can tell you that the remedy for propeller icing is not going to cut significantly into fuel economy. Competent engineers tell me that, and I believe it. What I'd like to know is, who leaked the word that we have a propeller-icing problem at all."

Estremoz glanced at Monforte. "I think we could possibly find out," he said. "Don't you, Mario?"

Monforte nodded. "It is possible," he said quietly.

"Is it important enough for us to postpone our return to Brazil for one more day?" asked Estremoz.

"I can't ask you to do that," said Lola.

"You would stay?"

She closed her eyes for an instant. "If you do, yes," she whispered.

"Then . . ." said Estremoz. He raised his glass. "No more business. To good wine! Good food. And exciting love!"

* * *

Lola Weiss and João Estremoz were in bed late the following afternoon when Mario Monforte returned to the suite. Joe insisted they need not get up but would just pull up the sheets and receive Monforte's report. He picked up the telephone and ordered champagne from room service.

Monforte entered the bedroom. "Senhor Estremoz, Senhorita Weiss," he said briskly. Then he smiled. "João, Lola . . . I have had what I believe I may call a successful day. At least I have obtained some information that may be of value."

Lola was almost beyond caring. They had hardly left the bed, all night and all day. She had done things with him that she had never imagined doing, never in her life—that now she would always want to do again. During brief intervals when he slept she had allowed herself to fantasize an impulsive proposition by this lovely man that she return with him to Brazil, to live as his mistress, maybe in some intriguing little apartment with a view of the beach. She would resent every minute that Monforte was here as a minute in which that impulse could not move Joe. Tomorrow he would leave, for certain. They did not have many more minutes.

Rude, realistic thoughts had intruded. She was a mature Jewish woman from Queens, an overeducated businesswoman with a reputation for shrewd judgments abrasively expressed. He was a Latin American businessman who was accustomed to arranging quick and temporary affairs with whatever woman happened to be handy, wherever he went. He would remember her. But that was all: just remember.

Monforte sat down comfortably in an overstuffed chair by the window and lit a cigar. "What shall I tell you?" he asked.

"Tell us everything," said Estremoz. He pulled himself up and energetically pounded his pillows into a comfortable support for his back. Then he pounded Lola's and offered her his arm to help her sit up, too. "Lola," he said with a sly smile, "has waited all day to hear your report."

Monforte smiled and nodded. "I was introduced during the day to selected officers at four banks. Indeed, I had lunch here in the Waldorf, in the Bull & Bear, with a vice president of Manufacturers Hanover. An interesting story emerges."

Lola leaned forward to see past Estremoz, to look straight at Monforte as he spoke.

"To date, Colonel Stirling has only explored the possibility of applying for major financing. He has spoken with two British banks, including Caledonia, which is interested because of the possibility that the Nimbus may be manufactured in Glasgow."

"Ah," said Estremoz. "Glasgow."

"Nothing has been settled," said Lola. "Brazil is at least as likely as Scotland. More likely, I think."

Estremoz smiled and gently patted her hip.

"The word is abroad in the financial community," Monforte continued, "that Powell Industries will one day soon seek many millions of dollars to fund the manufacturing of the Nimbus. Analysts are looking at the company—not just bank analysts but stock-market analysts. Powell Industries is a small, privately held company, but its impact on the general-aviation market is significant and may become more significant. Many people are interested. Many are anxious for every scrap of information."

"We know that," said Lola tersely.

"Of course," Monforte agreed smoothly. "You know also that these analysts are decidedly unwilling to reveal their sources."

"So if you managed to get one to reveal, we will be in your debt," she said.

Monforte nodded. "You will forgive me if I do not tell you which one revealed his source?" he asked.

Conscious that she had reverted to her hard business self—which was almost comically inconsistent with the circumstances of this conversation—Lola smiled. "Of course. Certainly," she said softly.

"Ah, then—"

They were interrupted. A waiter had arrived at the door to the suite, bringing the champagne Estremoz had ordered: two green bottles of Piper Heidsieck in silver ice buckets on stands. Monforte received the order and carried the stands into the bedroom. Estremoz swung off the bed as soon as the waiter was gone and took charge of pulling the cork from one of the bottles. Nude and unembarrassed, à la Winston Churchill—though in his lean, dark body very unlike Winston Churchill—he popped the cork under a napkin and proceeded to pour. He handed Lola a glass of champagne, then poured two more, for Monforte and himself.

"To my most dear Lola," he said, raising his glass. "Health. Happiness. Success."

Lola laughed. She had never before been toasted by a naked man. But neither he nor Monforte was embarrassed. Monforte seemed not even to notice that the satin sheet had slipped down to her waist. He had, after all, seen her breasts before. She had the impression that the two men would have flung the glasses into the fireplace if there had been a fireplace.

Estremoz poured a second glass apiece and sat down beside her, casually covering his hips by a tug on the sheet.

Monforte sipped and set his glass aside. "Hammond, Schwartz & Gottlieb have issued a new research report on Powell Industries," he said. "It does not contain all the information that came to the firm. They have withheld certain information—though they will use it in confidential analyses for selected clients. This information goes to the very question we talked about last night: the fuel-consumption effect of propeller icing and other problems necessitating design changes."

"What are they saying?" asked Lola.

"They say that the cumulative effect of the several changes so far made, plus others contemplated, is an eight per cent increase in fuel consumption."

"Worst case," said Lola. "That's Mac's limit, the most increase he would accept. It's not insignificant. But it doesn't require the company to revise its claims for efficiency. Twenty per cent would. Eight per cent would not. And they hope to hold it down to five per cent."

"Yes," said Monforte. "But the question I set out to answer for you is not whether there is in fact an eight-percent problem or a twenty-percent problem— or even whether the analysts believe there is. The question is, where did Hammond, Schwartz get the numbers? And that I think I can tell you."

"That's important," said Lola.

"I must have your word that you will not disclose the source—I mean, the source in New York, either myself or Hammond, Schwartz. It must not be disclosed even to Colonel Stirling."

"Mac—"

"Colonel Stirling," said Monforte evenly, "is an extremely intelligent and effective man—but he can also be an extremely precipitate one. I am in his debt for his ability and willingness to act fast and forcefully, but I am a bit concerned about what happens in the first half minute after his temper flares. You can use the information I have for you. Use it any way you want. But promise me you won't tell anyone your source."

"I promise."

Monforte picked up his glass and sipped champagne. "Six years ago a young man named Thomas Litton was employed by Hammond, Schwartz. He was regarded as brilliant. Indeed, he proved to be far too brilliant. It was discovered that his attaché case was not a simple repository for assorted papers and perhaps a sandwich or two but a highly sophisticated electronic listening and transmitting station. From time to time, he 'accidentally' left this innocent-looking briefcase in various offices and conference rooms, and when people talked there later they unwittingly spoke for his clandestine radio station, transmitting to his recorder not far away. He escaped prosecution only because people wanted to prevent disclosure of what he had learned."

"A democracy has only ineffective ways of coping with such people," remarked Estremoz casually.

"After he was fired, he established his own industrial-security agency," said Monforte. "He proposed to a variety of prospective clients that he be employed by them to do just what Hammond had fired him for doing. Enough of them hired him to give him almost instantaneous prosperity. He is a junior partner today in a firm called Dayton Industrial & Financial Security Services, which is supposedly a firm engaged in the business of securing companies *against* the kind of thing that is Litton's specialty. It gives him, I suppose, a front and a kind of respectability he would otherwise lack. I mean to say that Dayton is an ethical agency—if the term 'ethical' can be said to apply to that line of business."

"And Hammond, Schwartz still takes information from him," said Lola. "What they wouldn't let him do as an employee, they are happy to have him do as an outside consultant."

"Something like that," said Monforte. "But don't tar the whole firm. Only one or two people at Hammond have any contact with him."

"And he spied on . . . ?"

Monforte nodded. "Yes. Happily, my contact at Hammond, through Banco do Brasil, was able to supply a photograph—from their personnel file. They even had it enlarged for me. It may be an important key for you, Lola. I hope so. I hope we have been able to be of service to you."

"Yes," said Estremoz. "It is cynical, I know, but perhaps not entirely inappropriate to suggest that Powell Industries may wish to weigh our service in the balance when the decision is made to come to Brazil or not come to Brazil."

17

MAC STIRLING SETTLED himself wearily on a barstool at Dan's. Both Dan and Valerie broke away from a laughing group at the far end of the bar and came to him.

"Don't look like being a big biz executive agrees with you, ol' buddy," said Dan. "Don't like to bring it up, but you look *tired.*"

"By Christ, I *am* tired, Dan," Stirling admitted. "Maybe one of your special martinis will revive me."

"Well, it won't do that, have to tell you," said Dan. "But it might do somethin' else, like relax you a little."

"I'll settle for that," said Stirling.

He did in fact look tired: hollow-eyed, pale, slack-shouldered, disconsolate. He had been in the air constantly for two weeks, flying the many and varied tests the certification process required: airplane loaded heavy, loaded off center, loaded nose-heavy, loaded tail-heavy; cutting off one engine during takeoff, during flight, during a landing; plus endless fuel-economy checks. Shorty Bellows could have flown these tests, but Stirling wanted to fly them himself, sometimes four flights a day. Between flights he had to cope with all the problems of management, from minutiae to major decisions. And most of all, he had to deal with the issues of financing, settling on a manufacturing center, and the increasing possibility of new government regulations to discourage American companies from manufacturing overseas.

He wore khaki pants and a checked shirt with his old Air Force jacket. His eyes followed Valerie as she went to the other end of the bar for a fresh bottle of Beefeaters.

"Maybe you ought to spend a night with Val," Dan suggested under his breath. "Maybe that Powell woman is wearing you out."

Stirling grinned. "Thanks, Dan—for the suggestion. That girl's first-class, anyway. You and I ought to try to do something good for her."

"I did try," said Dan. "Then you wandered off the reservation."

Stirling nodded and blew a short, noisy sigh. "I did better, Dan. Val's a great little girl, but this is something different." He glanced around the room. "Look, I came in to show you something. I want you and Valerie to look at a picture, but I don't want everybody in the place to know."

"We can go back in the office," said Dan.

"No. Just slip this under the bar and have a look."

He handed Dan a manila envelope containing a 5 × 7 print of the picture Lola Weiss had brought back from New York—the photo of Thomas Litton.

Dan squinted and nodded. "I've seen the fellow. I suppose that's what you want to know, have I seen him. Yeah. He's been in here two, three times."

"Alone?"

Dan nodded again. "Eastern-type fellow. Friendly. Lots of jokes. The girls liked him. Haven't seen him lately."

Valerie returned with Mac's martini, and when she

looked at the picture she agreed that Thomas Litton had been in Dan's Silver Wing several times, always alone, always a fun fellow, full of jokes. He had propositioned her. She had turned him down. He had propositioned at least one more of the girls. She wasn't sure, but she thought Judy had maybe gone out with him.

"We can by God ask," said Dan. "Judy's—"

"No," said Stirling. "I'd rather you didn't. Please don't. Did he talk much with anybody else, like maybe with any of the pilots from MARC?"

"Talked to whoever happened to be on the next barstool," said Valerie.

"If he comes in again, let me know, will you? Quietly. Don't let him know. And, just for your information, Val, he works for Horn."

"Mornin', sir," said Jim Malloy. "Flying her this morning?"

"Maybe," said Stirling. "More likely this afternoon."

"I wish I had some word for you," said Malloy. "It's been quiet, nights. I was afraid someone would try . . . you know what I mean. But it's been quiet."

"No problem, Jim," said Stirling. "Keep the eye open. Call me anytime."

It was a little after six. He walked into Hangar One, where three airplanes now filled nearly all the space— 87SP, the veteran, now essentially inactive because most of the test-inspired modifications had been made to 88SP, 88SP itself, and the unpainted, unnumbered third Nimbus, the one that had been nearly wrenched apart by the static tests. He stopped for a moment just inside the doors to look at the three airplanes. Radical though they were, their lines were beautiful; they were three engineering marvels, to be admired, appreciated, even loved.

Bill Carey walked around the nose of 88SP. "Mornin', Colonel," he said. "Flying 'er this morning?"

"Maybe," said Stirling. "She ready?"

Carey nodded. "Yeah, she's ready. Y' know . . . makes me think of the days when Mr. Powell—I mean Mr. *Stanley* Powell—was getting ready for certification flights with the Cirrus. 'Overload 'er forward, Bill,' he'd say. 'Overload 'er hard.' And we would."

Stirling nodded. "Right. To satisfy the FAA. We have to face it, Bill. Some of the pilots who fly these planes will load them way outside the specifications. So do they kill themselves and all their passengers, or will the Nimbus take the abuse?"

"She'll take it, Colonel. I never saw an aircraft more likely to take it."

They walked around the airplane. Toward the rear, leaning against the wall, was the yellow-painted propeller blade fractured in the stress tests on the unnumbered Nimbus. Stirling gave it a kick. "Let's get this thing out of here, Bill," he said. "I don't even want to be reminded of what can happen when the engines are spun up to two-point-five."

Carey, too, gave the long thin blade a kick. Someone had sprayed it with yellow paint, to be sure everyone knew it was the blade with hairline cracks.

"All under control," said Stirling. "Sandbags . . ."

"Sandbags in the front," said Carey. "She's overloaded forward of the center of gravity. I mean, she's *way* overloaded. I wouldn't want to fly 'er that way if I didn't know. It's going to take some job of piloting, Colonel. If it wasn't you—"

"Thanks, Bill, but it's no big deal. The engineering specs say she'll take fifteen hundred pounds overload forward. You've loaded eleven, right? Let's see how she performs with that load. Then we'll do the same aft."

"I'm for it, Colonel," said Carey. "But take it careful, man. A lot rides on this flight."

"All I want to know," said Stirling, "and for sure, is that nobody has tampered with the airplane."

"That's why I'm here before dawn," said Carey. "I've been over everything about this airplane. I've got two other guys crawling through every inch. We've pulled seals and replaced them. We've stress-tested cables. We've drained and replaced lubricants. And so on. We're still at it. We'll be at it until you run her up and shoot down the runway. I'll go with you, Colonel. I'm willing to fly in this plane."

"I don't need that kind of testimony from you, Bill," said Stirling. "Forget it. I've taken crew chiefs on missions, in years past; but this isn't one of them; I have no problem with you."

"Your choice, sir," said Carey stiffly.

Stirling patted his shoulder. "One thing, Bill. I want to show you a photograph, sort of secretly." He took out the 5 × 7 and showed it to the mechanic. "Recognize the man?"

Carey shook his head. "Never saw him in my life. Swear to you, sir. Never saw him."

"You don't need to swear to me, Bill. You never saw him, you never saw him."

Carey nodded. "'Bout ten o'clock, sir?" he asked.

"Ten suits you?"

"Ten suits me, Colonel. I'll have her ready to go at ten."

Stirling reached for Carey's hand. "You've got a deal, Bill."

A meeting assembled in Stirling's office at eight o'clock. Present were Stirling, Terry Powell, Walter O'Connell, and Lola Weiss. A big pot of coffee blurped on a hot plate; a round tray of pastries filled one corner of Stirling's desk. Eggs, sausages, bacon, toast, butter, marmalade, and glasses of orange juice filled a tray that covered his coffee table.

"What I want to know is, is it dangerous?" Lola asked.

"Flying with the airplane heavily overloaded forward of its center of gravity? We'd ground a commercial pilot who did it," said Stirling.

"How much is it overloaded?" she asked.

"Eleven hundred pounds," said Stirling. "We've flown it eight hundred pounds overloaded forward, but never this much."

"Lola," said O'Connell. "Test flying involves doing what you shouldn't do. The Nimbus should not be flown eleven hundred pounds overloaded forward. Neither should any other airplane. But some pilot, some idiot, somewhere, is going to do it; so we have to know how it will fly. Then again, some idiot is going to overload it aft. Pilots are trained to worry about loading, not just how much the airplane carries, but *where* it carries it: forward of the center of gravity or aft. It's a big part of airplane safety. So Mac is going to fly the Nimbus with fore and aft overloads—while the FAA watches. He's going to perform specified maneuvers with these overloads. It has to do with the safety of the Nimbus when it's not flown by pilots like Mac Stirling and Shorty Bellows."

"It's no damn good, Lola, if it has to be flown by guys like those two," said Terry.

Lola walked to the window. Nimbus 88SP was being pulled out to the ramp. It was an exceptionally beautiful airplane, she decided. She had entertained doubts about these people's commitment to it. Their commitment was based on something besides the numbers. It was easier now to understand.

"Dan and Valerie have seen Litton," said Terry. "Anybody else?"

O'Connell shook his head. He knew he was the only one who had not reported on the subject.

"We owe you a debt of gratitude, Lola," Terry said solemnly.

Lola shook her head. "All I did is what any director of any corporation is obligated to do in the circumstances. Ethical obligation to—"

"Well done, Lola," said Stirling.

"The assault is coming," said O'Connell. "It had to come someday; in fact, I knew it was coming from the day I heard that Mr. Powell was dead. I knew Bob would come on strong. In fact, Terry, I have learned respect for you because you held it off so long. You have *guts*, Terry. More than most of us. Mac . . . Welcome to the war. You've got guts, too. Like she has."

Involuntarily, all of them glanced at the LeRoy

Neiman painting, the bold swirl of brilliant color, half abstract, of Terry as a Las Vegas showgirl. Mac had hung it on his office wall, as he had promised. It was too big, too vividly colored, not to dominate the room, and it spoke defiance, as he meant it should.

Lola spoke. "I've tried to be objective. Stan hired me because he was confident I would always be objective." She stopped, sighed. "I don't know if I am anymore or not."

"I had a college professor years ago," said Walter O'Connell, "who said that objectivity is the characteristic of an intellectual eunuch."

"There is an evil conspiracy inside this company," said Lola.

"In spite of that," said Mac Stirling, "in spite of the article in the *American Defiant,* we have sixty-five firm orders for the Nimbus. On the basis of the figures—"

"On the basis of your reputation," interrupted O'Connell. "They count on you, Mac. They take your word. When Terry brought you in—"

Stirling shook his head. "Look at the damn thing out there," he said. He stared down at Nimbus 88SP, now sitting on the ramp, surrounded by armed guards from Horn & Company. "Stan Powell." He nodded. "Stan Powell. And don't let us forget it."

"Mac . . ." said O'Connell. "You said ten o'clock. I think it would be well if the rest of us got out of here and let you have an hour's rest before you fly. I'm not going to kid you, man; you look *beat.* I'm not sure an air force doctor would let you fly today."

Stirling gulped coffee. "Don't mother me, Walt. I'm flying this test. I don't know how many of you know this, but the imbalanced-flight tests are vital. The FAA will never certify a plane that doesn't allow an idiot pilot to load it wrong."

"Mac . . ."

"No. Don't even suggest it."

Terry had stayed behind after the others left. She stood beside him, where he sat in the big leather chair behind his desk, and stroked his forehead and eyes.

"Somebody has got to goddamn well suggest it," she said acerbically. "You are *pooped,* Mac. I can see it, Walt saw it, Lola saw it; and you just throw out your hands and refuse to acknowledge it. You're goddamn *tired,* honey baby."

"I'm not sending Shorty out to fly—"

"You saw Shorty this morning," she said. "He slept all night—and probably all day yesterday by some swimming pool. He's *up,* Mac! Shorty's rested, ready to go. At least let him fly left seat. Fly copilot, honey. What the hell's—"

"I'll think about that, Terry," said Mac. "Left seat—"

"Let him have it, honey," she pleaded. "He's a good pilot. Christ, you've called him the best you ever worked with! And he's fresh. He—"

"Okay, okay," snapped Stirling. "I'll think about it."

She stood at the window. The sun was well up, but the shadows were still long, from the mountains and across the ramp and over the Nimbus. The light was still red. It was the kind of morning she had learned to love when she came to Las Vegas and later to Powell, California. In Pennsylvania, when you woke in your hillside bedroom, you might have a view of half a mile of woods or highway or city. Here you looked out over a hundred miles. It was a hundred miles of not much, but it was beautiful, a spectacularly beautiful vista of desert and mountain, sun and shadow, red and purple.

"Other people have two kinds of reasons for telling you you're tired, that you ought to let Shorty do some of the flying," she said quietly. "One reason is that people don't want to see you bend the airplane, as pilots say. They've got too much invested in it. The other reason is that some people have a hell of a lot of respect and affection for you. Don't accuse Walter O'Connell of mothering you, Mac. The man's your *friend*."

Stirling frowned. "Right. I . . . I'm grateful. I guess I don't show it very well."

She smiled. "And some people love you," she said softly.

"It's got eleven hundred pounds of sandbags forward of the center of gravity," Stirling said to Shorty Bellows. "It's going to fly like a—"

"Like it was never meant to fly," said Bellows. "Doesn't bother me, Mac. I figure the son of a bitch can take it."

"I wouldn't fly it if I didn't think so," said Stirling.

"Let's say she does okay on takeoff," said Bellows. "Then up to ten thousand for a couple stalls. FAA like that?"

The two pilots turned to Jerry Goldstein.

"Good enough for me," he said. "In fact, you didn't have to overload that much. You're up three hundred pounds from your last overload flight. You could increase in smaller increments."

"We can finish these tests faster if we go with eleven

hundred this morning," said Stirling. "If she handles reasonably well with the eleven, we might go to fifteen this afternoon. You agree, Shorty?"

"I have no problems," said Bellows.

Goldstein shrugged. "Wish I could go with you."

"You got that much confidence, Jerry?" Stirling asked. "I mean, in a test pilot that humps the chairman of the board of his company? A test pilot who got drunk and jumped out a window in Phoenix?"

Goldstein shrugged dramatically. "I got confidence in Shorty," he said. "*He* didn't do all that stuff."

"I would've if I'd had the chance," said Bellows. "'Specially hump the chairlady of the board. Some guys have all the luck."

"Hark! Who comes?" laughed Stirling.

Robert Powell had come out from the office building and was striding across the ramp toward the Nimbus. Dapper, bustling, he seemed to hurry whether he hurried or not.

"Bob."

"Mac. Shorty. Uh, Jerry. I, uh . . . I came out to wish you good luck."

"Luck ain't gonna be the point of it, Mr. Powell," said Shorty Bellows. "In test flyin', you rely on luck, you're dead. For sure."

"Oh, sure. I understand that. I just want to say I'm glad our airplane is being flown by the best two pilots in the business. I'll be in the tower, listening to the radio transmissions. So, once more . . . uh, well, if good luck is not the right thing to say, then anyway . . . uh, you have my best wishes. I wish I could go along with you."

"Could be arranged," said Stirling dryly.

Powell grinned disarmingly. "I throw up when you

do stalls," he said. He put his hand on the wing. "Beautiful airplane, as it turns out. I wish my father could have seen it fly."

As Powell turned and walked back toward the office building, Stirling and Powell exchanged glances. Goldstein pretended not to notice.

Carey let down the door and came out of the Nimbus, followed by two more mechanics. "I don't know what more we could check," he said.

"It's ready then?" asked Stirling.

"No, it's not fueled," said Carey. "I, uh . . ." He paused and glanced at Goldstein. "I did something a little odd. I sent a truck over to MARC this morning and bought a load of fuel out of their tanks. I mean, you know, if somebody wanted to do something bad, they could contaminate the fuel. The wing tanks have been drained absolutely dry. We pulled the filters. We're ready to fuel 'er now. Give us fifteen minutes."

Stirling glanced at his watch. "You got it. Gives me time to run back to the office. Got a couple things I could be doing."

"I'm glad you came back," Terry said when he returned to the executive offices. "Valerie's here. So's Dan. They've got something to tell you."

They were waiting in his office, both in blue jeans and the red T-shirts with DAN'S SILVER WING printed across front and back in white letters—which on the gray-haired, leathery Dan was so incongruous as to approach the ludicrous.

"Pleasant surprise," said Stirling distractedly, hurrying to the window to watch the refueling of the Nimbus. He turned back toward them. "You'll get to see us fly."

"Didn't know you had a big test this morning," said Dan.

"Glad to have you here," said Stirling. "But I guess you came for some reason."

Dan nodded. "Yeah. Val . . . you tell him."

Valerie sighed, put her hands to her mouth, frowned, and took a moment to organize her thoughts. "Mac . . ." she said. "Dan's telephone bill came in yesterday's mail. He was looking it over last night and found a charge for a long-distance call to Los Angeles. He asked me yesterday afternoon, to call that number to find out who'd been called. I dialed the number. A receptionist answered—'Horn & Company.'"

"So—"

"That's not all. Dan and I put two and two together. You told us Litton works for Horn. Litton made a play for Judy. Late last night we twisted Judy's arm a little. Dan asked her if she intended to pay for the long-distance call she made to L.A. She's not too smart, and she sort of fumbled and blushed, and then she said, sure, she'd pay for it. So I asked her why she was calling Charlie Horn. She got her back up and said it was none of our business, that she'd pay for the call, and that was the end of it."

"I told her she was fired if she didn't explain herself," said Dan.

"And . . ." Stirling prompted, anxious to get to the end of the story.

Valerie went on. "Litton had told her to keep her ears open and call and report anything she heard about the Nimbus project, especially from pilots. He said he'd pay her if she came up with anything good. Well, one night a couple weeks ago, Marty Dodge was at the bar, drinking, shooting off his mouth about how you wouldn't let him fly your pet airplane. He said there must be something wrong with it, or you'd let other pilots fly it. He—"

"I told him to shut up about it or get out of my bar," said Dan.

"Judy called Horn & Company and gave them Dodge's name," said Valerie. "If he's working for you—"

"He could be the leak," said Terry.

Stirling nodded grimly. "He's got a contract with us," he said. "Bob asked for him as test pilot for the Mink Bat. Now, isn't that odd? That contract is worth a little money to Marty."

"Besides, it gives him a reason to be around here," said Terry.

"The puzzle is getting itself solved, little by little," said Stirling. "Well. I can't tell you how much I appreciate the help. But I've gotta go fly." He looked down at the ramp. "The plane is ready. I've got four FAA inspectors out there, who expected to see a go at ten o'clock. It's ten twenty-five. I can't keep them waiting any longer."

He strode to the door, but when he opened it his secretary was standing there, reaching for the knob, about to enter.

"I hope you're not leaving," she said. "I took a call a couple of minutes ago from Senator Goldwater's office. They wanted to know if you'd be available to talk to the senator in the next half hour. I knew you are going to fly this morning, but I supposed you would want to wait a few minutes to take a call from—"

"Mary! You told them I'd be available?"

"Yes, sir. I . . . I guess I could call back and say—"

He shook his head. "No." He sighed. "I can't do that. The man's doing me a hell of a favor to call . . . Uh, well. I'll wait for the call."

"Did I do something wrong?"

"No, no, Mary. You did just right. Thanks."

Stirling returned to his desk. He dropped wearily into his chair. "I can't . . ." He shook his head. "I've asked Barry to try to get Senator Meredith off our backs. Plus, he's in our corner in opposing limitations on overseas manufacturing. I just *can't* fail to return a call from him—and return it now. Shorty—"

"Let Shorty do it," Terry urged.

Stirling picked up his telephone. He punched in the number for the line shack. He watched Bellows trot from the Nimbus to the shack.

"Shorty? I can't go with you. I've got an important phone call coming in, one that I just can't walk away from. I'm afraid you'll have to do the flight by yourself. Okay? Listen, don't do anything stressful. Just take her up and run through some maneuvers with the front-loading. Don't try a stall unless she's responding pretty close to normal on the controls. We've just *gotta* fly 'er right now. Jerry brought those other FAA types, and we—Right. Thanks, Shorty. Good luck. Come up as soon as you're on the ground."

He put the telephone down and stood at the window, watching regretfully as Bellows returned to the Nimbus, climbed in, and shortly started the engines.

"Overloaded forward of the center of gravity," he said to Terry, Dan, and Valerie, who stood to either

289

side of him at the window. "That's a little tough and a little dangerous, don't let's kid ourselves."

While they watched, Bellows ran out the flaps and retracted them, cycled the ailerons, elevators, and rudder. The Nimbus moved forward slowly, its strobe lights flashing in the morning sun, and gained speed after Bellows made a right turn into the taxiway. It seemed to diminish in size as it moved almost a mile away on the taxiway. Bellows stopped for a minute just before turning into the runway. He was cycling the propeller, setting his altimeter and gyrocompass, speaking to the engineers who were watching from the tower on top of the building.

Finally the Nimbus turned into the runway. It stopped again for a moment, then it rolled forward, accelerating rapidly. Stirling clenched and unclenched his fists nervously; in his mind he was flying, performing every step that Shorty Bellows was performing in the cockpit. Because the airplane was nose-heavy, Shorty let it accelerate a little beyond liftoff speed before he raised the nose. But when he did, the Nimbus responded instantly, lifting gracefully off the runway. As it passed the ramp and the hundred people who had come out of the hangars and offices to watch this test flight, the gear were coming up. It was climbing fast, and Shorty lifted the nose just a bit more.

And then . . . Mac saw it instantly: an ugly black spear of steel cartwheeling wildly into the air above and behind the Nimbus. A propeller blade, broken. With a blade missing and the massive propeller spinning totally out of balance, the tail of the Nimbus shuddered violently and began immediately to disintegrate. It was spewing parts as the airplane, now with no power at all, nosed over and plunged toward the earth. It struck a desert road just off the end of the runway, just outside the airfield fence, where it exploded in a boiling mass of fire and smoke, with debris hurled for hundreds of yards.

_____ **18**

THE BOARD OF directors of Powell Industries met three days after the crash of the Nimbus. Robert Powell had called for a meeting two days sooner, but Mac and Terry had refused to participate until after the funeral for Shorty Bellows. Mac had wept at the funeral, and he had not been in the office since the crash. Now the board was assembled around the conference room table, in a mood of grief and subdued anger.

Terry Powell presided, solemn in a gray cashmere dress with a rope of pearls around her neck. Mac Stirling sat to her right, looking across the table and out the window to the ramp and runway, as if what was happening in this room were not of much concern to him. He had a small stack of file folders before him.

"Madam Chairlady," said Robert Powell. "If I may . . . ?"

Terry nodded at him, and Powell rose from his chair. He opened a manila folder of notes and documents. His eyes snapped, a small, controlled smile was fixed on his face, and he shrugged to settle his dark blue suit over his shoulders.

"Ladies and gentlemen," he said quietly. "I regret that this meeting has to come so soon after a tragedy such as we suffered a few days ago. You will take note, however, of the fact that I had sent to the chairlady a request for a meeting of the board before the crash occurred. It was on her desk, indeed, the morning of the crash—though she tells me she had not yet opened it when . . . Well, in any event, the business of the corporation has to continue."

He paused and looked down for a moment at his open file. "This may not be the most pleasant of meetings," he went on. "In fact, I'm afraid it won't be. It may, on the other hand, be the most important meeting this board has held since my father died." He looked up and glanced around the table.

"The time has come to raise certain issues that we have allowed to lie dormant for a long time. It has been my thought that we should allow our new management to have its head, to make its experiments, reserving our judgment until they had a chance. Now they have had their chance. They have had, in fact, several months to demonstrate whatever it was they thought they could demonstrate. The time has come, I think, to review what they have done, in terms of accomplishment and non-accomplishment. That is why I asked the board of directors to meet today. I have no wish to seem precipitate, but I have a responsibility. Unlike the rest of you, I can never forget whose name is on the sign on top of the building."

Walter O'Connell frowned. He did not like this speech. Lola Weiss simply looked miserable at the outset of a confrontation she had dreaded. She was flushed, almost tearful.

"There are a number of issues to be discussed," Powell went on, flipping through the papers in his file as if to suggest that each one represented an issue. "I—"

The door opened and Charlie Horn entered. He carried a briefcase and a glass ashtray, and he sat down behind Powell in a chair with its back to the wall. He blew a stream of smoke toward the ceiling and settled himself more comfortably.

"Uh, Madam Chairlady," said Lola Weiss nervously. "Is it appropriate for Mr. Horn to be present during a meeting of the board of directors?"

"I asked him," said Powell curtly, dismissing her question with an abrupt gesture of his hand.

"Even so," said Lola. "This is a meeting of the board of directors—"

"What's the matter, Lola?" sneered Powell. "You afraid he'll tell our secrets? What do you want to do, make a motion that our security consultant be excluded from this meeting?"

"Precisely," she snapped, her eyes flashing anger. "And so moved."

"I think you owe Charlie Horn an apology," said Powell loudly. "We—"

"Excuse me," said Horn. He stood. "This is not one of the issues you are here to discuss. I'll wait outside. And no offense whatever, Miss Weiss."

Powell glared at Lola Weiss as Charlie Horn picked up his ashtray and briefcase and left the room. "All right," he said curtly. "The first issue I want to raise is the death benefits payable to the widow and child of Eugene—uh, Shorty—Bellows. I understand that because his tenure with the company was so short, his benefits did not vest. I am advised by counsel, however, that the board of directors has the power to waive that consideration and direct the insurance company to pay full benefits. It will increase our premiums a bit, but I so move."

"Without objection, the secretary will record a unanimous vote in favor of the motion," said Terry. "Hearing no objection, it is so ordered."

Lola Weiss, acting as secretary of the board of directors, scribbled the motion and vote into her minutes.

Powell nodded. "I hope we can dispose of the remaining issues as smoothly," he said without expression either of voice or face. "At this point I would like to ask the president how many orders we have lost because of the crash of the Nimbus."

"Twenty-one," said Stirling, looking up at Powell from beneath his brows.

"Almost half the orders we had," Powell suggested.

"No. More like a third."

"And how many new orders have we gotten since the crash?"

"We haven't solicited any, so we couldn't have gotten any."

"*Could* you have gotten any?" Powell asked.

"Not before the cause of the crash is determined and announced by the National Transportation Safety Board," said Stirling.

"And how soon will that report be ready?" Powell asked. "They sometimes take years."

"This one is being expedited," said Stirling. "We'll have it in a few more weeks at most."

"How about financing, Colonel Stirling?" Powell went on. "Is there a bank in the world that would fund a plant to manufacture the Nimbus?"

"We haven't applied for it," said Stirling, "so we don't know how the banks will react. Caledonia has shown interest. Bank of Scotland. Banco do Brasil—"

"Because you've suggested to those banks that we

might manufacture in their countries. Is there an American bank that would back this venture now? Dick? What do you think?"

Richard Deering, the director from California United Bank, pursed his lips and drew his brows together. "Well . . ." he said very tentatively. "I think it would be rather difficult right now. Putting the crash aside, there are other questions."

"Yes," said Powell. "Such as . . . ?"

"Well," said Deering, tipping his head to one side. "There's the problem of the propeller icing and the resulting increase in fuel consumption."

"Let *me* ask you a question, Dick," said Stirling. He folded his arms and leaned back in his chair. "Just how much more fuel do you think we'll burn because of the several small changes we've had to make to the design?"

"I understand it's six-point-eight per cent," said Deering. "Is that figure correct?"

"It's exactly correct," said Stirling. "And if you don't mind, Dick, I'd like to ask how you know, since we've never used that figure in a board meeting."

"Are you accusing Dick—" Powell demanded.

"*Bob*," snapped Stirling gruffly. "Cool it. I'm not accusing Dick of anything. But that figure hasn't been circulated, even within the company, and I'd like to know how he got it. As a board member, he's entitled to know. But since I didn't tell him, and Walter O'Connell didn't tell him, I'd like to know the source of the information."

"Uh . . ." Deering mumbled. "The, uh, figure's out, Mac. It's known."

"I see it is," said Stirling. "But how? I mean, look,

Dick, it's fine that you know; there's no reason why you shouldn't; but I would like to know where you got the figure."

Deering sighed. "There's a confidential analyst's report . . . I can't say more than that."

"Hammond, Schwartz & Gottlieb," said Stirling, nodding. "Not in the published analysis, but in the confidential report furnished for a premium fee to selected clients. Right?"

Deering nodded, at first hesitantly, then emphatically. "Yes. And the major banks have access to it."

"Okay, Dick," said Stirling. "Thanks."

During this exchange, Powell had stood impatiently, leaning on his knuckles, which were planted on the table. "Regardless," he said now. "Regardless of how, uh, whoever you say it is . . . how they got the information is immaterial. They got it. And are you denying it's accurate, Colonel Stirling? Have we or have we not got a six-point-eight per cent loss of fuel economy?"

"Yes. At the moment, that's where we stand."

"And there may be additional loss?"

"No," interjected O'Connell. "No more than another point-two per cent. Seven per cent maximum. The Nimbus may burn seven per cent more than we estimated. And with some work we may be able to cut that to six or even five per cent."

"Have you advised the companies that ordered airplanes that they can expect to burn seven per cent more fuel than you promised them?"

"No," said Stirling. "The figure is not firm. They will be advised, and they can cancel their orders if they want to. But they won't, because even if the Nimbus burned twelve per cent more fuel than we originally estimated, it would still achieve remarkable—and thoroughly marketable—efficiency."

"Assuming the FAA ever certificates it," mumbled George Binghamton.

"We don't have to fear that, George," said Stirling. "The certificate will be issued when the tests are completed."

"Hope so," said Binghamton. He was Stanley Powell's shirt-sleeved old loyalist, sitting on the board as a representative of the company's employees, a minor stockholder who had received his stock through bonuses and options given for long, plodding service. "Those Washington fellows were damn sarcastic after Eight-eight Sierra Pop went down."

"I'm afraid I have less than unlimited confidence in the issuance of an airworthiness certificate," said Deering. "At the very least it's going to be delayed interminably—until the NTSB issues a report on the cause of the accident. That's the talk in the financial community."

"Yes," said Powell. "And tell us what else the financial community is talking about."

"Well . . ." said Deering. Drawing a breath and sighing, he withdrew from the conversation. "I'll let you talk about that, Bob."

"All right," said Powell curtly. "It looks as if I'm going to have to. If nobody else will, I'm going to."

He opened his folder and withdrew a clipping of the article from *American Defiant*. He tossed it in the center of the table.

"I am advised," he said, "that the financial community is talking about *this*. I'm told it's the subject of conversation in Washington, from which must come not just the airworthiness certificate for the Nimbus but

298

also the export license for the Mink Bat. I'm told that this article and other information has been circulated among foreign governments, prospective customers for the Mink Bat. I need hardly point out that our employees have passed this newspaper around, that it's the subject of an endless string of jokes."

"So?" said Walter O'Connell. "Do you have a point?"

"I do," said Powell brusquely. He turned directly to Terry and stared at her for a moment; then he did the same to Mac Stirling. "The chairlady of our board is a mature woman, widowed, and perfectly well entitled to have whatever love affair she may wish. The president of our company is divorced and free to do the same. The question arises, however—and is being widely asked—as to whether or not Colonel Stirling's managerial judgments about the Nimbus project are colored by his anxiety to redeem Terry's judgments, the ones she says reflect my father's judgments, and his desire to do a service to a woman with whom he is passionately in love. We all have to wonder—do we not?—whether Terry brought Colonel Stirling to this board and secured his appointment as president of Powell Industries because she judged him the best-qualified man for the job—or because she thought him handsome and likely a passionate lover."

"You are treading very close to the edge of trouble, Robert," Stirling warned. "I advise you to be very careful what you say."

Powell smiled. "You see?" he asked, turning up his palms. "An emotional reaction. I can't help but wonder how often emotion has clouded business and engineering judgment. Love—" he grinned and shrugged—

"Passionate, devoted love. It's a wonderful thing. But does it belong inside the executive offices of a corporation?"

"I disassociate myself from the way you have chosen to express your concern, Bob," said Deering. "I do, however, share the concern itself. I need hardly remind this board of what happened at Bendix when it was learned that two of its chief officers were involved in a love affair. I am afraid it is true that an emotional entanglement between two corporate officers—any two corporate officers, in any corporation—raises questions of objectivity in judgment. And when that entanglement is spread across the pages of a scandal sheet, it simply cannot do the company any good."

Deering sighed. "I'm sorry, but I have to raise a question that may be no less emotional," he said. "I think one that may be of even greater concern to the financial community." He reached for the clipping and put his finger on a paragraph toward the end. "Terry, would you mind commenting on this reference to a Mafia kingpin? To whom does that refer?"

"Ask Bob," she said coldly. "He knows."

"Why should I know?" asked Powell, reddening.

"The man to whom it refers, Dick," she said to Deering, "is Vincent Strozzi. Before I met Stan, I lived for a while in Vince's penthouse in Las Vegas. You can inquire, if you want to, as to who Vincent Strozzi is and as to whether or not he has a Mafia connection. Or maybe you can save time by asking Bob."

"Why the hell should I know?" Powell demanded.

"Didn't Charlie Horn report to you?" she asked. "If you didn't send him to Las Vegas to ask questions about me and about Vincent Strozzi, then who did? Or is it just a coincidence, Bob, that the man you recommended for this company's security consultant had been in Las Vegas only a short time before, asking very pointed questions about me? Who prompted him to go to Las Vegas and ask all over town if I'd been a prostitute?"

"*I* want the answer to that," said George Binghamton, scowling at Powell.

"Well, maybe the thing to do is just call Charlie Horn in here and ask him," said Louis DiAngelo.

"I wouldn't believe him if he said the sun's coming up tomorrow morning," said Terry.

Powell pointed a finger at her. "Now, just a minute here. You've accused me of . . . whatever it is you're accusing me of. You've called Charlie Horn a liar. I'd like to see you confront Charlie himself with that accusation."

"All right," said Stirling abruptly. He rose to his feet. "Madam Chairlady, I suggest that Mr. Powell has had the floor quite a while and that it's time he sat down and let someone else speak."

"I've been interrupted re—"

"Chair recognizes the president of the company," said Terry.

"Now, just a damn minute!"

"Is this the way to run a meeting?" asked DiAngelo.

"You want to appeal from the ruling of the chair?" Terry asked Powell. "Have a vote on it?"

Powell glanced around the table, maybe silently counting votes. He dropped heavily to his chair. "But we're going to settle a few things before this day is over," he growled through clenched teeth.

"I can promise you that," said Stirling.

"There should be a motion on the floor," said DiAngelo. "Otherwise, we just ramble from one subject to another. I thought we should—"

"You are absolutely right, Lou," said Lola. "I move that we discontinue the contract with Horn & Company."

"You interrupted before I could . . ." DiAngelo complained. "I was going to move—"

"We have a motion before us," Terry interrupted firmly.

"Is this meeting orchestrated?" asked Deering.

"I second Miss Weiss's motion," said Walter O'Connell.

"Is this proposition to be discussed?" Powell asked. "Will Charlie Horn be given a chance to speak?"

"He will," said Terry. "But right now the president of the company has the floor."

"I want to hear what Charlie Horn has to say, myself," said Stirling. "But first, there's somebody else outside. If you'll excuse me a minute, I'm going to bring in someone who may be able to shed some light on the question of whether Horn & Company should be continued or dismissed."

Stirling left the room and in half a minute returned, leading a reluctant Martin Dodge by the arm. The test pilot was dressed for a meeting, not for flying: in a light blue plaid jacket, a white shirt and blue tie, and dark blue slacks. His face was flushed, and his breath smelled of whiskey. He sat down in the chair Stirling pulled out for him.

"Why is it any more appropriate for this man to be here during a meeting of this board than it was for Mr. Horn to be?" DiAngelo asked.

"Because he's not settling in for the whole meeting," said Stirling. "All he's going to do is answer a couple of questions."

"I don't know if I should object to this or not," said Powell. He stared at Dodge for a moment, then shrugged. "He's one of our test pilots. He's been flying the Mink Bat. Are the questions about the Mink Bat?"

Stirling shook his head. "All I want to know from Marty is this," he said, tossing in front of Dodge one of the 5 × 7 photographs of Thomas Litton. "Who is that, old buddy?"

Dodge looked unhappily at the picture. He shook his head.

"You don't know?"

Dodge shook his head.

"Funny," said Stirling. "I think if a man had taken *me* out to The Clock and paid for my hour with one of Fiona's girls, I'd remember him. I'd recognize him when I saw his picture. C'mon, Marty."

Dodge looked up at Stirling. "Shit's in the fan, ain't it?" he mumbled.

Stirling nodded. "Who is the guy, Marty?"

Dodge picked up the photograph and frowned over it. "His name is Tom Litton," he said.

"He paid you for information, right?"

Dodge nodded. "No big secrets," he said quietly. "Nothing about design. Nothing like that."

"Fuel consumption," said Stirling.

Dodge nodded. "Right. That's what he wanted to know: how much fuel the Nimbus burned."

"And you asked . . . ?"

"Guys around the hangars," said Dodge quietly. "Nobody really knew. But you could figure it out from looking at the loadings and the tach times on the airplane. Once I was hired as a pilot here, it was easy enough to pick up what Litton wanted to know."

"What'd you think Litton was going to do with the information?" Terry asked.

"Give it to another company," said Dodge. "That's what he said."

"Which he did, apparently," said DiAngelo.

Stirling shook his head. "No. There was a direct conduit from him to Hammond, Schwartz. He sold them the information directly—and they in turn sold it to banks, securities brokers, our competitors, to anyone who'd pay the price. Straightforward theft and sale of confidential business information."

"Oh, man, I—" Dodge fumbled.

Stirling turned and confronted the test pilot. "Tell me something, Marty," he said. "You've been flying the Mink Bat. Is it any good? Is it worth building? The real poop. No foolin' around."

Dodge stared at the surface of the table for a moment. "It's a good enough airplane," he said. "For what it's supposed to be. Not a bad idea, really."

"Yeah," said Stirling. "Well, we're going to finish the tests on the Mink Bat and sell it. So, I'm not going to fire you, Marty. If I fired you, you'd never get another job as a test pilot, not anywhere. You go on flying the Mink Bat, and you can go out with the salesmen and demonstrate it. But you stay out of the hangars. You stay away from the facts and figures in this company. You fly. That's your job. Now get out of here and get the whiskey out of you. You fly tomorrow. I'm giving you your last chance in the whole aviation industry, so don't screw up again."

Dodge looked up at Stirling for a moment, then nodded, pulled back his chair, got up and left the room.

Powell nodded and sniffed. "Cute," he said. "Most dramatic. So that's—"

"I'd like to know something," Deering interrupted. "How did you know this fellow Litton took him to The Clock, which I assume is a . . ."

"It's a whorehouse," said George Binghamton.

Stirling chuckled. "Charlie Horn is not the world's only private investigator," he said. "Retired air force security men make damn good investigators—efficient, ethical, and competent. The photographs of Mr. Thomas Litton have been widely distributed. He's been around our town a good deal."

"So who *is* this Litton?" asked DiAngelo glumly. "What's the connection?"

"Maybe Charlie Horn can tell us," said Stirling. "Why don't we call him in?"

"It's about time," said Powell, "that he got a chance to defend himself."

Stirling opened the door and invited Horn in. Once more, Horn brought his briefcase and his big glass ashtray, now filled with butts and ashes. Stirling offered him a seat at the conference table, instead of one behind, and Horn thanked him with a broad smile and sat down.

"I have a question for you, Charlie, if you don't mind," said Stirling.

"Not at all, Colonel," said Horn, dragging deeply on his cigarette. "Shoot."

Stirling flipped the picture of Litton in front of Horn. "Who's that?" he asked.

Horn picked up the photograph and studied it for a

long moment. Then he turned down the corners of his mouth and shrugged. "No idea," he said.

"Never saw him?"

Horn shook his head. "Not that I recall."

"Never heard of Tom Litton?"

"No. Not that I recall."

"He doesn't work for you?"

"He doesn't work for me."

"Okay," said Stirling. "Then did you ever hear of a firm called Dayton Industrial & Financial Security Services? In Boston?"

Horn's face darkened. "I have heard of the organization," he said quietly. "They are engaged, I believe, in the business of securing corporations against . . . industrial espionage."

"Exactly," said Stirling. "So, may I read you part of a letter I have from that firm? Uh . . . the most interesting paragraph says, 'This will confirm the substance of our telephone conversation, in which I explained to you that, although Mr. Thomas L. Litton is indeed a junior partner in this firm, he is at present on an extended leave of absence at his own request and at the request of Mr. Charlie Horn, of Horn & Company, Los Angeles, to enable him to work on special assignment for Mr. Horn. Any inquiries as to his current activities should be directed to Mr. Horn or to Mr. Litton personally.' The letter, Charlie, is signed by Emile V. Dayton, president, Dayton Industrial & Financial Security Services."

"I question the authenticity of that letter," said Horn aggressively. "I'd like to have a lab analysis of—"

"Bullshit," said George Binghamton. "You got egg on your face, you lying son of a bitch."

306

"Just a goddamn minute here!" Horn growled, rising from his chair and leaning across the table threateningly.

Stirling spun and chopped Horn hard on the jaw; and as Horn fell back, Stirling reached inside Horn's jacket and pulled the pistol from his shoulder holster. Horn dropped into his chair, grabbing at his jaw with both hands. Stirling slid the pistol across the table toward Binghamton.

"Hang on to that, George."

"What the hell's going on here?" Powell yelled. "The man is our security consultant! He's damn well entitled to have a gun on him!"

"Not when he's about to hear what he's about to hear," said Stirling.

"What—"

"Sit down, Bob," said Stirling in a low voice. "Your security consultant is about to be charged with the murder of Shorty Bellows. There are deputies outside. The district attorney was good enough to let us air some of the issues in this meeting before the arrest is made. This company is important to a lot of people, so they gave us an hour to settle some of the things we have to settle before criminal proceedings begin."

Horn shook his head violently. "You're crazy, Stirling," he muttered. "You're goddamned crazy. I've got enough on you to—"

Stirling cast a brief, hard glance at Horn, then ignored his muttering. "Let's start off with the cause of the crash of Eight-eight Sierra Papa," he said. "I went out with our own plant guards and searched for pieces of that broken propeller blade even before they'd removed Shorty's remains from the wreckage. We found two big hunks. But we didn't touch them. I left guards on them until the investigators from the National Transportation Safety Board got here. They took them in charge. They've done lab tests. Guess what they found? Hairline cracks in the blade. I mean, besides the cracks where it broke apart."

"So?" said DiAngelo. "That's the second blade that's failed."

Stirling shook his head. "Guess what else they found? Microscopic quantities of yellow paint that had seeped into those tiny cracks. And the blade that was left in Hangar One, all covered with sprayed yellow paint—guess what they *didn't* find in *that* blade? Cracks. No cracks at all. Any kind. Any size."

"Then somebody . . ." DiAngelo whispered hoarsely. "Somebody *substituted*—my God!"

Stirling nodded. "Somebody pulled a blade off Eight-eight Sierra Pop, sprayed it yellow to look like the blade we'd purposefully cracked in the static tests, cleaned the yellow paint off the cracked blade, and put it on the airplane. When Shorty hit the throttles for a fast climb, the cracked blade broke. And Shorty died."

DiAngelo turned toward Powell. *"Jesus Christ!* Bob, did you have any idea—"

"Hell no, goddamnit! What'd you think? What are you trying to suggest?"

"Who substituted those propeller blades?" Deering asked. "It's all very well to say it was done; but the point is, who did it?"

"I'm going to let somebody answer who knows," said Stirling. "I have a witness. She'll be testifying in court. For now, she just has a story to tell us."

He left the room again, and in a moment he returned, leading Ruth Powell by the arm. She was pale, and her eyes were red behind her spectacles, but she entered the room with her shoulders drawn back, her chin high, her mouth firmly set. As she sat down in the chair that Stirling drew back for her, she cast her husband an angry, scornful glance.

"What the hell is this?" Powell demanded. *"My wife!* A witness? Witness to what? What kind of story? Lou! You're my lawyer. You tell her she can't be a witness against me."

"I'm not your lawyer," said DiAngelo coldly. "Anyway, what are you afraid she'll tell? I'd like to know."

"My wife! Whose side are you on, Ruth? Ours? Or—"

Ruth Powell shook her head. "Up to the point where you killed a man, I was always on your side, Bob. But you see, I overheard everything you said that night when Charlie Horn and Tom Litton and that fellow Clark came to the house."

"Killed a man . . ." Powell breathed, twisting his mouth into a sneer. "She's crazy! She's a certifiable lunatic. Has been for years. There's plenty of evidence of that. Her own father would testify that she's mentally unbalanced."

Ruth settled sad, pitying eyes on her husband. "Someplace, Bob, it comes to an end," she said. "Someplace I have to forget our marriage and start to think about the kids—and myself too, if you don't mind. I could go along with everything . . . well, you know. We've talked about it. Until you conspired to kill a man." She sighed loudly and shook her head. "And that's what you did, Bob: you and Horn and Litton and Clark," she whispered tearfully. "That's what you did."

"You're crazy!" Powell shrieked. "You are *insane!*"

"He signed over a quarter of his stock in Powell Industries to Charlie Horn," she said. "I know it hasn't been reported to the corporation for the purpose of transfer on the stock register, but he did it; they agreed that the transfer on the books of the corporation would be deferred until he was president; and there's a document that says so, somewhere."

"Secret documents," muttered Horn, chuckling scornfully. "Imaginary . . ."

"They gave Thomas Litton a post-dated check for a hundred thousand dollars," she said. "That was a check on Horn & Company. It was to be his security, to assure him they would pay him that amount in cash."

Powell tried to grin but succeeded only in creating a grotesque twist to his face. He shook his head. "Loony . . ."

"And they gave Robert Clark fifty thousand dollars in cash."

"I owe you an apology, Bob," Horn said to Powell. "You told me she was nuts, and I didn't believe it." He turned to Stirling. "I don't think I have to stay here."

Stirling shrugged. "That's true. You don't. The deputies are outside. You can go with them any time you want."

"Maybe I better hear what insanity is being said against me," said Horn, settling back into his chair.

Stirling smiled sympathetically at Ruth. "Maybe you should tell us how you came to hear all they said."

She nodded. "Charlie Horn had come to the house before." She hesitated for a moment, then looked squarely at him and said, "I wrote him down from the first time I saw him as a vulgar, sordid little man—"

"Oh thank you, Mrs. Powell," sneered Horn.

"And I couldn't understand why my husband associated with him," she finished her sentence.

Powell had closed his eyes and lowered his head. He sighed.

"Anyway," Ruth continued, "that night—it was just last week, of course—they came to the door: Horn and Litton and Clark. It seemed to be a big thing. Bob was all excited. He told me he was going to have a business meeting and that I should stay in the bedroom or in my hobby room and not bother them. I didn't like that. If Charlie Horn was in my house, meeting with my husband about something important, I wanted to know what was going on. I decided I would listen to what they said." She shot an indignant glance at Horn. "I'm only sorry I didn't have a recorder handy."

"What'd you do, hide in a closet?" Horn asked scornfully.

"It's my home," she said. "I went in my hobby room and sat down at my loom, so if Bob checked on me he would think I was weaving. But I left the door open, and I could hear the talk from the living room." She tipped her head to one side and spoke to Horn. "It was easier to hear after you'd had a couple of drinks and your talk got louder." Then she looked at Powell. "And, of course, you didn't have enough respect for me to suppose I could understand what I might hear."

"And you heard them talk about the stock transfer and the post-dated check," said Stirling. "And what else?"

"I heard them talking about a propeller, about how to take off a blade," she said in a small voice, breaking with a sob. "I didn't understand it, and it didn't mean

311

anything to me until I heard that a blade had broken on the Nimbus. That's when I called you, Mac. Then I knew—" She drew a deep breath. "Then I knew," she said firmly, "that I'd heard them plotting murder. If I'd had the least idea that was what they meant, I'd have called somebody immediately, and Shorty Bellows would be alive."

"In your statement to the NTSB," said Stirling, "you said you heard the voices of four men, whom you identified as your husband, Charlie Horn, Thomas Litton, and Robert Clark. And you said one of them was assigned to switch the propeller blades."

"Clark," she said. She took off her glasses and rubbed her eyes. "He was the one who knew how."

Stirling nodded. "Robert Clark went to Harmon, the company that makes the propellers we use on the Nimbus, used his credentials as a reporter for *Aviation World,* and asked to be shown how to remove and reinstall a blade. It's no very big deal, of course, if you know how. A couple of wrenches . . . a couple of strong backs."

"But how did he get into Hangar One, past our security?" asked Binghamton.

"Charlie brought him to Hangar One about three A.M., in the uniform of a Powell Industries security guard, telling Jim Malloy he was a new man he'd hired and was showing around. Jim called me, but I ordered him not to interfere. I figured that when Bill Carey and his team went over it the next morning, we'd find anything Charlie and Clark had done to the airplane."

"You've got no witness to—" Horn muttered.

"I figured we'd find what you'd done and have you by the short hairs, Charlie," Stirling interrupted. "The boys did go over it, too—obsessively. But they didn't find anything wrong." Stirling shook his head. "You were too damn smart for us, Charlie . . . repainting, cleaning, switching blades. And Shorty died because I underestimated you. I blame myself—"

"The idea was to kill *you*," exclaimed Deering.

Stirling nodded. "If Senator Goldwater hadn't called to tell me about a talk he'd had with Senator Meredith, I'd have been sitting in the left seat when Eight-eight Sierra Pop took off."

"Clark—" DiAngelo said.

"Clark's dead," said Stirling. "The Arizona highway patrol found his body on a road outside Kingman. Somebody's going to have to answer for that one, too."

"The authorities . . . ?" Deering asked.

"Called the afternoon of the crash," said Stirling. "It was beyond us, this kind of thing. Murder." He shook his head. "Besides the district attorney and the NTSB, the FBI is active in the case. Except for going to Shorty's funeral, I've done very little the last three days but meet with investigators. The whole case is coming together. The evidence . . ." He shook his head at Powell. "You were stupid, Bob. How stupid could a man be?"

"What a lot of crap," Powell scoffed, though his voice was dry and thin. "You think you can make all this stick, you and my father's hooker? You'll play hell!"

"We'll see, Bob," said Stirling. "The deputies are waiting for you, too. You and Charlie. Litton has been picked up in Massachusetts. We'll see what sticks."

19

ARRESTED OUTSIDE THE conference room, Robert Powell and Charlie Horn were charged with aggravated murder and were held without bail in the county jail of San Bernardino County. That was on September 18. Thomas Litton was extradited from Massachusetts and brought to the same jail on October 1. The three of them came to trial on March 3. They were convicted and sentenced to life imprisonment. They entered San Quentin on April 11.

Ironically, the Federal Aviation Agency issued an airworthiness certificate for the Nimbus on the same day, April 11. It had passed every test.

By then the company had orders for more than two hundred aircraft. The publicity resulting from the trial of Powell and Horn had demonstrated to the world that the Nimbus was in no way flawed, but represented a major jump forward in the design of business aircraft.

By then, too, the name of the company had been changed. The new name was Nimbus, Incorporated.

As part of her divorce settlement, Ruth Powell acquired her husband's stock. She was elected to replace him on the board of directors.

On August 18, Mrs. McDonald John Stirling gave birth to a baby boy, which she and Mac named Stanley McDonald.

As soon as Terry was able to travel, she and Colonel Stirling flew to Rio de Janeiro to inspect the plant where Nimbus do Brasil was to manufacture the Nimbus. They made the trip in a Nimbus, which required only two refueling stops between Powell, California, and Rio de Janeiro, accompanied by Senator Barry Goldwater, who took the controls and flew the leg between Mexico City and Bogotá.

In Brazil they were the guests of Mario Monforte. Mac and Terry visited also with Lola Weiss, who had moved to a beachfront apartment in Rio. She was the liaison between the North American and South American companies.

Lola's executive assistant in the Rio office of Nimbus, Incorporated was Valerie D'Angostino, who had demonstrated a marvelous facility for languages and was already fluent not only in Portuguese itself but also in Brazilian slang. On a trip to the jungle to the north, she had shot a fourteen-foot caiman and was regarded as something of a prodigy by Brazilian hunters who saw the photographs of her with her trophy. João Estremoz had suggested that he would expedite her application for Brazilian citizenship if she wanted it; and she had expressed her gratitude and told him to go ahead.

Senator Goldwater flew home by commercial jet, and Mac and Terry flew the Nimbus on to Buenos Aires, then over the Andes to Santiago and up the west coast of South America to Lima, Quito, and Bogotá. They sold eight Nimbuses to South American companies, plus forty Mink Bats to governments.

On their return to California, they found themselves portrayed on the cover of *Time* and the subject of a story that described them as "the most successful husband-wife team in American business today."